ECHOES OF ABANDON

**Echoes in Time
Book Two**

Paula Quinn

ARE YOU SIGNED UP FOR DRAGONBLADE'S BLOG?

You'll get the latest news and information on exclusive giveaways, exclusive excerpts, coming releases, sales, free books, cover reveals and more.

Check out our complete list of authors, too!

No spam, no junk. That's a promise!

Sign Up Here

www.dragonbladepublishing.com

Dearest Reader;

Thank you for your support of a small press. At Dragonblade Publishing, we strive to bring you the highest quality Historical Romance from some of the best authors in the business. Without your support, there is no 'us', so we sincerely hope you adore these stories and find some new favorite authors along the way.

Happy Reading!

CEO, Dragonblade Publishing

Additional Dragonblade books by Author Paula Quinn

Echoes in Time Series
Echo of Roses
Echoes of Abandon

Rulers of the Sky Series
Scorched
Ember
White Hot

Hearts of the Highlands Series
Heart of Ashes
Heart of Shadows
Heart of Stone
Lion Heart
Tempest Heart
Heart of Thanks
Forbidden Heart

Dedication

Thank you for blessing my work, Lord. It's because of the creative mind You have given me that I can do this.

$$\blacklozenge\cdots\bullet\quad\bullet\cdots\blacklozenge$$

CHAPTER ONE

Manhattan, NY
Autumn 2019

A SHAFT OF sunlight broke through shadows and found Detective Michael Pendridge sitting on his bed in his boxer briefs, his dark hair falling around his face, catching on to the scruff on his jaw. An empty bottle of Jameson Irish Whiskey rested in his lap. A thin layer of sweat covered his body. His heart drummed loud in his ears, making his blood rush through his veins. His eyes were squeezed shut while his teeth bit down on the barrel of his gun.

He didn't have to think about all he'd lost since the day he put on the uniform eleven years ago. It was always there, fresh in his mind. This job had cost him his soul. It had taken everyone he'd allowed himself to care about. It made him a monster and robbed him of any woman he could have loved because of time, and danger, and his increasingly screwed up head. It wrenched compassion from his heart and replaced it with the hard shell of apathy. People were liars. They were capable of the worst crimes. He'd seen it all. It stopped turning his stomach and left nothing in its wake.

But he couldn't give it up. It was in his blood. His brother, father and grandfather were cops, and though he wasn't their biological son or brother, he felt the need for justice and right to reign.

There was only one way to stop being the deluded protector of the innocent.

He gripped his gun in his hand and slipped his index finger to the trigger. He took a deep breath. What was left? Whiskey. Just whiskey. The gun was already cocked. He groaned and pulled back on the trigger.

His phone rang.

He tossed the weapon onto the bed and picked up his phone. "What?" he demanded in a gravelly voice and raked his hand through his hair.

"Micajah Pendridge?"

He looked at the number. *Private.*

"Who's this?" he demanded. No one but his parents knew the real name left with him at the orphanage.

"My name is Mr. Green of Green, du Lac, and de Maris. I'm an attorney for the estate of Lady Eleanor Pendridge, Duchess of Glastonbury."

"Did she leave me money?" Michael asked and adjusted himself in his briefs.

"No. Detective, I—"

"You keep it then," he said and hung up. He tossed the phone over his shoulder onto the bed and stood up. He stretched his arms over his head then ran his hand over his prickly face. He needed a shower. And coffee.

His phone rang again. He looked at the number. It was private. He ignored it while he popped open a jar of instant coffee, broke through the seal, and poured some into a cup.

The phone continued to ring.

He muttered something unintelligible and snatched the phone. "Green—"

"Detective. Someone is missing and the item that was left to you could help find him. We need your assistance."

"What?" Michael asked, a little thrown off. He was sure all the whiskey last night wasn't helping his foggy head. "What are you talking about?" Did this have to do with the Kestrel Lancaster case he was working on? A young woman had gone to an office uptown and disappeared. Her friends, who were the only witnesses, said the fourth floor they'd been on had disappeared along with her. They said she'd received a letter and a phone call about an inheritance. They couldn't remember who'd called her, who the letter was from, or who they met when they arrived at the office. Michael thought it was odd. But it was proof of nothing.

"I cannot say much on the phone," Green continued. "You must come to the office on West Twenty-second. I will explain everything there." He gave Michael the address and hung up.

This had to have something to do with the Lancaster girl. It was the same M.O., just a different address. She got a call to go uptown to pick up an object that had been left to her. What was the object left to him? Too many questions. Now he *had* to go find out. He wasn't that far away.

He headed toward the bathroom, leaving the coffee. He'd pick up some on the way.

Ten minutes later, he exited the bathroom soaking wet with a yellow towel wrapped around his waist. He still didn't feel clean. He never did. He never would.

Jimmy Clements was twenty-two when he was gunned down by a perp robbing a bodega. Michael, Clements' partner, killed the shooter only to find out later he was a sixteen-year-old kid.

It busted him up and broke him down. A kid. A kid! There were days he couldn't deal with it. Days when he was close to putting bullets in the gun. He wished he hadn't shot it that night.

He missed Clements. Jimmy was more than just his work partner, he was Michael's closest friend, his brother, together every day for two years.

Michael pulled on a fresh pair of boxer briefs. These were a little tighter. He was gaining weight. There was a bit more meat around the muscle. He'd stopped caring about staying in shape. For what? So he could chase people down?

He found a bottle of whiskey with a mouthful left in the

bottle and guzzled it down. He dressed in black jeans and a black, short-sleeved T that hugged his long, tattooed torso. On his feet, he wore white socks and beat-up, black leather combat boots. He clipped his badge to his belt and snapped a magazine into his empty gun.

One day, one morning, it wouldn't be empty. But he put that thought behind him for now.

He wasn't worried about going to this address alone. It's how he did things nowadays. If he couldn't protect himself, then so be it. Whether he died at his own hand or someone else's didn't matter. But his instincts wouldn't let him walk into a spray of bullets. They made him fight back.

He'd be fine.

He threw on a leather bomber jacket to conceal his gun, slipped his phone into the back pocket of his jeans and walked out the door to his apartment.

Should he walk the two extra blocks to the garage to get his car or walk the six blocks to Twenty-second? He should walk. He needed the exercise. He'd come back later for his car and stop at a liquor store for some whiskey. The thought of it comforted him.

He thought about the cases he had to see to today. Files sitting on his desk, waiting for him. Why was he strolling up the street on his way to some address a guy on the phone gave him?

He should have taken the car. Why didn't he? He wasn't thinking right. Now he had to walk there and back. He shook his head at himself.

Clements had been buried by his family upstate. Everyone from the precinct had been there. Michael had been a pallbearer. Everyone had been kind and considerate to his family and to him. They asked him if he was okay. He smiled and said yes and they left it alone. But he hadn't been okay. First his brother, Geoffrey, rushing into the first tower on 9/11, and then Clements.

It had taken him a while to get used to having another partner—and a woman partner at that. He wasn't any chauvinist who thought women shouldn't be cops. If she wanted to, let her do it.

It was just hard for him to get used to being around a woman, the same woman, every day.

But Kelly Harkin had been easy to get along with. She was married with a kid. She'd transferred from the Twenty-sixth Precinct after her partner had been killed. They had a lot in common. She was capable and tough as nails. They remained partners for another two years before she died in his arms, shot by a son of a bitch who'd shot some neighborhood kids.

The ghosts haunted him. He'd seen a therapist twice a week for three months. Did nothing. He made detective by some miracle. At first, it was good, but it didn't take too long to discover his third partner, Langsley Hicks was taking bribes. Hicks was caught after a year. Michael went through hell over it because Internal Affairs believed he was taking bribes as well. For two years, he couldn't take a piss without someone looking over his shoulder.

He started drinking six months ago. He didn't drink during work, but when he got off, he could usually be found at Micky's Pub. Lately though, he stopped wanting to be around anyone, so he went home alone and drank himself to sleep. Depending on his stupor, it kept the ghosts away until morning.

He reached the building and looked up. Four stories—just like in the Lancaster case. What was he walking into…alone? But if this had to do with her case, it could be the lead he needed. Double doors. He went inside and took in his surroundings. There was a doorman. An outside elevator in a cage design, four doors leading somewhere else, and a stairway.

"Detective Pendridge?"

Michael spun around to face a big guy with an even bigger smile.

Michael looked him over with skeptical arch of his dark brow, and then followed him to the elevator. His heart pounded. Is this what they had done with Kestrel Lancaster? Was this guy a part of a human trafficking ring? When the cage door slammed shut, it jarred Michael's thoughts. He fought to hold on to the present as his mind screamed, *Shots fired! We need help! We need help!*

"Detective?" asked his escort. "Are you all right?"

"I'm fine," Michael answered.

This obviously wasn't the company strongarm. If anything, he offered his arm for help. And he hadn't patted Michael down to see if he had any weapons. Maybe this was legit.

"What's your name?" Michael asked him.

"My friends call me Luke."

Michael spared him a wooden glance. He didn't like when people were overly friendly or when they considered him a friend after a few minutes. "What do people call you who aren't your friend?"

"Luke," his escort said, his smile turning playful.

Michael ignored him.

They reached the polished wooden doors and Luke stepped forward, opening the door. He made way for Michael and held his arm out to an antique-looking chair.

"Mr. Green will be right in."

Michael offered him a light nod and looked around the golden-hued room. "Does anyone else work here? I didn't see any receptionist or—"

"It is Friday. We have a skeleton crew on Fridays."

Michael sat in the chair and waited. In front of him was a large wooden table polished until it looked like glass. "How do you keep dust off this thing?" he asked Luke, but a door opened off to the side and another man stepped inside. He was older than Luke, and bigger. His shoulders were wider than a baseball bat. He wore a suit but there was a dangerous air about him, as if his patience only went so far and then he would break you in half.

"Detective. I'm Mr. Green. We spoke on the phone. Let's get right down to business, shall we?"

"That would be nice."

"Your great-great-great-aunt Eleanor Pendridge left this for you." He leaned over and picked up a small briefcase. He laid it on the desk and opened it with the inside facing him.

Michael slowly reached for his gun.

"Detective, there are a few questions I must ask you before I can give this to you."

"What is it?" Michael asked, trying to look over the case to see the inside.

"Are you Micajah Pendridge, adopted son of Albert and Mary Davenport? And were you adopted when you were six months old by the Davenports?"

Michael held up his hand. "You've proven you know a lot about me. But what does any of this have to do with someone missing?"

Green's dark eyes shifted to the briefcase. He put both big, beefy hands in and lifted a small box so that Michael could see. "The contents of this box can lead us to a man we have been searching for for many years."

Michael narrowed his eyes on him. "How's it going to do that?"

"When you open it, you will see."

But when Michael reached for it, Green held the box away and slid a piece of paper and a pen to him with the other hand.

"Just sign here, please."

He placed the box on the desk while Michael read the document. It basically said he swore he was Micajah Pendridge.

"Would you prefer us to leave while you open the box?" Green asked.

Michael looked at the etchings on the box. Deer and a castle. He shook his head at them and opened the box.

He immediately felt drawn to the blackened brooch inside. He swallowed. He wanted to ask Green why someone had left him a charred piece of jewelry, but he didn't want to stop looking at it. The room seemed to pulse with a life of its own. Something was happening. He felt as if he had no control over his own thoughts. He lifted the brooch out of the box. There was a long pin attached to the back of it. "What is..." His mind drifted. He rubbed his finger over the surface of the brooch. The blackened char began to fall away. A shape began to appear. A dragon curled around a yellow stone. The air shimmered around it, coming from a light within the stone.

There was a small name in the stone. Michael looked closer at it. "Pendragon," he whispered.

The ancient brooch fell to the carpeted floor when Michael disappeared from the office.

Beddington, London
October 1724

THE CARPETED FLOOR turned into a paved street. Outside. What? How did he get out here? He shook his head. Did he black out? How? He wasn't drunk. Wait. He looked around in all directions, squinting under the sun. Where was he? None of this looked familiar. Where were the buildings, the skyscrapers in the distance? His heart began to accelerate.

He heard the sound of people around the corner, for he was on a street in the city, just not his city.

His hands flew to his belt. His gun and his badge were gone. No! His phone, his wallet. Everything. This couldn't be happening. *All right, pull yourself together, man. You'll figure it out and find your stuff.*

He followed the sound of the people while lifting his hand to his head. Had Green or his bodyguard hit him?

He turned the corner to find a crowd gathered around the middle of the street. All their eyes were set on the same thing. Some kind of traveling street show performing on a dais, with musicians and dancers. It looked medieval to Michael's eyes…and the people in the crowd…they were dressed oddly, too. Women wore petticoats and riding habits with tricorn hats and gloves. Men wore riding habits, also, with hose and—no. No. What was going on? Had he stumbled onto a movie set?

Someone—a woman, shoved her way past him and into the crowd. He watched her because it helped keep him from screaming that someone had better end this before he took them all in!

He knew that it was only because he was so used to examining things so closely that he saw the woman stumble into a well-dressed man wearing a monocle over his eye and slip her daintily gloved fingers into his pocket. She was robbing the man! Just as she had probably robbed him!

He hurried toward her.

He caught up to her, stopping her departure with his hand around her wrist.

"Give me back my things!"

She turned to face him.

He swallowed and fought to keep his hold on her. She was…breathtaking, a natural beauty with sable-colored eyes burning like embers on him and deep brown waves falling over her shoulders to the small of her back.

"Get your hand off me, you filthy swine," she snapped at him, her small, dimpled chin tilting upward. "I have nothing of yours. Why, I doubt you even have one thing to take!"

"You're right, because you robbed it all. Now, hand it over." He tugged on the small velvet pouch hanging from her wrist.

Before he could react, she fisted her small, silk-gloved hand and punched him in the jaw.

CHAPTER TWO

LADY CHARLOTTE WHIMSEY had been caught pickpocketing once before. She wasn't about to let it happen again. Her father, a high court judge and the Duke of Croydon, had warned her that if she was brought before him one more time, he would send her to his sister's house in the damp, lonely village of Otford.

Charlotte would rather be thrown into a vat of oil than live there with her Aunt Louise and her arrogant son, George.

She couldn't get caught she thought as she lifted her skirts and leaped over a small dog that appeared in her way. She cleared it with a smile and kept running.

Who was the flint-eyed stranger who accused her of emptying his pockets? She hadn't robbed him. She would have remembered if she had. His pockets weren't loose but sewn close to his tightly honed body. She'd looked when he'd accused her. He dressed strangely and the inflection in his voice was like nothing she had ever heard before. He clearly wasn't from London. Why, she doubted he was from England at all.

She wanted to turn around and see where he was. She smiled, sure she'd lost him. She'd been running since she was twelve. She was quick. Even quicker in her breeches and hose, which she never wore in daylight. She could out—

Her smile faded when she saw him step out from behind a carriage *in front* of her. She skidded to a halt and glared at him. Would she have to use her knives? She didn't want to kill anyone.

"Why are you chasing me?" she demanded, out of breath. "I don't have your belongings." She emptied the pouch tied to her waist into her hand. Two pocket watches and a large ruby ring fell out.

His eyes opened wider. They were rather pretty eyes, the color of sapphires, surrounded by long, lush, raven lashes. "How did you get a ring off a man's finger?" he asked, staring at the ring and then at her.

With his full attention on her, his eyes seemed infinitely deeper, less compromising.

Close up and with a clearer head, she thought he was older than she'd first reasoned. Perhaps he was in his thirties. He had the look of a weary soul, hardened to the point of not being moved in the slightest by her beauty.

Charlotte knew she was beautiful. Men told her often enough. They gave her special treatment. With a well-placed smile or a modest dip of her eyes, she could get anything she desired from them.

But she didn't think it would work on him.

"'Tis an art," she told him, holding up her shield of pride.

"An art that's going to get you tossed into jail. First though, tell me. Where are we? What year is it?"

"What?" She laughed at him. Was he mad?

Before she had a chance to respond, he snatched the ring and the watches right from her hand.

"What do you think you're doing?" she demanded.

"Evidence," he told her impassively and shoved the trinkets into a tight pocket in the seat of his trousers.

He quite boldly took her by the upper arm and started north. He stopped an instant later. "Where are we? Where's the nearest precinct?"

She eyed him. "The nearest what?"

"Police station."

She blinked. "Where are you from, Sir? You do not dress like anyone in England." She made the mistake again of dipping her gaze to his fine form donned in all black. His coat was made of some kind of hide. It was cut and sewn intricately to accentuate his body's masterful perfection, pulled tight around his upper arms.

"England?" he asked, the color draining from his face. "No. This isn't real. This isn't real."

"What in the world are you saying? What isn't real?"

"You! All this!" He let her go and held out his arms, stretching them forward.

"I'm real," she insisted. "You are the one who is dressed so oddly. What kind of breeches are you wearing? They...ehm...they appear to be made of one piece of heavy fabric, and they fit...well."

"Look, Lady—"

"Charlotte," she supplied with a well-practiced smile she almost instinctively gave him. "Lady Charlotte."

He didn't appear to be affected.

She looked around. If she ran away when he didn't expect it, she could make it through the alleyway between the butcher and the mill. She could—

"Don't even think about it," he growled close to her ear and took hold of her arm again. "I'm not letting you go anywhere until I get my belongings back."

She insisted she didn't have them and then kicked him in the shin. As expected, he let her go and almost went down on one knee, gripping his shin.

She lifted her skirts and took off running. She almost made it to the alleyway when his fingers clamped shut around her wrist. She spun around swinging her free hand. "How dare you continue to put your hands on me!"

With little effort, he grabbed her other wrist and put both hands behind her back.

"Let me go!" she shouted at him. No one had ever held her so. "You jackal!" She saw a couple passing by and screamed out, "Help! Someone help me!"

They gaped at the brute manhandling her and hurried away. She shouted again when more people happened by. Soon, a crowd gathered.

"I need a policeman," the man holding her called out. "This woman has my belongings. She may have robbed some of you, as well."

People began to murmur about it and check their pockets.

Charlotte knew that at any moment the people she robbed would call out—so she did first. "He is deceiving you! He robbed you. I saw him. When I confronted him, he put his hands on me."

Some of the people began hurrying away, hopefully to find the constable.

"You are going to regret meeting me, Stranger," she promised on a warning whisper.

"I already do," he replied succinctly.

"Look!" someone called out. "The others have returned with the constable. He'll get to the bottom of it."

Charlotte quickly thought of the death of her childhood cat, Ezzie, to bring tears to her eyes. She thought of every sad thing she could until tears streamed down her face.

"What's the meaning of this?" the constable shouted. "Young man, get your hands off her this instant."

"Officer," her captor began then paused, looked a bit green, and then corrected, still not letting her go. "Constable. I saw her—"

"He is lying," Charlotte wept. "I saw him picking goods from people's pockets. When I stopped him, he made advances toward me. When I refused, he said he was going to ruin me."

"Nice try," the stranger said in a low, menacing tone.

"I can prove it, Constable," she cried. "He has the things he robbed in his pocket."

"Empty your pockets, Sir," the constable commanded with his chubby cheeks burning red.

"You're joking," the stranger drawled in his emotionless accent. "This whole thing is a joke, right?"

"Empty your pockets," the constable told him again.

Charlotte turned her head and looked at the handsome stranger, for he was handsome in a dark, brooding, dangerous way. She smiled, slightly, so the constable wouldn't see. "He is not *joking*."

The man buried his hand in his back pocket. "*She* stole this stuff. Not me. I took them from her as evidence."

"All right," grumbled the constable, seeing the two watches. "I have seen enough." He put his hands around the stranger's wrists and pulled him forward. "You are coming with me."

"What?" the man gaped. "You believe her?"

"I will be the one asking questions from now on," said the constable, pulling him away.

The stranger let himself be tugged. He was bigger and taller than the constable, but he didn't resist. Instead, he turned one last time to pin Charlotte with a glare that promised retribution.

She looked away first, feeling chilled to the bone. Who was he? Though he looked like he could very well be an outlaw, she didn't think he was. He seemed simpleminded. Pity.

Preston would never believe what happened. That ruby ring would have made him proud of her. After all, she had to fall into a man's arms to get it. She had *lost her balance* and dragged herself down her victim's arm, taking his ring with her. There was a flair to it, of course. Something Miss Amanda Beasley, Preston's latest apprentice hadn't learned yet. Charlotte doubted she ever would.

Preston Bristol III, Viscount of Sutton, was Charlotte's mentor when it came to lifting and all things rebellious and defiant. Preston began his defiance by fighting the Whigs, the political faction in the majority since George of Hanover became king. Most were Protestant, though Preston didn't care about religion. He was a Tory—the other side of the faction, in favor of Catholic Stuart kings—in name only. He needed someone to hate and the powerful, dominating Whigs were perfect.

Charlotte didn't care who Preston hated. It was who he loved that drove her. Though, her drive was wearing thin of late.

He'd found her waiting outside her father's courthouse when she was just eleven. She'd worn her finest dress and ribbons in her hair. And she thought no one saw her when she lifted a small, silver box of powder from an old man in robes.

But Preston had seen her. He had been just a few years older than she and impressed with her skill. He met her at the courthouse every second and third day of the week from then on. They became quick, close friends. Quick, *secret* friends. Her father hadn't known how close until her name began to circulate in the courts. Petty crimes for which her father called in favors to other judges to sweep away.

She and Preston had never been intimate, but she'd fallen in love with him and the life he promised her when she was fourteen and never looked back. Not even when Lord Benjamin Adere asked for her in marriage last year and her father agreed without speaking to her about it.

Sadly for her betrothed, but fortunate for her, he died three months before their marriage. Dr. Lewis had said it was old age.

Since then, she had refused a dozen offers from noblemen with various titles. She wanted to marry the man who knew her better than anyone else. Preston. It wasn't always easy to convince her father to trust her to her own freedom. Though he always had before. When she was a child and it was most dangerous for her, when her mother had chosen the attentions of other men over her daughter.

She ground her teeth as she neared her four-wheel carriage and her driver. She hated thinking of her parents and her lonely childhood. These thoughts served no purpose other than to slip their icy tendrils around her heart make her angry. Make her hate.

"Take me home, Henry," she said, barely looking up at him in his seat where he waited for her. No need to let him see her tears. She cursed them as she gave them one more swipe with her gloved fingers.

"Aye, my lady." He waited until she opened the hinged door

and stepped inside. After she knocked on the panel in front of her, he tapped the horses on the flanks and made a sound with his mouth.

The carriage moved forward with a slight, sudden dip behind her. She waited to see if Henry stopped to see to the wheels. When the carriage continued on, she relaxed and pulled the pins from her hat that was hitting the roof of the carriage.

She leaned back against the cushioned bench and closed her eyes. She wished the ride home was longer. One of them might be there. Her parents. At home. Marriage to some dull noble was almost a temptation to be free of her parents. She'd actually let herself be promised to Lord Benjamin Adere to get away from them and stop living her days in anger. In the end, though, her betrothed had died. She couldn't bring herself to do it again unless it was to Preston. But he hadn't asked. Half the men who offered for her were old and fat, with red noses from too much drinking. The other half were young, pampered, high-wigged dullards who didn't care for conversation with her. Too busy were they singing accolades to her to learn anything substantial about her. She had no patience for any of them anymore.

What did the stranger think of her? He hadn't fallen at her feet when she smiled at him. What did he think she took from him? When the constable carted him off, her captor looked at her with determination sparking his gaze. Determination to make her pay.

Who was he? Why were his clothes and his speech so different than hers and everyone else's?

She must admit, she liked both. His clothes fit well and had drawn her eyes to parts of his body that made her blush. His derriere to name one. His trousers were fastened around his waist with a button and a strange silver clasp at the top of tiny silver teeth. She didn't think about the front and the way it had flattered the swell between his legs. His speech was slow, low, and sensual. The more she thought of him, the more she couldn't stop thinking of him.

Well, he was the constable's problem now. She smiled and patted her drooping curls. Standing before the justice of the peace would serve him well. Just as long as it wasn't her standing there.

She'd come all the way to Beddington, along the border of Croydon, where she lived, and Sutton, just in case she got caught. Today's stranger would likely be taken to the Sutton justice of the peace.

She decided she'd stop home for a few things and then ride her horse to Hayward House in Sutton. Preston was sure to be there. She wondered if Amanda Beasley would be there.

She had no right to say a word. Preston wasn't hers. Still, she didn't like it.

The carriage stopped. She plucked her hat off the bench and pushed opened the door. She stepped out into the sun, carrying her hat in her hand. It was good for riding and keeping her hair out of her eyes.

She walked to the house and thanked Old John when he opened the door for her.

"Are they at home?" she asked her family's long-time butler.

"Your father is in the library, Lady Charlotte."

"And Mother?" she added, stepping past him into the large foyer.

He shrugged his bony shoulders and shut the door. "She left this morning. She did not inform me as to where she was going."

"Well, don't tell Father I'm here. I'm going back out."

"Would you care to tell me where you are going, my lady?"

"To Sutton. But, John, you shall not tell my father that either, hmm?"

"If that is your wish."

"That is what I wish." She smiled at him, then headed up the stairs. She knew he would do as she asked. He always did. All the servants in the house adored her, helped raise her. They would never turn her in.

She hummed a little melody and headed to her room. When she got inside, she didn't call for Anna to help her dress but bolted the door and prepared herself for the rest of the day…and possibly the night.

She trusted no one with where she went and what she did.

Like her mother, she came and went with the wind. Her parents didn't notice.

CHAPTER THREE

MICHAEL HOPPED OFF the back of the carriage and rubbed his eyes after looking up at the rich, country estate house before him. Where was he? What was going on? The constable had been no help. When Michael asked, he was accused of drinking. Michael wished he had been.

None of this was real. It couldn't be. He must have stumbled onto the set of a huge movie lot. He was dreaming. Or dead. Something.

But everything looked real, sounded real, smelled real. They'd traveled a good twenty minutes to get here. No lot on any set was that big.

He wanted answers and he wouldn't get them in jail, so, when he saw Lady Charlotte Whimsey, for she was hard to miss even in a crowd, hurrying toward a horse-drawn carriage, he escaped the actor playing the constable and stepped up onto the back of the coach and hitched a ride to wherever she was going.

He wanted the things she'd stolen from him. His gun, his badge, and phone, and his wallet. She either had them or she would know who did. She was a skilled pickpocket and an even better liar, but he would get the truth from her, right after he got back his gun.

This must be where she lived. With her husband?

He rubbed his jaw. He needed time to think things through in his head. Nothing was right. Nothing made sense. He looked around and surveyed the area. There were gardens and trees surrounding the house. He would go sit for a minute and think about what to do next.

He assumed, while he hurried for the safety of cover, that someone wanted him to believe he was back in historic England. But why would anyone go through all the trouble? He must have been hurt, maybe shot. That was it. He was lying in a hospital bed somewhere dying…or recovering. This was all a hallucination. It would end as soon as he woke up or died.

In the meantime, there would be no baseball, no movies. There were no phones, or internet, or over-the-counter pain medicine.

He rubbed his scruffy face. Were there razors?

He sighed through his grinding jaw. Why would someone do this to him? Who was Mr. Green and where was he now?

Hell, the sun was shining, and bees were perched on flowers that scented the air. It all felt so real.

He heard a sound and looked to see the heavy wooden front door opening and Charlotte Whimsey stepping out. She went to the stable on the right side of the house. Should he follow her?

She still wore her riding gown and her hat was back on her head but now she carried a large satchel with her. He watched her disappear into the stable. He was about to step out of his hiding place and go after her, but she suddenly barreled out of the structure on a white and brown horse. She sat sidesaddle but she still traveled with speed. He knew how to ride, having taken lessons since he was eight and his best friend Richie Nolan had signed up for lessons, but he wouldn't catch up and he had no idea of where he was going. Best to remain here and wait for her to return instead of getting lost.

He eyed the stable. Another day, if God forbid, he was still here.

"May I help you, Sir?" someone called out.

Michael looked toward the house. An older man with gray hair stood in the large doorway waiting for his response. What was he to say? He guessed the truth was best.

"I'm afraid I'm lost."

"Where do you want to be?" the old man called out.

Michael almost smiled. Poor guy would never believe him. But *now* what was he supposed to say?

"No, I mean, I'm really lost. I was…beaten up last night by two guys. They must have knocked me out good, because I woke up some ways away from here, barely remembering anything."

He'd been around liars long enough to learn a little from them.

It seemed he didn't have to convince the old man because another older man, this one decidedly larger, called to the one at the door and then came forward.

"What's this?" he asked in a loud voice, peeping his head out the door.

He had a head of pure white hair, tied back at the nape by a black ribbon. Was it…George Washington?

"This gentleman is lost, my lord," the first man told him. "He was beaten by thugs and remembers little."

The lord nearly pushed him out of the way and moved in front of the doorway. "Come in, young man! Come in! Let me have a look at you, then I will send for a physician and have a meal prepared for you. What did you say you were called?"

Michael wasn't about to refuse. He felt like hell. "Michael Pendridge. Thank you. I could use something to eat." He rubbed his flat belly and went to the door.

The white-haired man's eyes opened wider, giving Michael a closer look.

He appeared to be in his early fifties. He was dressed well in flowing gold and scarlet robes. He was roughly five feet ten inches tall, two hundred pounds. Husband or father? Michael wondered.

"So, where am I?" He asked the most pressing question on his mind as he followed the men inside. The place looked like a palace inside, with antique furniture, paintings, and ornate lampstands scattered throughout. Props, Michael told himself.

George Washington's double went as white as his hair. "Ah, forgive John for not introducing me." The lord of the house threw an angry look John's way, to which John bustled in his black coat.

"I'm the Duke of Croydon, Judge Richard Whimsey of the High Court. You are in my home, Croydon House."

Judge? Duke of Croydon? Did the judge have any clue that the beautiful lady living under his roof was a common thief?

"Where's Croydon?" Michael asked, believing more and more that he was on an elaborate movie set.

The duke set his curious sable eyes on him—the same color of the woman's eyes. "England. Ehm, where did you say you were from?"

Michael didn't know whether to laugh or hold on to something to keep from falling over. England? Not just a movie set with people speaking in British accents? Impossible.

"Look, I get it. It's funny. I'm sure whosever idea this was is having a good laugh, but it's played out and is over now. Okay?"

Both men gaped at him as if he just sprouted horns. "What?" asked the duke. "Mr. Pendridge, come to my sitting room and have a seat. You need to rest. John, send for the doctor."

"I'm not sick or delusional," Michael argued, following him. But for the first time in his twenty-nine years, he felt like he needed to sit down. The duke was lying, of course. He knew what was going on. "I'm going to have you all thrown in jail if this doesn't stop now."

The duke produced a cloth from his robes and patted his forehead with it. "What has my daughter done now? John!" he barked an instant later. "Forget the doctor!"

Okay. She was his daughter. "I don't care about your daughter, Duke," Michael said, entering the sitting room with him. "Call this off now and I'll forget I ever met her." He probably wouldn't forget her. He could easily find out her real name and find her.

"Call what off? What are you saying? Where are you from? I have never heard your inflections."

Michael ignored his questions and gave him a warning glare. He threw one to John when he reappeared. "There is a gentleman at the door for you, my lord."

"Another one?" the duke remarked, excused himself, and left the room with the butler.

Michael looked around. Everything looked old, and yet, new. It was a comfortable room but there were things missing. Things like photos in frames, and electrical outlets. He searched for any camera or mics but found nothing. Not even dust.

The duke returned several minutes later and waited quietly while Michael rose up from his knees and palms in his search for any outlets.

"Did you find what you were looking for?" the duke asked him.

"No," Michael replied. Then he countered, "Something important? You look a little green."

"'Tis nothing."

"You said we were in England."

"That's correct."

"You're lying. How can I be in England when I was in New York thirty minutes ago?"

"*New* York?"

"That's right. You asked me where I was from. That's where. New York."

The duke's eyes widened. "You traveled here from the new world in thirty minutes?"

Michael narrowed his eyes on him. "New world?" Where had he heard that phrase before? "What—why are you all dressed like people from the past? Is this one of those historical movies?"

"Movies?" the duke asked, leading him gently to a chair.

"What year is this supposed to be?" Michael heard the panic in his own voice and took a seat. He caught the duke motion to John, probably to override the last order and get the doctor.

"'Tis seventeen hundred and twenty-four," the duke said softly.

"Okay," Michael said, holding up his hands. "I'm done playing along. I want my gun and badge back. For stealing those, I'll make sure your daughter goes to prison."

"Mr. Pendridge," the duke said as he smiled, though his color had not returned. "If you would calm down I could—"

"It's *Detective* Pendridge. But I think you already know that."

"Detective," the duke intoned, wiped his brow again, and accepted a cup from another servant dressed in brown and gray.

"That's right. You know, an investigator. Your daughter robbed me of my gun and badge this morning. She's a thief and I may begin a case against her. She robbed some people and then pinned the blame on me."

He reached for the cup being served to him. His eyes were quick enough to note John's slight smile when he heard about the lady. So then, the butler, or doorman, or whatever he was in this movie, was aware of what she was capable of and he approved.

"Are you telling me you don't know about your daughter's behavior?" He sniffed the cup. Wine. He needed it.

"That's correct. Have you gone to the local magistrate?"

Michael shook his head. He hadn't. He didn't know the laws here.

"Are *you* telling *me*," her father asked slowly with a methodical look, "that you don't know where you are or what the year is and yet you claim my daughter stole your gun and badge?"

Yeah, that sounded bad, Michael had to admit. He leaned forward in his chair and guzzled his wine. What was he supposed to do now? His instincts weren't honed for this. It was as if there were a gigantic joke going on and everyone was in on it but Michael. He put his head in his hands.

"All right, Pendridge," the duke said, seeming to take pity on him. "I will tell you this. There was a man at my door earlier, who claims to have seen my daughter this morning at a square near Sutton stealing from some gentlemen's pockets. A man in the crowd tried to stop her but she escaped."

Michael nodded and looked around again, thinking it no coincidence that things were working out in his favor.

"You were telling the truth."

"That's right," Michael muttered.

"Why do you not tell me where in the colonies you came from?"

"You wouldn't believe me," Michael groaned into his hands. "It's not called the colonies anymore. When I was there," he said, looking up from his hands, "thirty minutes ago, the year was—" why was he confessing? Why was he speaking as if this were real? He wanted to see the duke's reaction. Also, he had to tell someone.

"—two thousand and nineteen."

For a minute, the duke appeared to stop breathing. "You came from the future?"

"Yes," Michael confirmed.

"You understand all this is difficult to believe." The duke called for more wine.

Michael held up his empty cup. "What do you think it's like for me?" he asked.

"You sound mad," the judge told him.

"I wonder it myself," Michael admitted.

"You must keep this to yourself. Tell no one else."

"Why?" Michael asked, fixing his unblinking gaze on the judge while Whimsey dismissed all the servants but John.

The two of them sat opposite each other before a large fireplace. John the butler stood behind his lord's chair.

"People will not understand. They will think you demon possessed or mad."

"Oh, right." He wasn't sure at this point that he wasn't either one.

"But you may tell me. Let's hear your story," the duke allowed. "Start at the beginning."

Michael told him about his phone call from Mr. Green to go

to some lawyer's office to pick something up that was bequeathed to him by a distant aunt and would help aid in a missing person's case. "Well, I get there and this Mr. Green hands me an old, worn down, blackened brooch. I ran my finger over it." He remembered the strange light, the feeling of having no control over his thoughts. "Pendragon. That was the word on the brooch. I said it and then I was here."

"You spoke the name Pendragon and then you were here," the duke echoed.

"And he rubbed the brooch," John added.

The duke held up his finger and looked at Michael, not the butler. "Ah, but more important is the name Pendragon."

"You believe me?" Michael asked, astounded. He realized he needed someone to believe him.

"I have my own reasons why I believe you." the duke said in a mild tone. "For you, 'tis real, whether it truly is or is not."

"It's real," Michael told him in earnest. "I'm telling you the truth. I…uh…understand that it's hard for you to believe this crazy story. It's hard for me to believe and it's happening to me. I'm a New York City detective. I've been with the police force for eleven years."

The duke whispered, "An officer of the law."

"Yeah," Michael said and continued. "This morning, I woke up in the twenty-first century. I showered—you don't have showers here, do you?"

"You mean rain showers? Of course—"

"No," Michael said with disgust. "I'm not a plumber, but there are pipes behind the walls in my bathroom, with a showerhead, or a nozzle that comes out of it." He lifted his hand over his head to demonstrate. "You turn a switch and water comes out and you have a shower."

"Fascinating."

Michael didn't know what the duke thought was so enthralling, a shower or that Michael had come up with it.

"I touched some…I don't know…magic piece of jewelry and

supposedly came back in time almost three hundred years. I was at some square. Maybe I woke up there, but I don't remember that. Maybe I was drugged, brought to England and dumped on the streets. There was a crowd—all dressed like—do you have more wine, whiskey maybe?"

The duke nodded and turned to John. "More wine for our guest."

Michael was grateful and continued. "I saw your daughter pickpocketing some people. I realized my things were gone, too."

"Pickpocketing," her father whispered somberly. "John, is she home?"

"No, my lord. She left."

"Left? Where did she go?"

John shook his head. "You know she does not tell me where she goes."

"Yes," her father agreed, "because she is out being a criminal." He set his gaze on Michael. "I cannot protect her forever."

Michael's gaze hardened on him. "You should not have protected her the first time."

"Aye, you are correct. I have many regrets. But…" he paused to take in a deep breath, "we were discussing you. Go on."

"That's it. I told you everything."

"Well," the judge narrowed his eyes and squeezed his chin between his index finger and thumb, "from what you have told me, I believe this Mr. Green is a sort of wizard. It would seem he sent you here to find someone."

"Then you do believe me," Michael said, holding his cup up to have it refilled.

"Your story is compelling. I like a good mystery," the duke told him, receiving more wine in his cup, as well. "For instance, *Detective*, do you know who carries the name Pendragon?"

Michael thought about it for a minute. His head was mostly clear. The wine wasn't overly strong.

"The Excalibur guy?"

The duke smiled. "King Arthur, aye. King Arthur *Pendrag-*

on. 'Tis a Cornish surname with many variations in the spelling. Pendridge is one of them."

Michael sipped his wine. He wanted to make it last. He had a feeling he was going to need it. "What are you saying?"

"I'm saying, Investigator, I believe you are a Pendragon, perhaps even an heir."

$$\text{---} \blacklozenge \cdots \bullet \quad \bullet \cdots \blacklozenge \text{---}$$

CHAPTER FOUR

CHARLOTTE RODE THROUGH Sutton, alone, with a knife in each boot and four hidden in other places on her body. Pistols were too big and clumsy to use. She preferred blades. The deadliest being her tongue. The stranger learned that today when he interfered with her work.

She could have stabbed him but there was something so dangerous and mesmerizing about him. He seemed to have experienced much in his life. His eyes, though quick and perhaps once brilliant like lightning across the night sky, were void of fire and sunken in. He looked as if he could use a few good nights of sleep. She wished him well in her mind and also prayed to stop thinking about him.

She didn't want to stab anyone. Things had become so out of control in the past year. She didn't know how to stop the whirlwind, but she was determined to try.

It had begun with Preston and doing everything to make him happy. Things had to change. There was too much at stake. She wanted too much. A family. A sense of belonging. Preston promised to give them to her. She would do anything for him because she would do anything for a family.

She rode past beautiful springs and walnut trees growing around a giant pond filled with trout. Sutton was her favorite place on earth, with forests and farmlands, and homes of brick and wood.

She continued on to the scenic village with its beautiful cathedral church reaching up toward heaven.

She wanted to live here, near the trees by the pond. Or near Rosie.

She quickened her horse's pace, eager to reach Preston. She didn't slow again until she arrived at Hayward House, Preston's elaborately built hideaway for his men. She slid out of her sidesaddle and handed her horse off to Roddy, the stable boy.

"The stable is full, m'lady," Roddy announced, his already ruddy cheeks turning redder when he lifted his gaze from the ground and looked at her. "I can leave him outside with the two carriages. I will see to him personally."

She handed him two pence and a grateful smile. "My thanks, dear Roddy," she said and then left him for the house. She knew everyone would be here. They hadn't left for the last sennight. They were mostly the men who worked for Preston in some form or capacity. Some were moneykeepers (accountants,) some lawyers. Some were less law-abiding, from pickers to Horsemen. None of their wives were in attendance, though there were plenty of females wandering about, drinking and giggling.

When Charlotte reached the front door, she heard a sound coming from around the house. She followed it, recognizing the voice of her dear Preston.

She saw him speaking to Sebastian Alexander, Baron of Surrey. Sebastian was a dark-haired, handsome young devil with a silver tongue, and one of Preston's wealthy friends. Preston had many, and many of them broke the law. Most judges who knew Preston took bribes. Not all did, though. Her father didn't.

"The day has just become brighter," sang dashing Sebastian when he saw her.

Charlotte had to admit Sebastian was as beautiful as all the ladies gushed about. His hair fell in loose waves to his shoulders. The outer edges of his large, green eyes turned up, giving him a most sultry look. His smile was wide, his teeth, straight and almost white.

Aye, he was pleasing to the eyes, but he was her friend, and nothing more.

She quirked her mouth at him, and then at Preston. Had he nothing to say?

"I did not think you were coming," Preston told her with an even slighter smile than her own.

"Oh?" She cocked her brow at him then glanced around. "Whom did you invite when you thought I was not coming?"

Sebastian chuckled and shook his head at his friend. "You stumbled straight into that one, Sutton."

Preston angled his masterfully groomed blond head to sneer at Sebastian. "I did not stumble." He turned to Charlotte next with a glint in his blue eyes. "And your attendance had no effect on my invitation list, my dear Charlotte. You were and always will be first on the list." He let his smile shine full force on her.

She let him take her hand and bring her knuckles to his lips. Sebastian's silver tongue had nothing on Preston's. It's what had landed her in front of more justices of the peace than she cared to remember.

"I lifted a hefty ruby ring for you today," she told Preston. "But I was stopped by a man in strange attire. He accused me of robbing him. I did not. He robbed me, though. He took the ring and two watches!"

Preston's face grew bright red with leashed fury. "Where is he? I shall get the ring back!"

"He's at a justice of the peace by now. There was a constable—I did not get into trouble, Preston," she added quickly when he threw up his hands. "He did."

"The fewer constables crossing our paths, the better, Charlotte."

"This man took hold of me three times!" she snapped at him. She didn't look at Sebastian when he slipped away. "*Thankfully*, someone found a constable, else who knows what the man would have done next!"

"Forgive me," he repented when she pouted.

"What are you doing out here anyway?" She didn't want to ruin the rest of her day by thinking about the bold, pesky stranger from this morning.

"Lord John Eddren, Duke of Crawley, is traveling to London in a sennight," Preston told her. "Sebastian has his route. He wants to stop his carriage and rob him."

"And what did you tell him?" Charlotte asked, making her way toward the house.

"I told him to do what he wants. I have friends in Cheam who will keep him out of jail if he gets caught."

They stepped into the huge mansion, much larger than Bristol Manor, the house left to Preston by his parents, who died in a hunting accident six years ago. Preston took the deaths well, despite being only eighteen when he lost them and on his own.

He hadn't given up even on the hardest days when it seemed he fought his Tory fight alone. He rose to power by robbing for the poor and then running the largest criminal alliance in southern London.

"Charlie! So good to see you," said a woman in a gray, quilted riding suit. Black curls peeked out from beneath her gray, feathered cap.

Charlotte hated being called Charlie. None of her closer friends called her anything but Charlotte, and that was how she liked it.

"Maddie," she responded in kind to the Earl of Mitcham's daughter, Lady Madeline Evans. "So good to see *you*. We must get together."

Before Maddie could make any plans, Charlotte hurried off into the crowd. She lost Preston and saw Amanda—worse, she saw Amanda standing with her closest friends.

She stopped and, all at once, she felt her hopes and dreams floating away on a cascade of pale blond curls draping Amanda's shoulder.

Charlotte took a deep breath and put on her most practiced smile. "Amanda," she greeted, holding out her gloved hands.

"Charlotte!" Amanda's cornflower blue eyes grew as wide as any wild deer. "I thought you weren't coming!"

A pang in her chest. A hook of regret in her insides. "Aye, so Preston mentioned," she muttered. She bit down on her tongue until she tasted blood. "Well," she said, smoothing out her riding coat. "I was not planning on staying. I only stopped by to tell Preston about something."

"Oh, he just stepped outside with Sebastian. But I'm sure he will come running right back to me when he's through. Why do you not wait for him?"

"No, thank you. I saw him already." Charlotte kept her smile intact and turned it on her friends. She'd never let them see how their betrayal hurt her. It was better to see who her truest friends were, and Sophie and Eloise were no longer them.

She spun around on her heel. She wanted to leave. She didn't think anything could be worse than home. Perhaps she was wrong. Being here at Preston's with Amanda clearly spending her time with him was worse. Amanda's words followed her. *I'm sure he will come running right back to me.* Ugh. She'd like to give Amanda a bruised eye or maybe a swollen lip.

She thought she heard Sophie call out to her, but she didn't respond.

And to think of all she'd done for Preston! How many times she had gotten him out of trouble?

"Leaving so soon?"

She looked up and found Sebastian standing in front of her, blocking her path.

"Sebastian, I'm in a foul mood. Move out of the way."

"I love it when you're angry." He moved a bit closer and bent to inhale her hair. "Come to my bed and punish me."

She smiled. Would he never stop trying to get her to his bed? She produced one of her knives and held it to his groin. "What will you do to me in your bed after I slice your scrotum from your body?"

He closed his eyes and his smile faded. He stepped out of her way. "You are a savage bitch, Char."

"Always the smooth-talker, Sebastian." She smiled at him. She didn't mean it. None of her smiles were ever genuine. She'd just perfected them to make others think they were.

She slipped her knife back into its hiding place in a pocket of her riding skirts and left the house. She didn't look for Preston. She'd go home and lock herself away in her room and think about what a fool she was to care for a cad who promised her everything and meant nothing.

She found Roddy with her horse and thanked him for his care before she shoved her boot in the stirrup and hoisted herself up into the leather sidesaddle.

Why was she still wasting her time waiting for Preston to make a move in her life? Hadn't they known each other long enough for him to know if he wanted to marry her or not? He led her on while he entertained himself with other women like Amanda. Charlotte forgave him every time because, well, she wasn't actually anything but a friend to him, so she had no right to be jealous.

She cursed him for making her go home alone. She was thankful that the days were still a bit long. It wasn't that she was overly frightened of traveling in the dark. She'd been in dangerous spots before, but she had rarely been alone. It didn't matter. She couldn't stay here another minute. If Preston wanted her, he needed to prove it and come for her.

She put him out of her mind on the way home. Amanda and Sebastian, as well. She wasn't angry with the willful baron. He teased her often. He was never serious about anything. Nothing at all ever ruffled him. He wanted her because he knew he couldn't have her, that was all. He might be extremely handsome, but Charlotte pitied the woman who would become his wife. If there was such a woman.

She thought about her friend Rosie and Rosie's family just outside of Bromley. Rosie had once been her nurse, but she'd happened upon Charlotte's mother locked in the embrace of her then lover, Lord Roger Suthers, Viscount of Charlotte-Did-Not-Care. To keep her indiscretion quiet, Lady Lizette Whimsey sent Rosie away. Charlotte tracked her down when she grew older and had been helping her live. She could have brought Rosie money tomorrow if she still had those pocket watches. In a way though, she was glad she didn't have the ring to give to Preston.

By the time she reached the house, it was time for supper. She hoped her father was still busy and her mother was not home.

Old John wasn't at the door. Odd. "John?" She unpinned her riding hat and tossed it onto a chair in the foyer.

Her father peeped his head out of the dining hall entryway. "In here, Charlotte. Please, come inside. 'Tis urgent."

Heart pounding, she hurried to the dining hall half-expecting to see poor John lying on the floor. Instead, she saw her father heading back to his chair, John standing behind it, and…and…no, it couldn't be.

"Charlotte, dear," her father said, taking his seat. "May I introduce Detective Michael Pendridge. He is an investigator."

For the first time in her life, she was at a loss for words. She couldn't swallow, or think, or move. Investigator? How had he found her? What had he told her father? Had he told him anything?

"I believe you met him this morning," her father continued.

Instinctively, she looked at Old John, as the only comfort she knew in the hall came from him. She tried to slow her heart.

So then, the knave had spoken of her to her father. She could only imagine.

"Aye, we did *meet*." She turned her murderous gaze on the investigator. How much trouble was she in? He hadn't seen her picking pockets. He had no proof except that which proved *he* was the thief! "What brings you here?"

He appeared unconcerned about her rapid breath and flushed cheeks.

"You did, Lady Charlotte," he said.

Thank God for John, who pulled out a seat at the table for her. She wouldn't stay long. Just long enough to breathe.

"After I escaped the constable," he said without any fear of consequence from her family. "I saw you get into your carriage and I hopped on the back."

The bump on the road. She'd felt it! It was him! He'd traveled home with her all that time! Well, he'd certainly had the last laugh so far, hadn't he?

She stood up, revived.

"Father, I will speak with you after this scoundrel leaves."

"He is not leaving, girl."

Her heart dropped into her belly. She bit her lip. This wasn't happening. Since when did her father take in vagrants? "What do you mean he is not leaving?"

"Not until he can find another place to stay. He has traveled from afar."

She didn't care if he came from the moon. "Well then," she said curtly to her father, "he can keep you company."

"He has been doing just that for the last three hours now," her father informed her. "Telling me interesting stories."

"I have no doubt," she seethed, but managed a smile. "He told the constable interesting stories this morning as well. The wise constable did not believe him."

"The constable fell for your fake tears," her father's guest countered without bothering to smile. "As I'm sure many men do."

She hated him for being right. Her father knew it, too.

"Now, as I told your father…" He finally turned to look at her fully. "I want what you stole from me."

Not this nonsense again. "I have nothing of yours as I told you and the constable." She turned to her father. "I knew you cared little for me, Father, but to believe a stranger over me is—"

"A witness came to the door, Charlotte," her father interrupted her. "Now, sit down. There are things we need to discuss."

A witness. Did this witness ride on the other side of her carriage when she came home? She didn't ask her father. He wasn't in a humorous mood. "Will you not allow me to change out of my riding suit first?"

"So you can run away?" her father put to her, sounding as if he cared.

"Of course you understand," came the cool, deep voice of Investigator Pendridge, "if she doesn't return, I will have to hold you responsible, my lord."

"Of course," her father agreed. He agreed!

"I will not run away," she vowed in a low, trembling voice. She wanted to pluck one of her knives from her boots and fling it at Pendridge.

"Don't be long," he warned and then returned to his cup.

She practically growled and stormed away. She moved slowly toward the stairs, and even slower up them. How dare he tell her not to be long! Was her father afraid of him? What was a detective anyway? What damage could he do to her family? She might have to be pleasant to him for her father's sake, though she owed her father nothing. She didn't often do things for his sake, but Detective Michael Pendridge was here because of her.

She would try to be friendlier and perhaps do something with all this hair.

With the help of her maid, Anna, Charlotte changed into a shift with ruffled sleeves, small panniers, or hoops, and open-fronted stays of olive green. The stays were pulled tight, drawing back her shoulders and straightening her spine. She hated them so tight, but it accentuated her womanly shape and helped her get what she wanted. She pulled on petticoats and finally a gown of pale green.

Anna then quickly pinned up her thick waves by piling them on top of her head. She could only find ten pins, but she promised they would hold, and shoved them into strategic places and secured her beaded cameo around her neck.

Charlotte left her room sometime later, feeling more confident than before. She hoped both men were asleep, but if they weren't, she would handle them.

When she walked into the dining hall, her father stood up and smiled. His guest did the first, but not the second, though his sapphire gaze lingered on her before dropping back to the table.

"You are enchanting, my dear," her father admired with an indulgent smile.

John pulled out her chair, one in which she rarely sat these days. She sat but refused a plate of food and touched her hand to her belly beneath her taut stays.

She glared at Detective Pendridge instead. "I know what you are thinking—"

"Oh?" he asked, ready for her. "If it's that you took your sweet time testing not only your father's patience, but mine, as well. You're right."

In the firelight of the dining hall, there was something devastatingly beautiful about him. Was it the tilt of his head that shadowed his piercing eyes beneath his brow? The resolute cut of his jaw that belied his mask of indifference? He reminded her of a wolf, ready to bite off her hand if she put it too close.

"I wanted to look presentable," she defended.

"It doesn't take forty minutes for you to look the way you do."

"What is that supposed to mean?" she bristled.

As if to mock her, a lock of her hair escaped its pin and tumbled down her face.

She saw the investigator's eyes spark on her before she swiped the lock away.

"What I meant was…" He did his best to appear impassive, but the husky resonance of his voice exposed him. "…you're just as, um…you look fine without all the maintenance."

"Maintenance?" She relaxed her gaze on him and crooked her mouth. He certainly did not possess a silver tongue.

The investigator looked at her father and then at her again. "Attention. Upkeep."

"I see." So then, he did think she "looked fine". He hid it well.

"Do I call you Detective?"

"Call me whatever you want," he replied impassively and finished the last of his food.

"Ah, Detective, don't leave it open to me. You may not like what I come up with at times."

He glanced at her and she thought the power in his gaze was captivating.

"I can take it," he assured her. "Just watch out for retribution when it comes."

Her father laughed nervously, and the investigator winked at him again. Whatever it was meant to convey, it appeared to calm her father.

"Charlotte," her father said with authority, "you will control that tongue of yours. You are in no position to bicker."

She wanted to leave the table. She was sitting here for his benefit! But she offered her father a smile. "As you wish."

"Good," he said. "Now, I know that you are picking pockets. Do not bother to deny it. You have left me no choice. I'm sending you to your Aunt Louise in Otford."

"Father! No!" She bolted to her feet. "I will not go! I will go mad with nothing to do there!"

"Precisely," he countered. "There will be no one to rob. Now, Daughter, I have warned you."

"Aye, you have," she agreed, growing desperate. She cast her dark eyes on the detective and trembled. Another lock of hair sprang loose and bounced to her shoulder. This was his fault. Since she'd met him, he'd been nothing but trouble. "You have," she told her father calmly, breathing slowly. "And I have abused your mercy. But I will not touch another pocket. You have my word." She pulled on a ruffle along the cuff of her gown and a small hankie came out. She held it to her nose and sniffled. "Do not send me away."

"Charlie, what am I to do with you?" her father lamented. "Very well. Very well."

She looked up, her tears continuing to fall. "You will not send me away?"

"No," her father surrendered, letting out a loud sigh when she bowed her head and thanked him. "You will remain here, in the safety of your home, under the careful guard of Investigator Pendridge."

She blinked at him and let the last of her tears fall. "Pardon?"

"Yeah. Pardon?" Pendridge echoed.

"You have no place to stay while you visit," said the duke. "And I need an experienced eye to watch her."

"Watch me? What does that mean?" Charlotte demanded. "I refuse to be watched!"

"I will pay you in coin and also with a new pistol—"

"Father, you are aware that you are giving a stranger charge over me? You are giving him a pistol? You must stop this!"

"I accept," the stranger announced with a slight, triumphant smile.

She waited a moment until she could relax and unclench her jaw. "Very well." Let him think he won. Let her father think it, too. They would soon discover how wrong they were.

CHAPTER FIVE

OKAY, MICHAEL THOUGHT, his back pressed against the opposite wall, facing her room. This had gone on long enough. It had to end. He wanted to go home. Did he truly want to? For what? A gun in his mouth every morning? Memories he wished would die just like everything else in his life? Maybe being here wasn't the worst thing that could have happened.

He watched Miss Whimsey's bedroom door open. It felt as if his guts dropped to his feet.

Maybe going back to the future wasn't *that* important. He had a place to sleep at night here. And her to keep an eye on. He also had an offer from the judge to begin keeping law and order in Croydon. The duke must have decided that no one else would do it except this crazy guy. And Michael took the job.

"What do you think you are doing in front of my door?" she inquired with a stiff smile. Like all the others. A few locks of her dark hair dangled around her face.

"It's…it's, uh…the hour is late." He hoped to sound like he came from around here. Then again, it didn't really matter. He looked her over. She'd changed her clothes and wore a fresh riding habit. "Are you going out?"

Her gaze sizzled on him. "Not anymore!"

She slammed the door shut. The sound of it echoed off the walls. Michael gave the door a little smile. It opened again. She appeared a second time and gave him a dark glare.

"I do not know what you want or why you came here. Stay away from me. Leave while my father sleeps and I will not have the halls swarming with men who want to see you dead."

"I'm not leaving until you hand over my gun and badge." He realized he didn't need those things here. His gun would be useless the instant he ran out of bullets. But she didn't know that.

Her smile remained, so well-practiced was it. "I assure you, Investigator, if I had your gun, I would shoot you with it."

He wanted to smile. Were all the women in the eighteenth century this bold? Not that he believed he was in the eighteenth century. He didn't know what he believed. But he wasn't interested in Charlotte Whimsey. The last thing he needed in his life was a woman. He could use a drink though. He hadn't gone to sleep without being drunk in a long time. He doubted he'd get any sleep tonight. It was just as well. He had a feeling Miss Whimsey was going to try to leave the house without him.

He didn't really care where she went. He simply didn't want to lose her father's trust. He liked the Duke of Croydon, Judge of the High Court. Astonishingly, the duke believed him about the future and trusted him with his daughter. He was either a very good judge of character or he was a fool.

Michael appreciated having someone to tell. John the doorman/butler seemed to believe him, too. Michael had him swear he wouldn't tell Miss Whimsey. The less people who thought him crazy, the better.

But for a man who didn't consider himself crazy, here he was, standing in front of the door of the most beautiful woman he'd ever met, in her manor house in the eighteenth century. "Go to bed…my lady."

"I will not be told what to do by a man I do not even know." She took a step forward to leave the room. He reached his arm across the doorway, blocking her exit.

"Go to bed," he warned in a low voice, leaning toward her ear, "or I'll take you there myself."

For a moment, he actually thought she'd hold out. No one

ever had before. When he warned that he'd do something, he was known to do it. But he wasn't known here.

For an unnerving moment, she looked as if she would leap at his throat. But her resolve faltered when he didn't look away, and just an instant before he was about to make good on his threat and carry her to her bed, she spun on her heel and stormed away, kicking the door shut behind her.

Michael stared at the wood, a half-inch from his nose. She was a wild one. He shrugged his shoulders and sat on the floor. He knew she was going to try to leave without him. Well, not tonight, sweetheart. He doubted he'd sleep. But if he did, he wanted to make sure he blocked her path. He stretched his legs out before him, across the threshold of her door.

He realized he hadn't thought about his past or any of his partners since he got here. It was kind of nice. He felt himself relaxing. His eyelids were heavy. He sat up and leaned his back against the door. How was he so tired? Time traveling really took it out of a person. Time travel. It was all so…

CHARLOTTE PRESSED HER ear to the door. She heard a snore on the other side. No! He was asleep against her door? The rat! He was clever and she hated him for it. Pity his back would ache him in the morning for nothing. She hurried to the chest of drawers set against the east wall and pushed it aside. The small door on the other side gave her second thoughts about doing what she planned on doing. She'd never had to sneak out this way.

The tunnel had been built long before her family moved in. There were others throughout the house. Her father knew of one. Old John knew of this one and three others. There were cobwebs around the door, and it looked significantly smaller than she remembered. She'd never make it crawling on her skirts, so she changed quickly into her breeches and boots. She didn't like squeezing through small spaces and she cursed Detective Pendridge because she had to do it thanks to him. She wasn't about to be "watched" by anyone! She was a grown woman! She understood why her father assigned her a guardian. She knew she was trouble, but it was just like her father to hire someone else to handle his daughter.

Well, not this time. She took one of her lanterns and opened the door to the secret passageway. She'd been inside twice when she was a child with her cousin, Reggie. But she was much smaller then. She climbed inside and said a prayer. No insects, Lord. Just…do not…let there be…any insects. Something scurried by her! She stomped her feet and made loud noises letting all the crawlers know she was coming, and would they stay out of the way until she passed? She wanted to run but she had to control her air else she would lose it all. She couldn't let fear overtake her. Preston taught her that fear would slow her down, dull her senses, get her killed.

She thought of anything else to keep her mind off how long the passageway was and when she would breathe fresh air again. Anything like the glittering sapphire blue of Investigator Michael Pendridge's eyes, or the way they looked at her, like she affected him, and he did all he could to hide it. Or she was completely wrong and the detached nonchalance he showed her was genuine. One thing she knew for certain, her tears didn't affect him. He was probably going to hate her after this but what did she care? She'd prove to her father that this man was incompetent and unable to control her, just as Aunt Louise would be. She would only stop if her father sent her to France. Oui! That was where she wanted to be sent. Away from Preston. Away from her family. Away from Investigator Pendridge. Would her father do it? Would he let her go to France…or Italy…or anywhere but here?

Would she make it out of the passageway alive?

Finally, she smelled fresher air. It wasn't completely pleasant to the nostrils, but it was better than nothing. She hurried forward and climbed a small ladder to a door much like the one in her room. She pushed it upward and open, knowing what was on the other side. She climbed out into a shed about a half-mile from the house.

She looked around. She hadn't been here in years. She thought about what to do next. She actually wanted to be found. She would smile triumphantly. Sleep outside her door, will you? She wondered if she should try to walk back to the stables and ride to Preston's. The way things were going for her, Pendridge would track her down and tell her father where she was going and who she was seeing. Her father didn't like Preston. He knew about some of Preston's criminal activity, but he had proof of nothing. He'd likely tell all to his new friend, the investigator.

No. She had to stay away from Preston for a few days.

She disappeared into a dark corner in the shed and sat against the wall. There was nothing left to do now but get a few hours of sleep. She didn't want to walk around in the dark. Let them find her in the nearest village in the morning. If her father tried to send her to Otford, he wouldn't find her again.

She closed her eyes and smiled, satisfied in her victory.

She didn't sleep all that well, not because of her surroundings, or the sharp tool poking her in the back, but because she dreamed of Investigator Pendridge. She dreamed she was being led to the gallows in some town square. He was there, the only one who could help her, but he turned his disinterested gaze away from her and let her hang.

If her dreams would have stopped there, it would have been bad enough, but next he was in an odd-looking room with a bed. He held a sword to his throat. *Michael!* she cried out. His gaze met hers. There was no glitter in them, no…life. His hair was unkempt and his jaw was covered in dark hair.

What are you doing here? he asked.

I came to find you. Why? Why would she say such a thing?

She forced herself to wake up. She didn't want to look at him the way she was, as if she cared for him. She was happy to see sunlight streaming in through cracks in the wooden shed walls. It was morning. She would go to the town in Croydon. It was closest and likely the first place the investigator would look. She would make certain people saw her, so they'd tell anyone asking for her.

She sat up and stretched. She heard parts of her crack and pop. She pulled the remaining pins from her hair and ran her fingers through her thick waves. She didn't like wearing her breeches in daylight, but there was no choice.

She headed for the door, opened it, and fell over the body sprawled across it.

She landed in his arms on the ground. No, she thought, looking into his haunting dark blue eyes. No. He couldn't be here! Had Old John told him about the passageway in her room? Why would he?

"What are you doing here, Investigator?" she bit out, staring at him.

"I was obviously sleeping. Anyone would have seen me."

Her mouth opened into an "O" and she pushed off him. "Are you suggesting that I fell upon you on purpose? You are a fool to—"

"Are you telling me you didn't see me...me?" He looked down at himself, all tall and bulky, dressed in his black clothes.

"I was not expecting you to be lying at my door like a big oaf, blocking my path!"

He rose up on his long legs. The look he gave her warned that he'd like to throttle her. For a moment, she thought he might try. Could she fight him? She'd have seconds to do what she'd been taught...seconds before he grabbed her and used his strength to hold her down.

"Just watch where you're going next time. It's not a pleasant way to wake up."

She straightened, waiting for him to say more. He didn't. At least not about sleeping.

"What are you doing out here?" he asked her. "What are you

trying to prove?"

"I think 'tis clear. I will not stay where I am *put*. I will escape and, next time, I will not be so easily caught." She began walking the opposite way of home.

He went to the horse he had tied to a tree—one of her father's horses and untied it. He vaulted to the saddle and rode toward her.

"So you escaped," he laughed. "You've obviously been doing this for a long time. I knew not to underestimate you."

Was that a compliment? She smiled and nodded. "How did you know where to find me?"

"John told me about the passageway," he told her, keeping his horse at a slow pace beside her. "He was worried that you would never come back."

She smiled, knowing better. "He needed only look in my room to see that I did not leave for good."

"Oh?" he asked. "What would he look for that would help him know for certain?"

She shrugged her shoulders as if it meant nothing. "A bracelet my father gave me many years ago. I will never wear it, but I would never leave it behind."

"Why won't you ever wear it?"

"Did you follow me here and sleep in front of two of my doors to ask me about what I have in my bedroom?"

When he smiled and didn't answer, she continued. "Besides, 'tis you who is curious. Who are you? Where do you come from? You have not answered any of the questions I put to you so far."

"You know who I am," he told her from his saddle. "I'm Detective Michael Pendridge. I'm from…uh…York."

She stopped to rest her hands on her hips and squint her eyes at him. "You do not sound too sure. What are you doing here, Detective?"

"I was…uh…was beat up last night and left for dead. I woke up in the square. That's when I saw you."

"Hmm," she said and starting walking again.

It wasn't something she'd never heard of before. Men often got beat up. There weren't many constables to stop the attackers, or victims who wanted to prosecute them if they were caught. There wasn't any law here really. Lucky for Charlotte…and for Preston, and the rest of her friends.

"Why do you call yourself a detective and not investigator like the other investigators?"

"In York, that's what we call ourselves. Anything else?"

She looked up at him. "Now that you're here, what exactly do you mean to do?"

"About what?"

"Lawlessness."

He cut his glance to her. "You mean you."

"What?" She laughed a little. "Why would—"

"You're the only person I know here except for your father and your…what is John anyway?"

She thought about it for a moment. Old John was many things, she thought fondly. He was there for her when her father was too busy, and her mother had gone off to who knew where.

"A rat apparently," she answered, remembering that John had informed Detective Pendridge of where she was. "And a friend. To me and to my father."

"Okay then, and John, your friend. Out of the three of you, you're the only criminal. So what you're asking is what am I going to do about you?"

She felt as if smoke were coming from the top of her head. He infuriated her. She balled her hands into fists. "Since you are so clever," she said softly with a well-practiced smile. "Aye, what are your intentions with me? How long do you plan on staying here, following me?"

"I don't know. It's a nice set-up," he answered. "I'm getting paid to do nothing really. You're easy."

"Easy?" She thought about waking up this morning and thinking how clever she was to escape through a secret passageway.

But he was one step ahead of her. She grinded her teeth.

"I've had dealings with craftier, more elusive criminals than you."

"Oh." She lifted a brow at him. "I shall have to toss aside my pity for you and make you eat those words."

He chuckled. She would make him eat that, too, after she basked in the sight of him. The darker shadow of a dimple in his right cheek mesmerized her for a moment, along with the deep, throaty sound of him.

She blinked away and kept on walking.

"Where are you going?" he drawled, as if he would rather be doing anything else but this.

"Just going for a walk on this pleasant morning," she answered with a smile.

"At the pace you're walking," he informed her, "you'll need to get on my horse with me soon. I urge you to slow down."

He didn't want her to get tired and have to ride with him! Did he not want her near him? Why? Heaven forbid he got off the horse and let her ride alone. It was her father's horse, after all.

She slowed her pace anyway and looked around. She didn't know where in the blazes she was going. She was disorientated by being on foot and not in a carriage or in her saddle. She'd taken a wrong turn somewhere. Which way was the village?

He stopped speaking and Charlotte finally looked up at him. He'd removed his leather over coat and tied it to his waist. He wore a shirt that was dyed black. It fit him like skin. The sleeves were cut short and hugged his thick upper arms. He looked strong, as if he could use his fists to beat his way out of a fight.

She admonished herself for giving his arms or the rest of him any thought. He was her father's henchman. Paid to keep her whereabouts known to the duke.

He wasn't her friend. As soon as she thought she was getting comfortable with him, he reminded her of it.

"How did you do it?" she asked after another quiet moment. "How did you win my father's, and it seems, Old John's trust so quickly."

"I don't know. I was honest and they believed me."

That's it? There had to be more. Her father was a judge. It was his duty to be able to read people. But Old John was even harder to win. The tall, gray-haired butler trusted no one. To win him, one must first gain his trust. He could read just about anyone.

"Honest about what?" she asked.

"Everything I can remember," he said in a low voice.

Did she want to know? Did she want him to share his life with her? They might be spending more time together if he was going to continue following her around. It could be dangerous for him to grow fond of her. He wouldn't want to leave. But he was a law keeper and she broke the law. Preston and his friends robbed carriages on the roads and, twice, they'd killed. She wasn't sure she wanted to continue on as his friend. Their adventures and escapades picking the pockets of the rich and feeding the poor had gone dark. She was a part of it. She was in on it. Her life was going in a spiral. She felt as if she couldn't control it, just as she couldn't control her tongue.

"And what do you remember?"

"Nothing good."

CHAPTER SIX

MICHAEL WASN'T SURE what to tell her. He didn't think he
wanted to tell her anything. *Oh, by the way, I traveled
back in time yesterday morning. I'm from the future. There
aren't many women there like you.*

Sure.

She'd laugh all the way back to her manor house.

"So you told my father and Old John that nothing good happened to you and they believed you—and my father took you
under his wing. Just for that? Do you expect me to believe that?
You've had a hard life. Many people do. You are not special. Your
explanation about my father makes no sense. He would not—"

"There was more but I'd rather not go into it again.

"Oh, of course," she retreated.

He stared at her while she walked. "Why do you do it?"

"Do what?"

"Rob people."

She shrugged a delicate shoulder. "Why does anyone do it?
For the thrill."

He scowled. That was a dangerous reason. Someone who did
it for the thrill would likely continue to do it.

"Mmm," he grunted more than said.

"What does that mean?" She looked up, curious and a little
insulted.

"Nothing." He looked away as if she no longer interested

him.

"You speak strangely. I have never heard anyone from York speak like you."

He kept his expression impassive. He wasn't planning on telling her anything else about his past. She was cynical and critical. Unlike her father, she would never believe him. She would think he was a nut. On the other hand, what did he care what she thought?

"Did you ever think of putting your mind to work on something good? Like law enforcement?"

She laughed. "I'm a woman in case you have not noticed."

He had, he thought, groaning inwardly.

"Women," she sighed, letting her laughter fade, "do not do what you are doing."

"Why not?" he asked. "What's stopping you?"

She waved her hand and continued walking.

He watched her, examining, or rather appreciating her feminine frame wrapped up in tan, woolen trousers and a belted tunic. There were knives in that belt and probably some in her boots, as well.

Her rich, chestnut hair spilled down her back in glossy locks that begged to be touched, inhaled, tangled through his fingers…

"Where would you be going if I hadn't found you?" he asked.

"I expected you to find me, Investigator. I simply wanted you and my father to be aware that I cannot and will not be ordered about until I am forced to marry, and I will likely not change even then."

"Hmph. Is that what marriage is to you? Being ordered about?"

"That is indeed what it is!"

"Have you been married?" he asked her.

"No, I have not, but I was betrothed to Lord Benjamin Adere and he found great pleasure in my subservience."

"Betrothed…what is that, like engaged?" he asked.

She stopped and gave him a blank look. "Engaged? No, betrothed, as in promised to wed."

"Yes, right. So what happened?"

"He died," she told him, picking up her steps again. "He was older than my father."

Michael scrunched up his face. "Why would you promise yourself to an old man?"

"My father did. It was a solution to having me around."

He was quiet for a moment. Was she correct? Did her father want to get rid of her? Was she more trouble than she was worth? Michael shook his head on both counts. He didn't know the duke, except to have spent a few hours with him, but he seemed like an okay guy, not someone who hated his daughter or wanted to get rid of her.

"He could've sent you to your aunt's place," he pointed out, "but he let you stay here with him."

"With you as my shadow," she reminded him.

He shook his head. "One thing has nothing to do with the other. You're his kid. His daughter," he corrected when she gave him an insulted look. "If you weren't such a pain in the a—neck," he corrected again with an impatient growl, "he'd probably like having you around."

"You don't know any better, Detective," she smiled. "He is not your father."

He noted that she smiled often, even when she'd rather be shouting. He doubted her father, or any other man for that matter noticed the stiffness in her lips and the muscles around them, the veiled passion in her eyes that had nothing to do with happiness. She was a tempest cloaked in apathy.

He was trained to see things like this in people. Tells. Something that gives them away.

And now he knew that her issues likely stemmed from her father. But he didn't want to go into what they were.

Something flew by his head! What the—? He leaped from the saddle and snatched Miss Whimsey clean off her feet. She weighed little. She smelled like lilac. He let the scent fill his head and used his body as a shield while he rushed her to a large tree and set her behind the thick trunk. "Are you okay?" He wanted to run his fingers down her face.

"Aye, are you?"

"What was that?" he asked her, peering from behind the tree.

"An arrow," she replied as if he should know.

He should, since he was in the eighteenth century. He knew how to fire a gun, but an arrow was a different monster.

And speaking of monsters, what was with his pistol? A flint-lock. Seriously? With a 9" long steel barrel, it was heavy and awkward to hold compared to the guns in his century. It was in working condition with a finely raised acanthus leaf finial. The entire thing was embossed and engraved with markings that meant something to gunmakers of its time. It was a nice piece of handiwork, but none of it meant a thing. Why? Because Michael had no bullets. When the duke had given the pistol to him, it was on the condition that Michael become the lawman here. The duke didn't give him any bullets, he was to earn them. Michael's first assignment was to keep his eyes on his boss' daughter so why did he need bullets? Besides, the duke didn't know if Michael was a lunatic—whom he'd sent to watch his daughter. Michael shook his head while he looked into the bushes across from him. Someone was there.

Maybe Miss Whimsey was right. Maybe the duke was a bad father.

Whatever the case, Michael had to earn his ammo or get it himself. A lawman with a useless pistol, a couple of knives, and a pair of fists. Great.

He turned and looked at Miss Whimsey. "Stay here," he whispered. "I'm going to go around and take him hand to hand."

She nodded, though it seemed to be taut with uncertainty. It didn't matter as long as she listened to him.

Crawling across the ground, he made his way like a serpent to the edge of his covering. So far, the archer had not seen him. Getting across the road would be—a shot rang out. *From his side of the road!* Miss Whimsey? No time to consider it. The shot came close to their attacker and made him run. Michael took off after him. He chased the assailant for a minute or two and finally overtook him and tossed him into the currant bushes.

The assailant's mistake was to come up swinging. Michael ducked low, avoiding a fist to his jaw. He straightened with a jab to his opponent's cheek and a bone-crunching right hook that lifted the man off his feet and landed him on his back, legs twitching.

"Is he dead?" Miss Whimsey asked, rushing to them and leaning over the man.

"No. He's knocked out. Do you know him?"

She stepped back, looking surprised and a little offended. "Why would I know him?"

He shrugged. Then he asked, "Why didn't you tell me you had a pistol—and bullets?"

"You did not ask." She turned to walk away, moving her dainty hips. "Well, you caught him. Now, I'm leaving."

"You can't leave yet."

She stopped and pivoted around to him. "Who says?"

"I say," he ground out. "I have to find a place to take him."

"Leave him here."

He gave her a foul glance. "So he can shoot the next unsuspecting traveler? No. Not while I'm here." He bent down and hefted the man up and over his shoulder. He carried him to his horse and tossed him over the saddle. "Your father said there's been an increase in robberies on the road. An earl was killed a few months ago after he was held up by a highwayman who calls himself The Dark Horseman. Well," he turned to her behind him. "He'll be The Locked-up Horseman when I'm through."

Her smile changed just a bit. It became hollow and cold almost instantly. He thought she might be a master at veiling her emotions, controlling her reactions. She knew things about these Horsemen. He'd have to watch her more closely.

"What about *criminals* like me?" she put to him, one hand on her hip. "What would you do to me?"

"Same as him," he replied blandly.

She pouted her lip in an effort, he guessed, that drew many a male gaze to it. It worked on him, as well. For a moment.

"It might sound cheesy," he said setting his eyes on the road. "I don't care. I've always wanted to make the world better where I am for my kids. If I have any. My job hasn't changed. I'm afraid it never will. I must catch thieves and killers and bring them to justice."

"I like that you want to make it better for your—what I hope you meant as children, and not goats—if you have any."

He turned to her and laughed softly.

"But...I am a thief, as you know."

He shook his head and looked down at her hands. He lifted his finger and held it close to hers, barely touching her. "Don't be a thief anymore."

"Michael?"

"Yeah?"

"What does cheese have to do with wanting a better world for your children?"

He laughed softly and drew his fingers closer until they touched her, rattling his heart and making his nerve-endings burn. He traced her palm to the tip of her fingers and then pulled away.

"I need a place to put him."

"The town is close." Her voice came to him softly. "To the right and straight ahead."

He raised his gaze to her. Her rich, dark eyes had grown warmer on him. It made him want to smile warmly—or turn away again. He wasn't about to risk losing what was left of his heart to love.

He motioned for her to hop on the horse in front of his captive. She refused. He took the reins and walked beside her.

"You seemed to be remembering something a little while ago," she said in her dulcet voice. "Something that...perhaps broke your heart. Would you like someone to talk to about it?"

Someone like her? Why was she offering him her ear?

"I have been told I'm a good listener," she said, her gracious smile intact.

He'd gone to a therapist from work. He'd helped others, but not Michael. Talking about stuff didn't help. It only opened closed wounds and made him feel worse. "No. I'm fine."

"Are you wed?"

He cut his glance to her. "I said I was fine."

"Of course. I was just trying to start a conversation." She kept her eyes on the distance and didn't speak again.

"And no. I'm not wed in my century."

"Pardon?" she stopped walking and waited for him to stop as well. "Why did you say *in my century?*"

Did he? He was so used to thinking of things in the future as *his century* that he automatically said it. "I meant city, in my city." He laughed, but it was as disingenuous as hers.

"Then you likely would have said city, if that is what you meant," she challenged.

"Just a misstep of the tongue, Miss Whimsey," he said stiffly.

"Of course."

They reached the village. It wasn't as large as the city of Beddington, where they'd met yesterday morning. Most people here knew the duke's daughter and bid her good day. Michael was surprised that she got along so well with the commoners. He thought the duke's daughter would be stuffier with them.

He took a quick look around at the small cottages with thatched rooves. They were quaint, but small for the most part. There was a church, a mill, a few shops and some larger manor house-looking buildings.

He stopped thinking it was a movie set and started thinking Green and his friend knocked him out and brought him to this place…in England? There were mountain ranges he didn't recognize from America. How was it all possible? When he thought about it too much, it made him feel ill.

He felt eyes on him and noticed most of the villagers staring at him or the unconscious man hanging over his saddle. Some of them smiled. He didn't smile back.

He heard her sigh beside him and dipped his chin in her direction. "What?"

"Are you always so solemn?" She wasted no time asking him. "Does it pain you to smile?"

He turned his head to stare at her more fully. "I don't think about it."

"You have to think about smiling?"

He shrugged and picked up his steps once again. Her hand on his arm stopped him. He didn't know what to tell her. Should he lie? He preferred not to, but he didn't want to share his life. "I'll make more of an effort to smile in the future." He turned and kept walking.

When he reached the center of the village, he stepped up onto a wood gazebo of sorts, with a raised wooden floor. *It was all real. It was all real.*

"Can I have everyone's attention?" he shouted. His voice boomed, loud and strong. People on their way to the mill, or to the baker or the butcher stopped and did as he asked.

"My name is Investigator Michael Pendridge. I have been sworn to duty as a law keeper here in Croydon by Judge Whimsey, Duke of Croydon."

"Where do you come from?' someone called out.

"Never saw you before today!"

He nodded. "I'm from York." It was close enough. "Judge Whimsey has entrusted me with keeping the law and that's what I intend to do. I'm not here to explain myself to you. I'm here because I need someplace to put this man who tried to kill us on the road."

"He tried to kill Miss Whimsey?" Some of them began to shout angrily. Miss Whimsey had to quiet them down with few well-placed smiles and reassuring words.

"You can put him in the cellar of the mill," a young man who looked to be in his late teens called out. "There are rooms with iron doors down there. They are very old."

"Take me to it," Michael told him and then pulled his prisoner out of the saddle and hauled him over his shoulder. He followed the man to the mill, surveying him as they went. "What's your name?"

"I'm called Colin of Ipswich."

"Well, Colin, I'm called Michael. Do you have experience dealing with criminals?"

The young man shook his golden-curled head, but he appeared more confused than untrained.

Michael sighed. "Right…um…have you ever been in charge of bad men like this?"

The unconscious man draped across his shoulder opened his eyes somewhat and tried to lift himself off his captor.

Colin immediately stepped back and smashed his fist into the man's jaw, knocking him out again.

"Forget my last question," Michael said, readjusting his prisoner. "You just answered it. Do you want to work for me, Colin?"

"Aye," Colin answered without hesitation. It made Michael very pleased. Only one problem. Where was he going to get money to pay Colin?

First, he had to get the man off him and into a cell.

Hidden behind baskets and barrels of grain, the dark, gated rooms in the cellar were perfect for what he needed. He went to one and stepped inside. He dumped his prisoner to the floor and smacked his hands together, as if he were ridding himself of unseen germs.

"I'll pay you…um…" What did one pay his employee in seventeen twenty-four? "I'll let you know."

Colin nodded. "What do you need me to do?"

"Guard him. I'm going to go back to speak with Judge Whimsey about what to do with him." He patted his back pockets then audibly sighed. "I could use my phone right now." He smiled halfway and shook his head when Colin asked him what a phone was.

"Forget I said it. I'll hire another man or two to take shifts watching him and help you out. I'll return later with everything we need to know. For now, you stay here with him, okay?"

Colin quirked his mouth at him. "Okay."

"I have to escort Miss—" He realized she hadn't followed him in. He ran for the exit of the mill with an oath on his lips.

She wasn't outside. At least, not anywhere he could see her. No one knew where she'd gone. He checked the baker's shop, a shop with a guy making leather shoes, a blacksmith outside under a tent, the tavern, everywhere in the village.

Damn it! He'd let her escape him. He probably wouldn't have a job when he told the duke. What should he do about paying Colin? Securing his prisoner? No. She wouldn't cost him this. If he was stuck here, he needed a means to make money and live— what if he wasn't stuck here? When he thought about it, there had to be a way back. He wasn't cut out for this life. He liked the gritty, fast-paced life of New York.

Didn't he?

His brother wouldn't have died here in this time.

What he should be doing was investigating how he came here and why.

But there was no time for all that now. He had to find Miss Whimsey. Of course, his horse was gone. She was no fool.

Someone had to have seen her take off on the horse.

He hurried back to the gazebo and called out. "Whoever saw Miss Whimsey leave this area had better speak up now or I'm going to lock you *all* up!" He repeated his warning a second time when he had all their attention.

A young man wearing tattered brown trousers and leather shoes on his feet stepped forward. Immediately, an older man pulled him back by the shoulder and shook his head.

"I'll lock you all up for the night and return for you in the morning," Michael called out. He had to do something to get someone to talk. "Maybe."

"Why do you want to find her?" the young man who'd stepped forward called out. "What do you mean to do to her."

"I don't mean her any harm," Michael told them quickly. Time was running out. She was getting away. "Her father hired me to keep an eye on her. From what I was told, Croydon needs some law and order. I can keep them. I know how to do it, and I will, but I can't go back and tell the duke I lost his daughter. He'll kick me out on my ass."

"She rode west."

"Liam!" the older man scolded. "We do not aid strangers who seek to find her."

Liam turned his gray-blue eyes to his companion. "You said it yourself, Sir, the roads are becoming more dangerous day by day. This man is willing to do something. I will not let our cowardice stop him."

"Come with me," he motioned for Michael to come. "We'll need horses. I can track her."

As he hurried back to the stable, Michael called out for two men to help Colin inside the mill.

He had a chance. He had a horse. And he had an escort, one who knew how to track. Talk was sparse for a while, both of them comfortable in the searching silence.

They finally found her about twenty minutes in, though Michael had no Apple watch to tell.

He didn't want to come upon her right away but rather, watch her and see where she was heading. Liam agreed to help, though Michael hadn't asked for it. They let her ride forward and tailed her from about a quarter of a mile away.

"What should I call you?" Liam asked him as they rode. "Constable? Are you the new Governor?"

"Michael. Michael is fine."

Michael was quiet for another thirty feet. Then he asked, "Why did you defy your friend and call out?"

Liam shrugged his broad shoulders. "It was the right thing to do. I know how dangerous it has become to travel anywhere.

People cannot get food in some places. Once they are on the road, they are game for the thieves. No one will step up to help. Everyone is afraid."

Hearing this made Michael angry. "Who or what are they afraid of?"

"No one knows. Anytime someone seeks justice from one of them, the victim turns up dead. His family sometimes dies with him. None of the thieves have been caught or killed. You are the first man to capture one of them."

Michael wasn't afraid. He was challenged to make this right. Get rid of the Horsemen first and then whoever leads the thieves. The prisoner would need to be interrogated then. Michael knew how to do this, too. For now, though, he kept his gaze on the long, dark locks bouncing down Miss Whimsey's back as she rode away.

Madly, he wanted to smile or smirk at her attempts to escape him. She kept him on his toes, his mind alert and focused. He liked it. He thought less about other things like Clements and Kelly and his brother...and a sixteen-year-old kid.

She turned a bend in the road and Michael and Liam couldn't see her. Michael sped up his horse and didn't see the two riders coming at them from the right.

$$ \text{\textbf{———} ◆··• •··◆ \textbf{———}} $$

CHAPTER SEVEN

MICHAEL HAD TO leap from his saddle to avoid being cut in half by a swinging blade. He was going to have to learn how to fight with a sword! The rider came around again. Michael was ready and waiting for him. He leaped at the assailant before the man had time to position his sword for a strike. He grabbed at his ankle and calf and dragged the man off the horse. Next, rid him of his weapon. After a right hook to his nose that left it broken and bleeding, Michael kicked the hilt of the sword out of the man's useless hand, but the assailant had another, smaller knife. He came at Michael with it. Michael retrieved the sword and drove it deep into his opponent's belly. He turned quickly to see how Liam was doing.

The young man had managed to avoid getting killed and fought off his assailant with double-fisted punches to the face and chest. Ah, a brawler. Michael wanted to smile.

His opponent went down, throwing himself down on a knife he held in his hand.

Liam turned to offer Michael a bloody smile.

"What now?" Liam asked, swiping his sleeve across his mouth.

"We get them back to the mill."

"We should leave them here," Liam told him. "Someone will come for them. 'Tis what the Horsemen do with thieves and killers. You go and get Miss Whimsey. We will meet up later."

Michael took one of the thieves' pistols. It had one bullet in it. Liam took the other. Michael thought it odd that he liked two people in one day. But it was good because he was going to need help at this, and Liam and Colin seemed to be perfect.

He didn't want to think about the future plans he was making here. His life was in the twentieth-first century. This was all temporary until he found a way back.

At the next bend, he sped up his horse and came upon her.

At the same time another man did.

OH, THANK GOODNESS! Preston! She knew he'd be here in the area. Whenever they had squabbled in the past, they would meet here the next day. He'd come. He did care. She was about to call out to him when she saw *him*. Investigator Pendridge. Her watchdog. He'd tracked her down. No. No, she hadn't left a trail. How did he know which direction to take from the mill? Someone must have told him! When he saw Preston, he rode toward him slowly, like a dark wolf on the prowl. He looked at her and cocked his brow ever so slightly.

What was that supposed to mean? Was he judging Preston on his stature? His appearance? She wasn't sure, for an instant later his expression went blank and detached.

Preston pulled his pistol from his belt and pointed it at Pendridge. "Whoever you are, if you want to see another sunset, you better kick that horse and get running."

"Is this how you greet everyone you come across on the road?" the detective asked calmly, but she knew Preston's freedom depended on his answer.

"Old friend," Charlotte interrupted and smiled at Preston before he opened his mouth. "This is Investigator Pendridge. He is from York and is here under my father's order."

Preston's tirade came to a halt. He cast her an angry glare

instead. "Why have you led him here?"

"He followed me," she defended, tired of having to do so.

He rolled his eyes and sighed toward heaven as if she were the biggest fool ever to be born.

"What do you want?" Preston turned back to the investigator.

"Her."

Charlotte didn't know why his claim, spoken somewhere on a deep murmur and a throaty command, went straight through to her bones, her veins, her blood. But she wanted to obey. She almost went to him.

"Well, you cannot have her," Preston defended, pointing his pistol, "and if you put your hands to her, I will—"

A shot rang out. It came from a pistol the investigator held, produced from someplace behind his back. He shot Preston! Preston! She leaped from her saddle and ran to him. He was alive. Shot in the leg!

"Why did you shoot him?" she demanded, reaching Preston.

"I don't like being threatened, especially when there's a gun being waved in my face."

"He shot me, Charlotte!" Preston looked down at his bloody leg and appeared a bit queasy. He looked up and glared at Pendridge. "I'm going to have your head for this, you peasant!"

"Do you really want to threaten me again?" the investigator asked, riding up to Preston's horse and snatching Preston's pistol from his hand. "Next time I shoot, it won't be your leg."

"Come, Preston, let me take you home." Charlotte hurried back to her horse, but the investigator's fingers closing around her wrist stopped her.

"You're coming with me, Miss Whimsey."

"Get your hand off me!" She tried to yank her wrist away, to no avail. "You have no right!"

"I have every right. Your father paid me."

When she cursed her father, he wanted to let her go. He wasn't sure he wanted to work for a guy who paid a stranger, a potentially crazy stranger to watch his daughter. A guy whose daughter hated him enough to curse him.

He expected her to slap him or claw at his eyes. But she did neither. "Detective, I have to help Preston. You must let me go."

"He can ride by himself."

She shook her head. "I will not leave him."

"Charlotte, do not let him talk you out of staying by my side," Preston cried from his horse. "I feel faint!"

"I must care for him. Tell my father you never found me. Please."

She wasn't trying to sway him with tear-filled eyes. She didn't think there was any way of getting away from him other than perhaps appealing to his kinder, gentler side. If he had one.

"I'll escort you to—"

"No," she said, shaking her head.

"He can't protect you and I'm not leaving you out here basically alone to fend off some arrow-shooting asswipe."

She narrowed her eyes on him and gave him a confused look. "Sometimes I can barely understand your speech. But I can take care of myself."

She watched his gaze cool on her like frost on sapphires. "That's good to know," he said. "But if I don't escort you, you'll be coming home with me."

"Fine!" she said through clenched teeth. The man was insufferable. "You may escort us." She stepped around him and mounted her horse. "Come, Preston, Investigator Pendridge will escort us to your home. There is no use in arguing. You can direct your formal complaints to my father when you are well. Now, say no more lest he shoot you again."

She had to shut Preston up. Who knew what he would say! Between him and the detective, she was up to her thighs in mud. She had to keep them from killing each other. Why should she care if Preston killed the investigator? He always seemed either melancholy or detached. Dark and dangerous, or barely giving his attention. She'd stopped Preston from shooting him, only to have him shoot Preston.

She came to the horrifying conclusion that it was her fault Preston had been shot!

"Wait!" the investigator called out. "Where are we heading?"

"Sutton," Charlotte told him, not missing Preston's angry stare.

"I can't go."

"Why not?" she asked.

"Pity," Preston drawled out.

"Someone is waiting for me to return."

Charlotte actually felt her hackles rise. A woman? Did he just remember someone he loved waiting at his home for him? Did he meet someone since yesterday morning? What was he like to this girl? How did he—

"Oh?" she asked as lightly as she could. Why was she even entertaining thoughts of him with someone else, and why did those thoughts hurt a little? No.

"You will have to bid him farewell," he said, his eyes simmering beyond a veil of indifference.

"I cannot," she insisted softly. "Will you truly shame and humiliate me by dragging me back to my father?"

He looked as if she had just kicked him in the guts. He even ran his hand over his flat belly and groaned a little.

"Please," she pleaded. "Just tell my father you lost me."

He was quiet for a moment, looking as if a hundred different things were going through his head. Finally, he nodded. "Okay. Go then."

Go? She wanted to kiss him! No. No. She laughed at herself. She didn't truly want to kiss him. Did she?

Why was he letting her go? Did he not think her as important as this other woman he had to get back to?

"Come on then, Charlotte," Preston urged, pulling her along.

"Thank you," she said with an appreciative nod to Michael, then followed Preston toward Sutton.

The moment they were alone, Preston turned on her. "You were drooling over a man who shot me, Charlotte!"

"I was not drooling, Preston. Do I not always tell you that the best way to catch flies is with honey?"

"He is no fly. He is not like the others who swarm about you."

Aye, she had noticed it also.

"He will be nothing but an ant when I'm finished with him," Preston wore on. "An ant I will smash with the heel of my boot."

Charlotte shook her head. Why did Detective Pendridge have to shoot him? Did he wish to start a war with Preston? It was unwise. Preston knew too many people. The detective would lose.

He'd left her. He'd voluntarily left her. She looked back over her shoulder. He wasn't there.

"Charlotte!" Preston barked. "What has come over you?"

"Nothing. I am surprised he did not shoot you in the heart. I think he could have."

"Do you?" Preston sneered.

Charlotte marveled that someone so handsome could look so ugly. He wasn't always so ruthless. Before his involvement in the Tory/Whig wars a few years back, he was more of a romantic rebel, at least, that was how she had seen him. He'd had noble ideals of stopping the Whigs from taking over Parliament and taking back from the men in power. Helping the poor and finding ways, legal or not, to feed them. She was all in—with about thirty others. But as the Whigs grew more powerful, his hatred of them grew with it, and he changed. He fell in with a band of thieves who robbed for the pleasures of being rich. They were mostly highwaymen who mercilessly robbed carriages belonging to rich, old duchesses. They worked in packs, like wolves strategically positioning themselves in the most beneficial places. Even after noblemen…and women began traveling with guardsmen, Preston's *associates* took them down in the dark, from the left and the right, in front and behind. They were terrifying. Everyone knew of them. The Horsemen.

They'd become so notorious that Preston had to purchase a

second house, Hayward House, just to meet with them. He did not want to be associated with nefarious Horsemen, for it would damage his image when he ran for the office of Mayor of Sutton next autumn.

Her belly sank. What if the investigator found out? What if he found out that she was one of forty-five petty thieves who worked for him?

"Who is he anyway?" Preston pushed. "Where did your father find him?"

Did she dare tell him that it was the man who had taken the ruby ring she had meant to give to him? That he was the one who caused her trouble yesterday morning, that he hopped onto her carriage and followed her home? She thought of the rest and her heart pounded.

"He was beaten and left for dead in Beddington."

"Where you were yesterday morning. Did you bring him home, Charlotte?"

"No! Of course not! If he followed me, I was unaware!"

"I have no doubt about that," he jeered, then shook his head. "All that beauty wasted on a simpleton."

She closed her eyes and prayed silently for patience with him. She wanted to admonish him, but he was correct. She was going to get him into trouble by being so careless. First a constable. Now an investigator. "Preston, there is no need to be so abrasive. I—"

He closed his eyes and grasped his bloody leg. "Ah! I am in pain!"

"All right. There now," she tried to console him with her hand on his arm. "Let us keep riding. We will arrive at Bristol Manor soon, and then you will feel better. 'Tis a good thing you kept your physician on. 'Tis not a serious wound."

He slapped her hand away. "Not serious? Is that what you think? 'Tis all right that your friend shot me because 'tis not serious?"

"He is not my friend, and I did not say that 'twas all right for him—oh, for goodness' sake, Preston, you are bring impossible!"

He looked aghast. Horrified that she could say such a thing. "I am being impossible? I have an iron ball in my leg. Put there by a man you became breathless over. Do not deny it. I know you, Charlie."

She could have felt sorry for him. But he called her Charlie.

"After you bring me home," he continued, "you may hurry back to him."

"Will Amanda tend to you, then?" Charlotte asked him with a charming smile, as if nothing were wrong in all the world. She'd perfected the smile, so much so that even Preston didn't know it was feigned.

"Now that you mention it, she might."

When had he become so cruel?

"Very well, Preston. I will give you your wish, but I will leave now. Get home on your own."

She pulled left on her reins and turned her horse around. She kept riding away as Preston's voice faded on the wind. She could imagine his look of stunned disbelief and she smiled. It felt good to shock him. It felt even better not to care if she did.

Investigator Michael Pendridge had nothing to do with it. He had nothing to do with her riding home—or that she was eager to get there. She was angry with Preston. She'd had just about enough of his underhanded dealings. With him, there was no honor among thieves. But more than that, his dealings with Amanda were the last she would take. She wondered if she should ride into the village first and free John deVille from his prison. She was certain poor John had only been trying to protect her from the stranger she was with. She hadn't told Preston about John because he'd be angry at John for shooting someone so close in proximity to her. His answer would be to "let him rot". Well, no, she would not let him rot.

She hoped the investigator hadn't gone back to the mill. She couldn't tell Pendridge she knew his attacker. He would ask her too many questions. And whatever he discovered, he would tell her father. She couldn't risk it, so she had said nothing. John would forgive her…once she let him out of his jail.

When she reached the village, she wasted no time. She knew he'd been put in the mill. She wanted to get home before the investigator if possible. If he was out entertaining a woman, she likely had time.

She thought about him as she entered the mill. These men certainly didn't waste any time when it came to finding women, did they. Why, the investigator—

"Miss Whimsey?"

No. Not him. Why was he here? Colin of Ipswich and Liam, the smith's apprentice, were with him. They both had pistols. Why did he have to ruin *everything again*?

She kept her voice light, though she wanted to growl. "Investigator."

"What are you doing here?" he asked.

She had to think fast. "I was looking for you. I suspected you would be here with your prisoner. I did not want you to face my father without me. He would be very disappointed." From the corner of her eye, she saw Liam nod his head.

"Yes," the detective murmured. "I had considered that."

One side of her lips quirked upward. "Did you?" she asked when he nodded.

"Before I came upon you and your friend," he said in a low voice.

Liam moved away and disappeared into one of the small gated rooms.

Was that where John was?

What did the investigator just say? Before? Then…he knew the consequences of leaving her with Preston, and he still released her.

Her smile brightened a bit. She would remember that. And the fact that he was not with a woman.

But first, she had to free John.

◆··• •··◆

CHAPTER EIGHT

CHARLOTTE TRIED TO see past the mask of indifference the detective wore. She knew much about masks, for she wore one every day. The more she looked at him, the more she wanted to see him feel something, to express it in his eyes, in the dip or the lift of his chiseled upper lip beneath his scruff. She didn't usually like a man with a mustache and beard, but his added to the air of darkness that covered him. How would she gain his affection if he wasn't affected by her? How would she mold him? Did she want to tamper with something so feral, so indifferent? What if beneath the mask there was something far more broken, something volatile and ugly just waiting to come out?

She breathed in and smiled at Colin. What were they doing here?

"What are you doing back here, Detective Pendridge?" she asked as lightheartedly as she could.

"I've come to interrogate my prisoner."

"Oh." She grew serious. "Will it be painful for him?"

"That depends on him."

"Shall I wait?" she asked, looking around, then giving him a wide-eyed stare. "He's not going to scream, is he?"

His gaze on her grew intense. He studied her for a moment, making her feel as if he were looking through her. "What are you looking for, Investigator?"

"The truth," he answered, and waited while she blinked and

breathed.

"The truth about what?" Could he hear her frantic heart beating?

"Who's your friend? The peacock I shot in the leg?"

"Preston Bristol III, Viscount of Sutton."

"Why were you fleeing to him? What could he do for you?"

"Do I get to ask questions next, Investigator?"

"If you call me Michael. What's your question?" he asked.

"If you do not remember your past, how do you know you were an investigator?"

"I remember my name," he told her. "And Detective is part of it."

She stared at him, looking for the truth in his eyes. He smiled just a little and nearly melted her heart all over her bones.

"Well, do you believe me?" he asked. Was that a hint of amusement flashing across his eyes?

"Why should I not?" she threw back.

"Because," he replied as he grew serious. "Trusting people could get you killed."

She didn't know if it was true or not. The only person she ever trusted was Preston and it hadn't cost her her life. "Will trusting you get me killed, Michael?"

"I hope not."

She smiled and covered her mouth to yawn. "I'm sleepy. Take me home."

He thought about it for a moment, then nodded and called out to Colin. "We'll leave the interrogation until tomorrow. You and Liam can go home. William and what's-his-name—"

"Gerald."

"Gerald FitzSimmons is here?" Charlotte called out loudly around Michael's arm.

Colin nodded with a smile.

Charlotte turned her most innocent smile on Michael. "May I ask him how his wife is?"

"Tomorrow," the investigator said and turned back to Colin.

"William and Gerald can guard him tonight."

Colin nodded and promised to leave soon.

Charlotte followed the investigator out of the mill and to their horses. William and Gerald FitzSimmons would be guarding John tonight. Perfect. It was in Gerald's hands now. Many of the men in the village and nearby towns worked for Preston and his band of Horsemen. Gerald knew she would tell Preston if he did nothing to help his brother-at-arms. Perhaps she'd return to the mill later, just to make sure John was free and William wasn't dead. Hopefully, her father's hound dog would not be sleeping in front of her door again tonight.

"How would your friend, Preston, get along without you tonight?"

"Another of his friends will attend to him. Amanda."

"Ah."

"What is that supposed to mean?"

He glanced at her and leaped onto his horse. "What?"

"You said '*Ah*'. What are you implying? Do you think that is the reason I left him? Because even if it is, why should you care, as long as I left, correct?" She mounted her horse and gave the reins a gentle flick.

"You say that as if to imply that I wanted you to leave him," he muttered, passing her.

"Am I incorrect?" she called out.

He slowed and made a sour face, at which she smiled. "No. He's bad news."

"You have a strange way of saying you think he's no good for me," she told him, catching up and keeping pace with him.

"Well, I have been charged to keep my eyes on you."

"To spy on me."

"To keep you out of trouble. And he seems like he'll get you into trouble."

How did he know so much about Preston after meeting him just once? She'd heard her father once say that investigators thought differently than the rest of us. He'd met enough of them in his early years of being involved in the law to know. Michael Pendridge didn't behave like other men. He seemed completely unaffected by her wiles. He certainly dressed and spoke differently than anyone she'd ever known. If he figured out Preston so quickly, what did he make of her? She thought the best thing to do was be as honest with him as she could—without revealing too much. Anything else and he would see right through it.

"I do not need help finding trouble, Investigator, as I have no doubt you will discover." She slowed her horse. He slowed his and rode alongside her. "You will eventually have to cage me. You will have to, Detective. I cannot escape you. I do not know where you came from, but I think you came here to catch me."

He stared at her without saying a word or moving his horse. She guessed he was figuring things out about her. She was practically confessing to living a life of crime.

"Why don't you stop now then?" he asked, perhaps softer than he meant, for it almost sounded like a plea. No. Not from him. His jaw was set. His gaze hard and resolved.

"Because then people I know would go hungry. Their children would go without care."

He blinked and his gaze actually warmed on her. She was glad she was sitting.

"You steal…uhm…rob people's things and then, what? Sell it to get money?"

"That's correct."

"All right," he said quickly, looking around. "Don't say anything else." He let out a long, deep sigh, and then tugged his reins and trotted away.

Charlotte watched him go. She hoped and prayed that she'd done enough to soften him toward her. Though there was a purpose for her words and actions, they were honest and true. They were the only things that would work on him.

The trouble was they did something to her, too. She'd removed her mask for a moment and confessed to breaking laws. He could have taken her captive and brought her to a justice of the peace tonight. The prospect of it frightened the wits out of her.

But he either chose the law or he chose her. She had to know. It was risky, but Charlotte wasn't as afraid of risk as she was of commitment. She knew very little of it, having to rely on the goodness of the servants' hearts to care for her while she grew up. She had Preston, but he had the things he loved to hate. He had his Horsemen. Now, he had Amanda.

She had no one and she needed no one. She was needed by Rosie and others that she helped. That was all. She wouldn't let them down, not for Preston, not for her father, and not for a clever investigator.

They rode back to the manor house in silence. After a bit of awkwardness, the silence became comfortable. In fact, she wanted to stay with Michael and his comforting silence and not be traded off to her father.

Was he going to tell her father?

"Good day to you, Old John," she greeted him at the door. "Are my parents in?"

"No, Miss. They are out."

Relief filled her. It didn't occur to her that they would be worried about her until Michael scowled and murmured to the old butler about a father who wasn't up all night worried sick that his daughter was out alone or with a stranger in the dead of night.

Charlotte gave him a thankful smile and then turned it on John. "I will freshen up and then we will eat.

"Aye, Lady. I am glad you are well and unhurt," John said and then shuffled away without another word.

"Did my father show you to your room yet?" she asked him when they were alone.

"Yes, last night. It's way too extravagant."

"Would you rather sleep with the horses?"

"No. I would rather sleep in a bed meant for one, not two…or three."

"Why?" she asked, looking up into his eyes. He was a curious one. "Why would you prefer a bed meant for one?"

He raised his eyebrow at her as if he couldn't believe she would ask such a question. He didn't look like he wanted to answer, but she waited for one. He pursed his lips, drawing her dark gaze there.

"I…uhm…I want to remain alone."

"Aye. But why?" she pressed delicately. "Which way is your room?"

He pointed and she led him down the hall and to the left.

"Why are you escorting me?" he asked her.

"You did not answer my question, Michael. Why do you wish to remain alone?"

"I didn't know we were exchanging our life stories," he mumbled and looked away.

"Very well," she sighed. "You will find it quite dull here. How long do you plan on staying?"

"I don't know. As long as I need to. As long as your father lets me."

Did she want him to stay? He meant danger for her and all her friends. She'd helped him today—well, she would have, that is, if her father had cared enough to know she was safe with him. But that was her father. Her mother was worse. Charlotte was lucky if she saw her.

"This is it," he announced, coming to a door she recognized. "My room."

She opened the door and looked inside. It was large with a king size bed and busts everywhere with silver wigs atop their heads.

"It looks like this was my father's room for his wigs," she said, stepping inside.

"He has a room just for his wigs?" he asked behind her. "And he sleeps in here?"

She nodded, then shrugged, and then, before she knew it, laughter bubbled up to the surface, kicking masks and veils to the wayside. She held her hand to her mouth as if she could stop it.

She couldn't.

But what was even more delightful than the rushing springs rising up in her was witnessing it happening to him, too.

Oh, how glorious it was to watch his stoic features brighten and his shadowed eyes spark with life. The sound of him was another matter entirely. Could the sound of someone else's abandon do odd things to the deepest chambers of one's heart? She wanted to make it her goal in life to make him laugh. To make him feel.

"Lady Charlotte." Old John stood in the doorway of the room.

She shook her head to clear it. What in heaven's name was wrong with her? What was she thinking? "Aye, John?" she asked, sobering up.

"You should not be in here unchaperoned."

She nodded and rested her hand on his arm. "Well then, 'tis a good thing you are here, old friend. Aye?"

"I—"

"John, is this my father's wig room?"

"Aye."

"And does he sometimes sleep in here?"

"He sometimes used to. 'Twas his dressing room, as well."

She set her gaze on Michael and let the hint of a furtive smile pass between them.

"I can assure you the sheets have been thoroughly washed and bleached."

"It's fine. Look," the mysterious stranger said in his odd way, "I don't want to impose."

"You are not imposing," Old John assured him. "My lord no longer uses this room or these clothes, and if he put you here, then here is where he wanted you. Mayhap he wants you to grow accustomed to the clothes, the wigs and—"

"I won't be wearing any wigs," their guest let him know, slipping out of his short jacket and tossing it on the bed.

Strangely, Charlotte felt like giggling. Goodness, what had

come over her? Was she feverish?

"The clothes then?" dearest John pressed. "You cannot wear the same clothes every day and those are not from—"

"This country," the investigator said quickly. "I know. Okay. I'll try something on."

Charlotte gave him an understanding smile when his gaze slipped to her. What was he hiding, and what did Old John know? She was going to find out. But first, she wanted to see Michael Pendridge's calves in hose.

CHAPTER NINE

THE DUKE OF Croydon had an endless wardrobe, all useless to him as it was all from his younger, slimmer days.

"He has a new wardrobe three doors down," John advised them, "but he refuses to get rid of any of this."

"Good thing for our guest," Miss Whimsey...Charlotte mused as he stepped around a wooden screen with an olive-green bundle of clothes dangling over his arm. John trotted along behind him.

"We'll see about that," Michael muttered and pulled his t-shirt over his head and arms.

He decided not to look at her over the screen. It was safer that way. She mesmerized him. Cast a spell on him that compelled him to consider her more than his boss' daughter. She made him forget. She made him feel heady, as though he'd been drinking. And she made him laugh.

He shook his head as he bent to untie his boots. John bent and tried to help, but Michael refused his offer, not wanting the older man to hurt himself.

He wouldn't let her in. There were too many ghosts inhabiting his heart. There was no place for a vibrant woman.

He grunted and pulled off one boot, and then the other. Why was he trying on eighteenth century clothes? Was he surrendering to this fate so easily? How had this happened? Didn't he want to find out?

Yes, but he couldn't do it walking around like a twenty-first century man. He pulled down his pants and John gave his boxer-briefs a strange look.

"What do you use for underwear around here?"

"Breeches mostly, and something like this." John held up something that looked like a diaper. "I'll keep these on for one more day."

Okay, what did he have to put on first? Some kind of ruffle-edged, thin, linen gown that fell to his waist, green, woolen breeches that stopped at the knee. When he saw the white hose, which were more like socks, and square-toed shoes, he almost decided against the clothes and sticking to what he had. But his jeans would get him into trouble.

Did they burn witches in this century?

"The hose don't fit," he grumbled, trying to pull them over his feet and calves.

"Just pull!" John advised, patting out the wrinkles in the em-broidered jacket.

Three pairs of hose later, Michael learned how to put them on without tearing them to shreds.

"I don't think these clothes fit me," he said, looking over the screen." I seem to be bigger than the duke was."

Charlotte smiled at him from her chair by the window. "We can have them altered."

"Great."

He put on his jacket while John tied the strings above his stockings. He looked ridiculous. He tucked in his chemise and put on his justaucorps next. The coat fell to his knees in folds of deep green and golden embroidery along the edges.

He slipped his foot into a black square-toed shoe. The shoe was just small enough to squash his toes.

"Bend please," John instructed, "so I can brush your hair and pull it back."

"Are we going somewhere? Why do I have to look all fancy?"

Someone was actually brushing his hair! Just when he

thought he couldn't take another moment, John tied his hair into a ponytail with a black ribbon at his nape and then stepped back to survey his work.

"Very good, Sir," the old man said, then moved in closer to whisper into his ear. "Now you look like one of us."

One of them. It made Michael feel like an alien, an outsider. It reminded him that this wasn't right. It wasn't his time. He might be sent back at any moment.

John stepped out from behind the screen and then waited for Michael to do the same. When he did, his hostess' eyes on him seemed to darken, from sable to obsidian. Her pupils were dilated. She sat up in her chair, her gaze taking him in from head to toe. "Oh."

He shifted under her scrutiny. "I don't look ridiculous?"

"Not at all," she breathed. "Nice calves."

He felt his face burn a little. He tightened his jaw. "Thanks. It's all a bit tight."

"It looks perfect," she insisted.

"I don't think I can go out like this." He wasn't cut out for this kind of fashion. His trousers were too tight on his thighs and crotch. The fit was almost indecent. If not for the knee-length coat, he wouldn't have kept it on.

"There is an off-white justaucorps hanging in that wardrobe," she said. "I think you should try that one on next. Just to see." Her eyes widened along with her smile.

He felt something in him—deep inside him—like a flutter, or a flicker. He didn't know. He only knew it burned a little. And it scared the hell out of him. Why was she making him feel this…this warmth? How could he stop it?

"Is there anything black?" he asked John.

Miss Whimsey looked Michael over, as if she hadn't considered black.

John disappeared into another alcove and fidgeted around for a minute. He reappeared with a different black coat in each hand. One was heavily embroidered with bright reds and forest greens.

The other had dark blue stitching and nothing else. He chose that one. It fit closely to his chest and waist and then flared out just a little, with a cut up the back for riding a horse.

"There are trousers to match," John let him know.

Michael held out his hand.

When he turned, ready to head back to the screen, he beheld a sight that branded itself into his head, his heart. Miss Whimsey was standing near her chair, wearing his leather jacket. She could have fit three more of herself in there with her. She smiled when she looked up and held her droopy sleeve to her cheek.

"'Tis very soft," she practically purred.

He nodded and disappeared behind the screen before he told her how much he liked looking at her in it. He was sure he smiled at her like a fool at some point. He changed quickly and stood before her again—she had taken off his jacket—in black breeches and a black coat to match. His jacket underneath was dark blue. Much more his style.

He looked at her from beneath his dark brows. Did she still approve? What did he care? He hadn't changed much from his own clothes. At least, not the color, or the lack of it. Of course, before, he didn't wear hose or shoes with heels on them that pinched and rubbed with every second that passed.

She was smiling. Was it genuine? With her, it was almost impossible to tell. No, that wasn't true. He knew her laughter with him earlier was authentic.

His was, too. His. He'd laughed. He was still trying to get over it in his mind. He hadn't laughed in three years. He hadn't found anything humorous enough to make him laugh out loud in that long. What had she done? It was as if she pushed a button and exposed his soul to the sun.

It felt wonderful. He wanted more, but he realized everything could change again in the blink of an eye. And even if he did stay here, if he gave her his heart, he would likely lose her as he lost the others.

He couldn't go through it again—or even take the chance of

going through it. But, oh, looking at her was like looking at a summer sunrise over Manhattan. She was beautiful and mysterious, with a pulse all her own.

"Detective, I fear that you are going to suffer the demands for attention from many different women tonight."

"What's tonight?"

"Wednesday," Miss Whimsey informed him as she slipped out of his jacket. "All the judges of the different districts gather together here for dinner. I do not usually attend but I wouldn't want to miss my father explaining you to his haughty friends…and their wives and daughters."

"So you wish to be amused at my expense," he quipped, slipping his foot out of his shoe to find some relief in stretching his toes.

She graced him with a confident, slightly provocative smile that made his blood judder in his veins and his legs feel weak. "I must confess, I do."

"John," he said as he turned to the old man. "Are there any shoes that might be bigger?"

"I will check, Detective."

"Thank you."

He watched the butler set about his task. His gaze slowly swung back to her. She was no longer smiling at him. She had gone to the window and was looking out.

"I should be going," she said softly, without turning to him.

He wanted to ask her what she was thinking about at that moment when her gaze seemed so distant, so set for the unattainable.

"Are you planning to run away again while I'm at this gathering with your father?"

She turned to look at him. "No, but now that you bring it up…"

"I would find you." He didn't mean for it to sound so husky. This wasn't some romantic thing. He worked for her father. He wanted to earn his bullets.

"Only if I wanted you to," she countered.

He examined her from foot to crown and chewed on his words before he let them go. "You would. You wouldn't stop me."

Her eyes opened wider on him. "I should storm over there and slap your face for your bold gaze alone."

His mouth curled at the corners. "Threats are weak, Lady."

She did her best to harden her smile, but she failed. "You mock me," she said softly on her way out of the room. "Everyone mocks me."

"Charlotte, wait." He stepped forward and stopped her with his hand on her arm, easily falling for her feigned somber mood. "I'm not—"

She turned with her fist already flying. She caught him in the nose, striking with all her might. It felt wonderful for all he'd put her through. His head snapped back. When he brought it forward, he was clutching his bloody nose.

"Threats may be weak, Investigator." She smiled victoriously. "But I am not." She turned on her heel and left the room without another word.

She had said enough. She wasn't weak. Holding his bloody nose, he believed her.

His smile began slowly and widened at the door through which she left. She was a hellcat. Could she get any more perfect?

RICHARD WHIMSEY, LORD Croydon, spared no expense for his little gathering of judges.

The large, linen-covered table in the dining hall was heavy with silver goblets filled with red wine, with silver bowls and plates to match. The flatware looked to be silver also. The spoons were shaped like leaves and the forks were long and two-pronged.

There were dozens of dishes being set down on the table.

Michael was there early with the duke and John. The servers were preparing for dinner. Michael didn't care what food was being served, he wanted some wine.

He tried to keep his mind off the duke's daughter and the shape of her lips. It was difficult.

"We have some time before everyone arrives, Detective," the judge said, "why don't you tell me a little bit about the future. What is the law like?"

It was a bit jarring how easily the judge believed him. He'd put Michael in charge of his daughter. She was right. What kind of father was he? This went beyond simply taking Michael at his word or liking a good mystery. It seemed as if Whimsey knew something—like something certain. But how?

Michael told him about the law in the twenty-first century and the judge seemed genuinely fascinated.

"What is it that you know, Your Honor? That makes you trust me? If someone came to me with my crazy story—"

"Oh, come and meet Robert Adarely, Lord Epson. He has arrived early."

"Wouldn't it be more beneficial if I was making certain Miss Whimsey was still in her room getting ready?"

Her father stared at him for a moment. Long enough for Michael to think he might agree and send him away to check.

"Aye, it might be," the duke replied with a growing smile. "But you know nothing about the laws here. Tonight, you will learn."

Michael had to admit that if someone should know how the laws worked here, it was him. Keeping the law was in his blood, no matter what it cost. But sitting with a bunch of old judges listening to lectures was not appealing in the least.

"Remember," the duke continued, "I must tell them you are from Brittany. If you claim to be from York, you should know the law. The French have a different judicial system than we. It will make sense when you hear ours."

Why was the judge doing all this for him? Lying for him?

"Epson!" Whimsey greeted with a wide smile. "Always the first to arrive,"

Michael wondered how he was supposed to greet people these days.

Lord Epson was a short, stout man of about fifty-five, maybe older, receding hairline, sharp nose, gray eyes. Michael thought he looked a little like Napoleon.

They spoke briefly about the spreading lawlessness and how things needed to change.

Michael wondered how the law worked and what could be done about changing it, but he was whisked off to another man as this one stepped into the dining hall.

The hour had come. The guests were arriving. There would be twelve in all, including three judges, the duke, and him. Three of those men had a wife and two of them brought their daughters, the Baxter twins, Miss Katherine Longsley, and Miss Whimsey. The daughters were younger than Miss Whimsey, maybe six or seven years younger than him. Too young to pay any heed to their sparkling eyes and glowing smiles when they addressed him at the dinner table, after they were all seated.

He hadn't been paying attention, too caught up was he on why Charlotte was late. Her empty seat was to the left of her father's and his was beside it. Dinner was about to be served and she hadn't arrived. Was she in the house? Where would she have gone? Back to Preston? It didn't make sense. If she wanted to be with him, she wouldn't have left him today.

He looked toward John. Did he know anything?

When it seemed even her father was tired of waiting, he stood up and looked over the table at them all. "Allow me to introduce to you my new *detective*, Michael Pendridge of Brittany. He is here to help Croydon in its quest to keep the law under control. But he does not know our laws or how our justice system works."

He motioned for Michael to stand. Michael hated this spotlight type of thing, but he stood quickly and then sat again.

"What, exactly, is a detective?" asked George Baxter while he dug into his meal.

It smelled like fish. When he was served, Michael had to admit it looked delicious. There was fowl and lamb and other kinds of meat, even meat inside cakes and pies. And endless wine.

"He is an investigator," Judge Whimsey continued. "He has pledged to keep the law in Croydon and since he did it in Brittany, I trust that he could do a fine job here."

"What will he be doing?" Epson looked up from the bread he was buttering.

"Catching criminals," the duke told them.

"And after they are caught?" Lord Longsley asked. "Who will try all of them?"

"Longsley, why do you not explain our laws to Detective Pendridge? Then he will know what he can do."

Lord Longsley chewed his food then sipped his wine before he spoke. "How much do you need to know?"

"Everything," Michael answered.

"Do you know any of our cities or towns, where any place is?"

"No," Michael answered honestly, realizing he might have bitten off more than he could chew.

Longsley stared at him, sizing him up and then looked at the duke for reassurance, which he received in the form of a nod. "Our system is badly broken."

"But there are many judges who do not agree," Epson muttered.

"If someone is robbed or the crime is petty thievery, the thief is usually never taken in. There are not enough constables, or men on the streets to keep them safe. Constables do not get paid, so there is no incentive to risk life or limb. If the thief is caught and taken in, it is up to the victim to prosecute, the cost of going before the local magistrate comes out of their pockets. They must then present evidence to the grand jury, and if the grand jury finds true bill, the victim, who is now the prosecutor, will provide evidence for a trial."

Michael sat quietly listening, growing more stunned as Longsley spoke. Finally, he could stand it no longer. "This is the most insane thing I've ever heard, not to mention completely reprehensible. There is no justice making the victim pay for his or her own trial."

"We agree," the duke told him, motioning to himself and the others. "Most times, the thief goes free. For crimes like murder and other serious offenses, we impose only two sentences on the convicted. Either we turn them loose or we hang them."

Michael shook his head. It was almost too primitive and unjust to comprehend. Why not turn to a life of crime for its benefits when you would probably never be punished for it while you were alive? As long as you didn't kill anyone, you were good.

"The law breakers are out of control."

Michael sat back in his chair and gave a short laugh. "I'm not surprised."

"We do not know what to do," the duke admitted. "I heard you captured a man who shot at you and my daughter today in the woods and you put him in a sealed room at the mill."

"That's right," Michael said. "And now you're telling me he goes free if I don't go to a magistrate, then hope the grand jury thinks I have a case, and if I do, I have to become a prosecutor."

"You see the problem then," Epson said, barely looking up from his plate of chicken fricassee and carrots.

"Yes, I do," Michael agreed. "You have many of them." The duke had one of his very own. Where was his daughter? She couldn't be fixing herself up for this long. No. She was out somewhere, doing whatever it was she did. Would he have to arrest her?

"We want to improve the system. But before we do, we need advice on what needs to be done to improve it."

"To start," Michael began, "you need police—constables on the streets, and they need to get paid. Second, you need prosecutors. People who know the law, and they need to get paid, too."

The men all looked around at each other. None of them noticed Charlotte stepping inside the dining hall. Her dark eyes found him immediately and she smiled. Real or not, it beguiled him.

He felt like smiling back.

CHAPTER TEN

CHARLOTTE HAD STOOD at the bottom of the stairs in the manor house a few moments earlier and ran her palms down her tight, satin stays then fanned out her skirts. She hoped she looked presentable and not like she recently returned from the mill on a frothy horse. She'd pushed the poor beast, but Kevin, the stable hand, had vowed to take extra care of it.

John deVille was free, Gerald FitzSimmons would keep quiet about her and what he'd done when he pretended to wake up from also being struck on the head, beside William sleeping soundly on the floor in the mill.

She'd made sure he wasn't dead before she left. She'd arrived at the mill after it happened. She hadn't stayed long. John was gone, and Will and Gerald were alive. It had been a successful night.

She'd made it back home a short while ago and managed to freshen up and look half-pleasing. At least, she felt that way when she stepped inside the dining hall and Detective Pendridge set his eyes on her. His stoic expression hadn't changed, but his breathing had. She smiled at him. He didn't smile back but his gaze warmed on her. Did he suspect?

Her gaze fell next to the Baxter twins, Sara and Cara, fawning all over him. She didn't blame them. With his raven hair pulled back from the strong angles of his face, and his long, black justaucorps, strong thighs and shapely calves, he was a sight to behold.

John hurried to her side. "He has been growing more and more fidgety all night, looking to *me* for answers as to where you were."

"Ah, now did I not tell you 'twas better that you did not know where I was going?" She patted his arm and smiled onward at her father.

"Father," she said as she held out her hands. "Please forgive me for being tardy. I began to come down and was struck by a terrible headache. I had to call Anna so I could lie down."

"My dearest daughter," he certainly didn't say for her benefit. "I'm so glad to see you feeling better. As usual, you look beautiful."

Her well-practiced smile remained.

"Just like your mother."

Her merry expression vanished and she walked to her seat and sat down. She wasn't sure if she was grateful that her chair was next to Michael's or not. Why would her father compare her to her mother? He knew she hated all things to do with Lizette Whimsey. Charlotte was nothing like her! She looked nothing like her! Once again, Charlotte sat staring at an empty chair across from her. It was as if her mother had abandoned her without leaving for good. Charlotte wished she had left for good.

She could feel Michael's gaze on her. And then it was gone. She breathed and reached for her cup. She wasn't sure why she had come. She glanced at the man beside her. His presence helped. Oh, aye. She'd come for him.

"Have my father's friends been boring you all night talking about the law?"

The men laughed. None took offense.

"I, for one," Lord Longsley said, "was just about to ask the detective what dialect he speaks. I have heard nothing like his speech before."

"Nor have I, my lord!" Charlotte agreed, smiling and turning to the detective.

"From where in Brittany did you say you came?" Longsley asked.

Brittany? Charlotte's smile widened as the detective's face went blank. Hmm, why would her father tell the others that Michael was from France?

"Pendridge," Epson said, eyeing him the way a cat would size up its prey. "Do you not know where you come from?"

"Dinan," Charlotte answered and blinked at the detective. "Is it not?"

"That's right," he said, raking his gaze over them all. "Dinan." He rested his diamond-hard gaze on Epson. "Anything else?"

The short baron shook his head and continued on with his meal.

Charlotte flicked her gaze to the baron and offered him a stiff, yet comforting smile. She wanted him to know it was insincere. She didn't like him. She'd never seen him show kindness to anyone.

"What brought you to our shore?" Lord Baxter asked next.

"I invited him," her father interjected. "After hearing about him from a friend of mine, I wrote to him, inviting him to come to England to meet with us."

"What do you think of our glorious land and its people so far?" Baxter held up his hand to her father, but there was no need. No one could answer the question but Michael.

"I've only been here for a day. I haven't seen much."

"And its people?" Longsley pressed.

His sapphire eyes shifted to her for a moment. She was looking at him, so she saw.

"Courageous and courteous," he answered.

Lord Longsley laughed, almost as if to mock him. "Aye, and beautiful, no?"

"Aye," Michael said under his breath. He nodded and reached for his cup.

"Tell me—" Lord Baxter began from across the table.

"Oh for goodness' sake," Charlotte interrupted. "Let the poor man eat his dinner!"

Everyone was quiet after that and enjoyed their three-course meal of chicken fricassee, stewed carrots, ham sliced cold into thick cuts, meat pie and pastries, and venison. The second course consisted of custard pudding, roasted vegetables, and smoking hot potatoes with melted butter.

They rested before dessert, everyone agreeing on the deliciousness of the food. Especially the rare potatoes. Her father was praised for serving other delicacies as well, like asparagus and venison. The duke soaked in his accolades, knowing his prestige gave him power.

Charlotte excused herself from the table, as had some others, and went to stand by the window. Agnes, one of her parents' servants, brought her a hot drink made of roasted oranges, sugar, and port. It was delicious.

"Where were you tonight?" Michael's voice came up behind her.

"I already told my father. I was overcome by a headache. Would you like to speak to my maid, Anna?"

He shook his head. "No. I'm sorry. My brain never stops working."

He smiled a bit lopsidedly and she thought he might be drunk. Her father was serving his best wine tonight.

"Did you know that if I want the man I put in jail to stay there, I have to pay for everything? Do everything?"

"Aye, I know the law," she told him and watched him down his hot drink. She cringed, but he didn't seem to mind the heat.

"I want to help them change it. Damn! That's good!"

"Oh?" she asked, her curiosity piqued. Her father never told her what they spoke about at his gatherings. "You want to help them change the law?"

"Yes. You need more constables and prostitution."

"Pardon me?"

He blinked. "What?"

"You said we need more prostitution." She grinned. "Is that

what you told them?"

He looked at her as if her nose or lips just popped off. "Prose-cutions." He closed his eyes and shook his head. "Pros-e-cu-*tors*! Yeah. That's right! What's wrong with that?"

"Nothing, Michael."

"People need to go to jail for their crimes," he suddenly brooded.

"Even me?"

He looked down at her and she felt a little lightheaded from the tenderness of his gaze. "If I catch you doing something."

Disappointment dressed her features. So, he wouldn't let her go, then. He was serious about this work. That didn't bode well for her friends—or for her.

She pouted and returned to her chair as she spoke. "Then I shan't let you catch me." She turned and offered him a sweet, yet challenging smile over her shoulder.

She almost regretted leaving him when she reached her chair and saw that he looked lost amid the guests and the servants moving swiftly about. Where was he truly from? Why had her father lied about him being from Brittany? Why had her father wanted him with the guests rather than watching her? Something was going on.

She looked over the faces and spotted Old John. She would speak to him later. She would find out.

She heard the music of Cara Baxter's laughter fill her ears. Cara's sister Sara's voice blended with it a moment later. She looked to find them flittering around Michael like butterflies around flowers.

Too bad the color of Cara's gown made her skin look ever paler. And Sara. Ha! Charlotte saw right through her charade of laughing, then patting his arm and keeping her hand there. In a moment, she would slip her arm around his. What would he do?

His gaze found her while the twins spoke softly around his ears, one on either side.

"You are making an impression on him," Old John muttered

as he came to stand behind her. "His eyes search for you while other women vie for his attention."

Hmm. It meant little. "He gives no one his full attention."

"Were you out with Preston?"

"John, you will stop this talk immediately," she warned softly.

"Of course, my lady."

"And no. I was not with Preston," she said quickly when everyone began to return to their seats. "I was suffering with a frightful headache and I hate to say, 'tis returning." She gave him a hard look and he stepped away.

Michael and the twins returned to the table. The girls were smiling. Michael looked as if his tight shoes had finally gotten the better of him. The twins either didn't realize or didn't care that he wasn't enjoying himself and went on giggling until they were seated, away from him.

"'Tis worse than I expected," Charlotte said for his ears alone.

"My ears are ringing," he confided.

She muffled her laughter with her fingers over her mouth.

"Most men would be enjoying the attention of giggling women in their ears," she remarked as she sobered.

"I didn't say I wasn't enjoying it."

Why would she feel the sting of such words from him? But she did, and she struck back. "Oh, then let me lend my aid." She rose from her seat and hurried around the table to Cara's chair. When she reached her, she bent to the young lady's ear and set her triumphant gaze on Michael. "Dear, it seems the detective would like to meet you tomorrow night, here in our garden. Do you agree to such a meeting?"

"Of course," Cara said breathlessly.

They whispered and Charlotte even giggled with her, though she wanted to be ill, afterwards.

She returned to her chair and Michael's frosty glare. "She has agreed to meet with you tomorrow night in the garden."

"Meet with me for what?" he demanded somewhere between a growl and a whisper.

"Knowing her, whatever you like."

"Charlotte."

She could hear the effort it took for him not to shout at her.

"Go back and tell her you're insane, or that I have a week to live."

"I will not, and I take offense to you calling me insane."

"I don't care." He gave her a stiff smile of his own. "You got me into it. Now get me out."

"Oh, but the poor thing is fond of you," she cried. "I just could not break her heart. Besides, you enjoy her company. You said so yourself."

"Oh, so you're jealous?" he demanded, but thankfully in a low voice. He sounded a bit incredulous. "Is that what this is about?"

She laughed in his face. "You are a clever man, Detective. Surely you realize how insane *you* sound right now."

One of his dark brows lifted for an instant as amusement hovered around his eyes. "Okay. I'll meet with her. Who knows, maybe she's the one."

"Maybe," she sang without biting her tongue.

He waved at the sisters and then turned to her. "Maybe I'll have two."

"Hmm." She took her drink and swigged the contents. She wanted to tell him to enjoy himself, but what she really wanted was for them all to roll around in poison ivy.

She watched him down two more cups of wine. *Good man. Get nice and drunk so I can get away from you again tonight.* She had to check on Preston and see how he was doing. What would she do if Amanda was there? She slammed her cup onto the table, then looked around guiltily.

She met her father's admonishing gaze and looked away. Mostly because he looked blurry. She didn't care if he was angry with her. Too bad for him that his daughter was disruptive! But she wasn't a child anymore and her days of seeking his attention were over.

She looked away and remained quiet because she didn't want to appear to be a drunk. Especially not in front of the Baxter twins…or Detective Pendridge.

She covered her cup with her hand when the server came around again.

Michael did not. He spoke to the others just fine, but some of his words were a bit slurred. Most didn't notice that his mood had grown grimmer and darker, since he was those things to begin with.

But she noticed. And when he finally rose to bid them all a good eve, she noted that he seemed extremely distracted—and not by the twins.

She watched him leave the dining hall. She wanted to leave as well. How obvious would it look if she followed him? He was her father's guest after all.

Her father put up a weak fight when she rose from her chair to go.

He left her. He left his post and the dining hall where her father wanted him to be and walked out of the dining hall as if there were no more reason to stay.

What she should she do? She could go see Preston without the detective on her tail. She could go find Michael.

She stepped through the doors when she heard him.

"Clements. No! Don't go inside alone. Wait for me…wait for me…"

"Michael," she called out and hurried toward the shadows. He was there, at the bend of the corridor, in the darkness. Was someone with him? Was he asleep? "Michael," she said again when she reached him. "Who are you talking to?"

"Clements," he said in a tone so filled with sadness it almost made her cry. "It's Jimmy. I thought he had gone away. But he's back."

She looked around. There was no one there with them. He'd had much to drink. He wasn't in a good state of mind. "Is Jimmy a memory?"

He was quiet. His breathing changed. She thought she heard his heart in the darkness.

"Yeah," he finally said and stepped forward into the light. She followed. His eyes were red, likely from all the drink…or from tears. She didn't think he was the crying type.

He stumbled a little and looked straight at her when she grabbed hold of him to keep him steady.

She almost saw a glimpse of him in the deep well of his eyes, of who he truly was. Protective, patient, weary.

"I'm sorry." He sounded ashamed. He looked away as if to prove he was.

"Why are you sorry?" she asked, helping him to the stairs.

"For this. It won't happen again. Things were feeling okay. I messed it up by drinking again."

"Again? Do you remember drinking often?"

"Of course I do. It was just two days ago. Before I came here."

She smiled. "Of course," she pretended to agree. "Do you remember your home, Michael?"

"Yes." They reached the stairs and began the ascent. "In New York." His gaze darted to hers from beneath his lush, black lashes. "Brittany," he corrected.

They were both lies. And why would he call York, *New* York? Who was Jimmy? "What are you doing here?"

"I don't know. Maybe it's my second chance. I don't have a bullet."

She smiled. "Do you want one?"

He didn't answer right away but then nodded.

She had no idea why a bullet would be his second chance, but it seemed as if he needed one. She pulled up her skirts and reached for the pistol tied to her thigh. She felt his eyes on her. Heavy, hooded eyes, watching her every move, staring at her thigh. Once she had the pistol in her hand, she emptied the contents and handed him a bullet.

"Thanks," he said in a thick, husky voice.

She led him to his room, opened his door, and stepped aside to let him enter.

Why was she here tending to him instead of tending to Preston? This was wrong. This man would see her or Preston hang.

"Goodnight," she said and shut the door. She certainly wouldn't go inside the room and tuck him in. She had to change into her riding clothes and hurry out, before the guests began leaving.

Of course she should be with the man she'd adored practically her entire life. If Amanda was there, Charlotte would fight for him. She was familiar with every feminine wile known to women...and men. Amanda had no chance against her.

She kept that thought planted firmly in her head as she hurried to her room, shut the door, and began to change.

Someone knocked. Old John? She pulled open the door in her chemise to find—it wasn't John.

CHAPTER ELEVEN

"I CAN'T SLEEP."

She blinked up at Michael, stripped of his justaucorps and jacket. He couldn't be here now, looking so appealing in his half-tucked in chemise, his black hair falling over his dreamy, bloodshot eyes.

"I just left you! How long did you try to sleep?"

He shrugged his wide shoulders, stretching his chemise across his chest.

His gaze fell over her from head to foot in her bed clothes. His jaw tightened.

"I was getting ready for bed," she let him know, hoping he didn't spot her muddy riding boots close by.

"Oh." His gaze fluttered to her bed. "Okay. Goodnight then. I'll be outside the door if you need me."

What? "No, Michael, go to bed in your room please," she insisted. "I will not be watched yet again. If I wanted to leave today, I could have gone."

He shook his head. "You know I would have caught you. I catch everyone I hunt. It's what a detective does."

"I do not like the thought of being hunted," she told him, covering herself up with her hands and arms. "You may find me, but I would never consider you anything but a most hated enemy. If that is what you want, then fine."

She shut the door in his face and turned for her bed. It was useless. She was not getting away from him tonight to see Preston, and she was afraid of him growing too curious of Preston if he followed her and perhaps found out more than he should.

Just how good of a detective was he?

She climbed into bed and sat up to stare at the door. Was he outside of it? Why did he take his duty so seriously? These days, no one else did. She should be furious—and she was. But another part of her didn't mind so much. She liked the idea that he fancied her and that he might be so diligent because he wanted to be near her. But even Old John had agreed that Detective Pendridge was unlike other men. He wasn't swayed by her wiles. They didn't affect him. Or did they? She just wasn't sure about him. About anything about him!

She decided that if he was outside her door, she might as well turn it to her advantage.

Slipping out of the bed, she hurried to the door and pulled it open. She didn't see him right away. She looked left and then right and then looked down. He was sitting with his back against the wall on the other side of her room, just beside her door.

"Looking for me?"

"Aye," she said, trying not to blush. "Why did you follow me home, Michael? Why did you come here and speak with my father as if you knew him, gaining his and Old John's trust? Why?"

"I don't know," he answered quietly.

"You have to know why you came here," she insisted. "Why you followed me."

"I saw you pickpocket some guy in the crowd. My things were missing, too. I figured you took them."

"Your badge and your gun."

"Right. My phone and my wallet."

"I do not even know what those things are!"

"I can tell you."

He could tell her. And just like that, they were speaking civilly to each other.

"I cannot sit out here with you in my chemise and you cannot come inside my room without an escort."

"Sit on the other side of the wall inside the room," he suggested. "We will keep the door open so we can talk and hear each other."

She nodded, feeling like a fool, and hurried back into her room to do as he recommended.

"You there?"

"Aye." She wanted to giggle. She didn't know why. She felt childish and silly, but she didn't mind this so much either.

"Okay, my badge is a small shield I wear on my belt or around my neck to prove I'm a cop...police officer. My wallet is a small leather flap with pockets to hold my ID...eh, identification, money, credit cards."

"What are credit cards?"

He explained them. They sounded delightful. So did he. She liked just hearing his voice and not seeing him. It emphasized things more clearly. Like his odd accent, his deep, breathy tones.

There was nothing like his credit cards in England. What was plastic? A chip? Where did he say he came from again?

"Brittany."

"You do not come from Brittany," she challenged "Why are you trying to hide it? I will ask Old John. He will tell me."

"You wouldn't believe me."

"How do you know? Did my father believe you?"

"Yes."

"Then it cannot be so unbelievable."

"Oh no?" he mocked. "I come from the future. From the year twenty nineteen, that's two thousand and nineteen."

She was quiet, then she made a small sound like laughter. "You are drunk."

He laughed with her, but it sounded stiff and flat to her ears, and since that was all she had to go on, she didn't think he was sincere.

"An amusing story."

"Yeah," he muttered. "That's what too much wine will do."

She smiled and shook her head at him. But he couldn't see. "So, what is next? Oh, aye, your phone. What is a phone?"

"That's a hard one to explain."

"Are you smiling?" she asked him.

"Yes. How do you know?"

"I can hear it in your voice," she said, turning her ear to the wall.

"I can hear it in yours, too," she heard him say softly. Did he want her to hear him?

"Funny," he continued, "because I don't smile all that much."

"I guessed that. You are infuriatingly impassive."

"That's okay," he mused. "You're dramatic enough for the both of us."

"Hmm. I'm not sure I understand how to take your impression of me. No one has ever called me *dramatic* before. I know of some dramatic plays, but—"

"Take it as a compliment and forget it."

"Dramatic. A compliment. Well then, thank you," she offered.

"Why did you leave Lord Nose-Up-His-Ass today?"

She laughed softly into her hand at the name Michael gave Preston. "He angered me."

"What is he to you?"

"Why? What does that matter to you?"

"I told you, he's trouble. I'm looking out for you whether you want it or not."

"He is important to me," she confessed. "Only Old John knows how long Preston and I have been the closest of friends. Preston helped me get through some very lonely times. He taught me how to take care of myself. How to live. He was there for me when my parents forgot I existed…and then my father thinks to stop him from being in my life? What does he know?"

"It's not what he knows, it's who. Your father knows a lot of judges and other important men."

She wanted to tell him that Preston knew important men as well. But the less Michael knew, the better.

"Who do you know, Detective? Who is Jimmy?" She wasn't sure he would answer or if it was too bold of her to ask. "You were quite drunk. Perhaps you still are. I do not mean to bring up—"

"I'm not. I've sobered up some."

"And Jimmy?" she pressed gently.

"I don't like to talk about him."

"Why not? Do you only talk *with* him when you are drunk?" She smiled and hoped he did to on the other side. "He haunts you. Why? Who was he?"

"Jim Clements," he said, giving in. "He was a cop…a law keeper with me. My work partner for two years. My best friend. After I lost my brother, Geoff on 9/11, I was doing poorly. Clements helped. Kept me busy. I spent more time with him than with anyone else. We had each other's backs."

His deep, gruff voice was comforting to her ears even though what he spoke about was not. She could hear that this came from a deep place for him by the rhythm of his breath and the slight quaver in his voice.

"You have my sympathies on the loss of your brother."

"Thank you."

"Go on, please. And later, you will tell me what is a nine-eleven."

"It was a day. A terrible day," he replied, sounding distant and sad. "But that's another story. Clements and I had been investigating a homicide and got a tip on a guy who lived above a bodega uptown. We drove up there. We weren't out of the car for five seconds when we heard the shots coming from the store. Someone ran out with a gun in his hand. Clements shouted for him to drop his weapon. The perp shot him. I shot the perp. It all happened so fast."

This was real. At least it was real to him. He used words

Charlotte had never heard before. Words like bodega, uptown, and perp. But she understood that his closest friend was hurt or killed while trying to uphold the law.

"Clements was down. He was who I cared about. I called it in, but I didn't leave my partner's side. He didn't make it.

"Neither did the killer. He was a sixteen-year-old boy. I ki...killed a...child."

"Oh, Michael," Charlotte whispered. She didn't know what else to say. This was tearing him apart. "That must have been very difficult."

"It was," he answered quietly. So quietly she almost didn't hear him through the wall.

"It still is," she added, wanting to go to him. She didn't move. Perhaps it was easier for him to open up this way, without seeing the listener.

"It still is," he echoed. "I lost others after that, but that was the worst thing that could have happened. But you know what they say, time heals all wounds."

"Who says that?" she asked.

"I don't know," he admitted. "Why? Do you think it doesn't?"

"Do you still feel the same as you did when this tragedy happened?"

"Some days I do."

"What is it that stops your wounds from healing?"

"I don't know. What do you think of me now, Miss Whimsey? Now that you know what I've done?"

"You mean the sixteen-year-old boy?"

"Yeah."

"Did you know he was young before you shot him?"

"No. Everything happened so fast."

This was what was stopping him from healing. He couldn't forgive himself. He was ashamed and filled with guilt over what he'd done. "I think 'tis a very sad thing. Sad that a boy carried a weapon that could kill. 'Tis too much power for one so young. He likely would have hanged even if you had not shot him. I feel sympathy for his family, but I do not blame you for shooting someone who just shot your friend and would have shot you next."

"Yeah."

She thought she heard him make a sound as if he sniffed.

She reached out with her left arm, the one against the wall and closest to the open door. "Michael, reach for—"

He took her hand in his. She was expecting it, but she didn't expect his warm, curious touch, and the way his big hand covered hers, to rattle her bones, her senses, her logic.

"What about you?" he asked. "What makes you break the law?"

She laughed. Ugh, she hated talking about it. But she guessed if he could do it, so could she. "I was forgotten."

"What do you mean?"

"An hour or so after my mother gave birth to me, my parents forgot me. My father continued to work, and my mother claimed to have a terrible headache. Too horrible to feed her newly born babe. So the servants did it—and kept me alive. It never changed. Whenever my parents were together, they fought, so they stayed apart. They came to visit me once in a while, but they never stayed long. I didn't know who they were so every time they came near me, I cried. My father hated it. As I grew older, I cried harder just to prick him.

"On Sundays he used to take me with him to the courthouses. We didn't spend any time together. I used to wait outside for him. That's how I met Preston. He became my friend."

"When did you start pickpocketing?"

"When I six."

"What?" He swung his head around the doorway and looked into her room at her. "Six? Charlotte!"

"I did what I could to gain my father's attention."

He returned to his position against the wall. "So, this is all to gain his attention?"

"I think it has grown into a bigger monster," she admitted.

"I'm so angry with my parents. I do not care if they live or die. They are strangers to me, especially my mother. It has left this wide hole in my chest, which no one has been able to fill. Not even Preston."

"Your father fooled me. He gained my trust by believing me."

"Believing you about what?"

"The future, Charlotte. He believed me about where I came from."

She let go of his hand and sat up straight, her spine off the wall. "How could you think my father was a good man when he hired someone to watch his daughter who believed he traveled back in time?"

"I did think it was odd," he said, scooting around the doorway. "I still do." He sat beneath the frame, now facing inside the room and in full view of her. "But I told him the truth. I don't know why he believed me. I know it sounds crazy."

He didn't seem like the kind of man who lied much. Unless he was so good at it, as she was, that he could fool even her. But why would he?

"Tell me what you told him." For this she wanted to look into his eyes. She scooted to the entryway and sat facing him.

He told her a mad tale about a man named Mr. Green, who Michael believed was involved in another "case" of a missing girl. He told her about the fourth floor Miss Lancaster's friends claimed had disappeared, with her. He told her about the old brooch and the name Pendragon. How rubbing the brooch and saying the name cast some kind of spell because he ended up here in the eighteenth century. "Are you real?" he asked her quietly, reaching his hand out to her.

"Aye. I'm real." She lifted her hand and touched it to his.

"What if you're not? What if none of this is?" he asked, intertwining their fingers, looking at them.

She gave him a worried look. "Oh, but I must be real. I remember my life! I have scars and memories of how I got them!"

His decadent mouth curled into a half-smile. "All right.

You're real."

She breathed a sigh of relief and then laughed softly with him.

"What in the world is this?" A woman's voice from in the hall. Her mother.

Michael sprang to his feet.

Her mother's tone changed. "Who are you and what are you doing in my daughter's room and with her wearing nothing but a chemise?"

"Oh, please, Lizette," Charlotte drawled, standing up while her mother lifted her violet veil off her face. "Do not shame yourself with such insincere concerns for my well-being. Did you just drag yourself home? Go to bed. You look horrid."

She severed her gaze from her mother's and settled it on Michael. She wanted to see his reaction, for Lady Lizette Whimsey was known as the most beautiful woman in England, even at the age of forty. She did not look horrid. Charlotte wondered if she ever did. She wore a close-bodied gown of violet damask with a pleated back and cool, full skirts of Indian cotton. Her hair was piled atop her head like a golden halo, and though securely pinned, some of her locks had come loose and fell around her shoulders beneath her veil. Her large violet eyes were surrounded by lush dark lashes that worked well with her coy smiles.

"Are you not going to introduce me to your friend, Charlie?"

Charlotte almost snarled at her. "If you must know, this is Investigator Pendridge. Father hired him to keep—"

"—to keep her safe," Michael finished for her and gave her mother an unimpressed smile—which meant nothing since he was impressed with very little. Charlotte appreciated that he did not want her mother to know why he was here, in this house. To watch her.

Her mother gasped at Charlotte and then laughed, though it sounded more like a witch's cackle to Charlotte's ears. "It seems you are keeping her from Sutton, which will please her father." Her gaze found her daughter's and her laughter turned quickly into a pout. "The roads are so dangerous in Sutton, are they not, Charlie?"

"Aye," Charlotte agreed, trying to calm her heart. How much did her mother know about the Horsemen? Then she asked, "Have you been drinking?"

Her mother's expression changed to hot anger. "Of course not, darling. Have you been keeping yourself out of trouble?"

Charlotte stared at her with traces of amusement and disappointment around her lips. Lizette Whimsey didn't know Michael already knew about her criminal activities. She turned to Michael, motioned to her mother and, with a mocking tone, said, "The woman who birthed me."

"Seventeen hours you took to get out," her mother sneered. "You have been nothing but trouble ever since."

Charlotte smiled at her, but it was difficult, perhaps because of Michael's nearness, to keep herself from crying.

"All right, that's enough," he said, stepping between them. "You've said enough, my lady. I think it best if you go wherever it was you were going."

"Oh, look at the shining knight defending his lady's honor!" Her mother laughed again.

"I can assure you," he said in low voice, "I'm no knight."

"You are positively terrifying, Investigator!" Her mother giggled at him.

He flicked his incredulous gaze to Charlotte. She was tempted to laugh. He had no idea what to do with her mother. Most men didn't.

Charlotte watched the panic in his eyes when she took a step away. "Why do I not go get Father and let him know you are here? Investigator, I'm afraid you will have to accompany me as my father ordered you to do."

"Charlotte, you go too far," her mother scolded mildly, seemingly too tired to argue. "I know when I am defeated."

She winked at Charlotte then spun around on her heel. Two more pins fell out of her hair. She came toe to toe with Michael.

She looked up. He stepped back. "Look out, snake charmer." She looked over her shoulder at her daughter. "Charlotte is a most dangerous serpent."

CHAPTER TWELVE

MICHAEL KNEW HE should say something. But what? Oh, hey, your mother is a raging bitch? He blew out a short whistle instead. "She's a real piece of work."

"Piece of work?" Charlotte asked, eyes narrowed. "I have heard the term here and there but what does it mean?"

"Oh, sorry. She's out there. Eccentric, you know?"

"You are kind."

She returned to her room. He started to follow her, but she turned and held up her palm to stop him. "Unless you intend to marry me, do not come into my bedroom in the middle of the night."

He stepped back. He certainly didn't intend to marry her—or anyone. Still, he knew the things her mother had said hurt her. How deeply he had no idea, and no idea why he wanted to help if he could. Strange. He was not one to go to when one needed comforting. But it was different with her. He found that he liked talking to her. He'd told her more things about himself tonight than he'd told anyone in years. He didn't want it to end.

"So then put some clothes on and come out here and talk to me."

She shook her head, smiling as an almost automatic response. "I just want to go to bed."

"Okay." Was she telling him the truth? Did she just want to get rid of him? He gave her a reproachful gaze. "You're not going to try to go out, are you, Charlotte? Your wall is fine to sit and talk against, but my back pleads for a bed to sleep."

She gave him a faint, more genuine smile. "No, I'm not going out. You have my word."

Did he trust her word? Was she a snake? She was beautiful but there was someone else behind her confident, unperturbed veil. Someone he started to get to know tonight.

"Michael," she said as he turned to go. "She does not know me well enough to call me a snake, but you are free to make your own judgments."

He pulled up his shirt, exposing his flat belly, tattooed with a large snake. "I like snakes."

Her smile widened and she opened her mouth to speak.

"Michael!" one of his new hired men called out. Gerald, he believed was his name. He came into view hauling weak and woozy William under his arm. Michael ran to them and helped support him.

"We were attacked," William groaned, cupping the back of his head.

"By who?" Michael asked him. "Did you see who did it?"

"He came out of nowhere," William answered.

"You did not see who did this?" It was Charlotte, still in her chemise, but covered in a long, velvet coat.

"No, Lady," Gerald told her. "It happened too fast."

But there were two of them. "How did someone come up on you without either one of you noticing?" Michael put to them. Something didn't feel right.

"I do not know," William said with a guilty frown. "He was just there."

"Who did he hit first?" Michael asked them.

"Me, I believe," William answered.

"What does it matter, Michael?" Charlotte asked him, sounding impatient.

He cast her a wry look. "I thought you said you were going to bed."

"That was before our men were attacked. Their wounds must be seen to. Who do you think will arrange that? That is correct! Me!"

"All right," he held up his hand. "Just keep quiet."

He didn't turn all the way around when she spoke again.

"How much longer do you think this will take?"

He looked at William, grinded his jaw, and then continued. "So this person smashed you in the head with something and you fell unconscious?"

"If you mean was I knocked out cold, aye," William answered.

Michael turned to Gerald. "What were you doing that you didn't see or hear this in enough time to stop him from striking you?"

"Perhaps there were two attackers!" Charlotte interjected.

Michael thought she might be right. That would solve it. "What do you think, Gerald? Was there another man?"

"Aye, Investigator, there had to be two."

"Aye," Michael mimicked, then turned them over to Charlotte. "Go have your wounds seen to with Miss Whimsey. I'm going to look for our prisoner."

Charlotte stopped and turned to him with a smile fastened on her lips. It looked clownish and artificial. He smiled back.

"'Tis dark out, Michael."

"I'll manage."

"Wait until morning. I will—"

"It'll be too late," Michael growled. "I want him back."

"But I may need you in the morning. My mother will be here, and I do not want to face her alone"

He smiled. He surprised himself by doing it, but he did it nevertheless. "I'll be back in time for breakfast. Now go, let me get done with what I must do."

She looked as if she had more to say, but she was wasting time. Every moment was precious.

"I'll be back in time."

She finally left the hall with Gerald and William. Michael watched them go. Who attacked them? Were the attackers friends of the captive? How did they know he was at the mill? They must have been with him when he shot at Michael. How had he missed them? He wasn't used to fighting on horseback in a forest.

He thought of the old saying, *as thick as thieves*. Thieves stuck together, didn't they. This guy's friends came and broke him out.

Michael left the hall, eyeing the way she had gone. She was a thief. Who did she stick close to? Preston Bristol III, Viscount of Sutton.

He hurried out of the large manor house and called for a stable hand to get him a horse. He'd get his attacker back and his friends as a bonus.

How was he going to get them without a gun…or rather, with only one bullet in his gun? What happened to his Glock? Was it with his other possessions? Was that guy Green holding on to them? How would he get them back?

The stable hand that brought him the horse was different than the first one. This guy looked like the owner of a well-polished genie lamp. He looked to be in his late forties-early fifties. He had long, black hair pulled into a ponytail and a beard that reached his collarbone. His eyes were large and dark. He was tall…or his demeanor exuded that of a big guy, not afraid of much.

"Ah, you wanted a horse?" he called out, reaching Michael.

Michael wondered if the horse was considered the first of his three wishes.

"Yeah. Thanks."

"What are you doing out here in the night, ready to ride off into the darkness?"

Michael stared at him. Who was this guy? "I'm going to catch a criminal."

"Alone and with no weapon?"

Michael's expression grew darker. "How do you know what

I'm carrying?" He didn't tell him he had a pistol with a bullet in it.

"I know many things, Detective Pendridge," the man said with a side smile. "I know that you met Sir Gawaine, or as he prefers to call himself, Mr. Green, in this realm, and were brought here to the past."

Michael forgot about everyone else but this guy. He knew! He knew the truth!

"Who are you?" He was tempted to grab him and shake him. "Who?"

"Why don't we go to the stable. We can speak with less chance of being heard."

Michael agreed and they walked together to the stable. "My name is Simeon. Roldan Simeon," the man told him as they went. "I'm a time traveler."

Michael laughed and threw his hands up in the air. Great. His first sign of hope is a nutcase.

"You don't believe me?"

"That would be a no," Michael replied, sobering as they entered the stable.

The man smiled, looking more like some weird version of Aladdin. And then he disappeared. There was nothing but air where he had just stood.

Michael blinked and rubbed his eyes. The man was gone. It was just Michael and the half-dozen horses lined up in their stalls. What? No. He was drunker than he thought. He ran his hand through the air and laughed at himself.

"Detective."

Michael spun around, wide-eyed. "What are you doing? How did you do that?"

"I told you." Simeon leaned in, wide grin intact. "I can flit through time, landing in this year or that. But I cannot stay in one place too long."

Michael gave him an incredulous look. "What are you talking about?"

"Detective, I'm telling you. I'm a time traveler, cursed by a hag to never settle down, to never have time for love."

"This isn't happening. I'm not standing here with a cursed genie who's pining for love and who can disappear."

The man laughed. "I'm not a genie. Would you like for me to get you something from the past or the present to prove to you the strength of my words?" Simeon asked, confident that he could, in fact, prove his words. "It can be nothing like a phone or something that could alter time."

"I'm still wondering if I really traveled back—"

The man disappeared and returned a few seconds later with a well-worn bicorne hat in his hands. "Napoleon's," was all he said.

Michael's head was reeling. This guy was actually disappearing and appearing right in front of him. Was he a wizard? He said he was cursed.

It could have been anyone's hat. How was Michael to know? But the guy was disappearing! It was difficult not to believe him.

"Did you just take it from him?"

"Yes," Mr. Simeon replied. "I went in, picked it up from where it was resting on a wooden chair, and left. He probably doesn't even know it's gone yet."

Michael shook his head as if to clear it. He couldn't be thinking of Napoleon now!

"Are you here to bring me back?" Michael asked him. Now that it might be a possibility, he wasn't sure he wanted to go back. Here, he didn't feel like ending everything. He didn't feel plagued with thoughts of Clements and his brother and the rest. His thoughts were more filled with Lady Charlotte Whimsey.

"I cannot bring you back," Simeon told him. "I had never met any who traveled through time until I met Kestrel. When I—"

"Kestrel Lancaster?" Michael gave it a shot. He didn't really think it would be the same person but...

"Why, yes," the alleged time traveler said with a smile. "It's Kestrel de Marre now. Married a knight. They are my friends, but I can only visit for a few hours at a time."

"So she was sent back here, too?"

"To fourteen eighty-five."

Michael drew out a long whistle that stirred the horses. Whatever was going on here was some serious stuff. His thoughts trailed off to Charles Lancaster, Kestrel's father. He was a decent guy, was always very cordial to Michael. He'd looked to be in his late forties, dark hair, silver streaks, expensive reading glasses perched at the end of his straight nose. "Her father was worried sick over her."

"Oh?" Simeon appeared curious. "You met him then?"

"A few times," Michael told him. "I'm a cop. I was put on the Lancaster case. I wanted to help him. He's a good guy."

Simeon nodded. "Yes, yes, he is. I like him, too. He knows where she is. Fear not."

Michael felt better knowing that but how did her father find out? Had she been returned?

"So," said the man who could disappear, "you know nothing about the brooch or how you got here?"

Michael leaned his shoulder against the wooden stable wall and shook his head. "Nothing."

"There's much to be told," said Simeon pulling up a stool and having a seat.

"I have much to ask."

"You have heard of King Arthur?" Simeon asked, narrowing his coal...or were they dark blue eyes on him.

"Pendragon. Yes, I know Pendridge is a variant of it. I'm a Pendragon. The duke already figured that out. What about the brooch? Where is it? Why was I sent here? Wait—did you say I met Sir Gawaine?"

"That is correct. You know him as Mr. Green, I believe."

"Yeah," Michael drawled out, recalling the tall, broad-shouldered man. He was Sir Gawaine of the Round Table? Wait a minute! Why was he acting like this was all real? But it had to be real. There was no other explanation. He thought it wouldn't hurt to hear this Roldan Simeon—time traveler—out.

"Okay," Michael pressed, "King Arthur—you were saying?"

"Yes, yes. He is real, same as all this, but from another realm."

"Another realm." Michael stared at him. "Yeah, you mentioned that before." Was he really supposed to believe all this? It was getting crazier by the second.

"Yes. You come from the future, I come from the past. *They* are not from *here*." He motioned back and forth with his fingers.

"They?"

"The king and all his knights, his wife, their wives, his wizard, the sisters. Avalon."

Michael assumed Mr. Simeon, if he was telling the truth, had seen many breathtaking things in his lifetime. His breathless smile when he spoke of Avalon revealed what he thought of such a place. "How do you know of this realm?"

"I have been there."

"You can travel through realms as well as time?" Michael asked him.

"I don't know. I'd never tried before. I didn't even know there were different realms until I followed Sir Lucan back to Avalon in my quest for the brooch, needed by Miss Lancaster at the time."

"Did you ever find it?"

"Of course, I did," the alleged time traveler said indignantly.

"It didn't work for her?" Michael wanted to smack his own face. He was actually buying all of it!

"Oh, it did," Simeon answered. "In the end."

"What end? What happened?" Kestrel Lancaster was his case, after all. He'd chased down empty leads long enough. He'd like to know what happened to her.

"She chose not to go back. Sir Nicholas' foster mother, of sorts, returned in her place."

It was a lot to take in. Too much. There was a chance of getting back. Getting back to…

"What I have heard is this," Simeon continued. "King Arthur recovered from what was thought to have been a mortal wound, and left Avalon. The brooch was made by one or more of the sisters to find him. But the king had his own power and tampered with the spell, causing the brooch to send people to where their greatest love awaited them."

"Their greatest love?" Michael lifted his shoulder off the wall and stared at Simeon. "How accurate is it?"

"One out of one. Pretty accurate if you ask me."

"What?"

"No one knows for sure," Simeon admitted quietly. "It's all just rumors and guessing."

Did that mean Charlotte was his greatest love or not? His belly churned. He hoped not. He didn't want her to be. What if she died? And chances of her dying young in seventeen twenty-four were pretty high. He could stop it. Nothing was written in stone.

"I have to get back to my time," Michael told him, feeling the new talons of desperation at his throat.

"I don't see how that's possible. I don't have the brooch, nor can I get it."

"Why did it send me here?" Michael argued. "Just to meet her?"

Simeon's large, almond-shaped eyes grew even wider. "Who is she? She lives here, I assume?"

"I thought you knew everything," Michael said skeptically.

"Not everything," the older man said with an indulgent smile. "I hate to spy. I didn't want to see you without being seen."

Michael shook his head and a strange, strangled, little sound escaped him. He had to pull himself together. He could. He had done it every night when he emptied his gun. But this...this was all too crazy and there was so much of it. "Let me get this straight," he said in an authoritative voice. "I usually do this in my head, but you've filled it with all this nutty stuff about traveling through time and—"

"How do you explain what has happened to you?" Simeon put to him soberly.

"I'm dreaming, maybe in a coma. I could wake up at any moment."

"Or you may not," the stranger added. "I have recently spent a little time with Kes and Nicholas. They are real. She is expecting his child."

Michael needed to sit. Why the hell had they come to the stable? He looked around for another stool. He found one and set it in front of Simeon's.

"Okay," he said, sitting. "So say this is all really happening, and time travel is real. Does my coming here have anything to do with King Arthur…or just her?"

"I think everyone tied to the king in some way might be going through the same thing."

"For what purpose?"

"I don't know. I thought there was no Duchess of Glastonbury at first. But the more I find out, the more obscure it all becomes. Sir Gawaine doesn't even know why the brooch began being sent out, it appears, to the king's distant relatives. It was made to find him. They have only recently discovered that it was tampered with by Arthur himself. I say, if he wants to be left alone so badly, leave him be."

"Where is the brooch now?"

"The knights likely have it."

"The knights. How many are there?

"Six. Gawaine, Kay, Lucan, Agravaine, Erec, and Sagramore."

Michael didn't care about their names. "How do we get to this realm they're on? We can take six."

Simeon laughed. In fact, he doubled over. "We couldn't take *one* of them. Do you hear me, young man? Not one. And besides, I can't take you anywhere with me. The curse doesn't work that way. I can do nothing to alter time."

"Just my being here is altering it," Michael pointed out.

"But I didn't bring you here. The king's brooch did."

"So how was Miss Lancaster able to return if she wanted to?"

"Sir Gawaine brought the brooch to her to send her back.

She'd been talking about future events and could have been responsible for Henry Tudor not becoming king."

"But she didn't." Michael knew enough about history and the War of the Roses in fifteenth century England. Henry Tudor won the war.

"She talked a lot. They were afraid of her altering the slightest thing."

"So I have to almost alter something to get Sir Gawaine back here to take me home."

"If that is what you truly want. From what I heard, you were at the end of your rope with life, drowning your sorrows in whiskey."

Michael couldn't deny it, but it was love that had led him to that dark place. More accurately, the loss of love. He loved and lost his brother, Clements, Kelly, his hope in mankind. All taken in violence. He lost his love for humanity. He lost his heart, and his soul. He never thought he could get any of it back again. He felt as good as dead. But recently—he looked toward the entrance of the stable—toward the house—for the last day or so, he felt the stirrings of life in him.

Could he find Michael Pendragon here? He shook his head. He didn't want to. He was safer this way. Sure, he remembered everything the police therapist had told him. He should step out, trust that he would be okay, blah, blah. He didn't want to. Weren't you supposed to want to? He wanted to stay detached. Yeah, the booze helped him forget, most of the time.

She appeared at the entrance as if his thoughts had summoned her. He smiled almost instinctually. Another thing he hadn't done in ages.

"What are you doing in here?" came her dulcet voice, her well-practiced smile illuminated by the lantern she held up to her face.

"Lady Charlotte, this is Mr. Roldan Simeon. He—"

"Who? Michael, there is no one there."

◆–·• •·–◆

CHAPTER THIRTEEN

H E SPUN AROUND. No one was there. He was alone, but Charlotte did note the two stools.

"You know what this is?" Michael raked his fingers through his hair. "He can disappear. He travels—man, I know how this sounds, Charlotte."

"He's like Mr. Clements," she offered, trying to be helpful.

"No. This guy is real flesh and blood. He's hiding. Simeon, show yourself!"

"Michael, I think you should let me get you back to the house and to your bed." It would be perfect if he would just follow her, too drunk—as he clearly was—to think straight. If she could get him to bed, he would forget about John deVille and finding him in the dark. He had no idea who he might run into. Perhaps the same men who beat him over the head the first time.

"I want to prove to you that I'm not nuts. Simeon!"

She corked her ear with her finger. "Come now, you are frightening the horses."

She took his arm with her free arm and led him out, counting her breaths to the front doors. "Tell me about him outside."

"No, no," he chuckled, but it sounded stiff. "Just forget it. I had too much to drink tonight."

She suddenly did not believe him. He did not want to speak of Mr. Simeon any longer. That was fine with her. How could her father believe him when he said he came from the future?

Michael was sadly not right in the head.

They walked back to toward house, with Charlotte thanking God that she was getting Michael away from trouble with Preston's men if they met in the dark. She didn't want to see Michael get hurt. Although, she thought with a slight smile fixed to her face, it would take many of Preston's henchmen to beat Michael.

"How are the boys?" he asked her, his handsome face cast in golden light from the lantern.

So, he was finished talking about his other friend, Mr. Simeon, then. "You mean Gerald and William? William was hit with the more serious blow. He was likely hit first."

She thought she might have underestimated Michael earlier when the young men arrived, and he began asking questions. He was clever, asking things none of them but William were prepared for, as if he had already discovered some truth that would implicate her. What if he caught her one day? What would he do? She could grow closer to him, hopefully making it harder for him to punish her. She would need his mercy because people would always be hungry.

As for tonight, she hated how their evening had ended but she was glad William had made a full recovery.

Still, her night with Michael had been…different. Usually, any man who courted her wanted to see her face or "bask in her loveliness". Ugh, they bored her until she wanted to start ripping strands of her hair out just to feel something. But Michael did not care about looking at her. He had sat on the other side of a wall and opened up to her about himself as she had to him. It had been thrilling. She wanted to spend more time with him, but she knew she shouldn't.

"I enjoyed our time together tonight," she confessed.

"You did?" he asked, looking surprised.

"Aye," she said, just as surprised. "You did not?"

"Yeah, I did. I'm just surprised you did, too. Usually, a girl likes to be wined and dined, not spoken to from the other side of a wall."

"Depends on who is speaking to her," she told him with the barest of smiles when he cut his glance to hers.

"Or to him," he muttered, taking the lantern from her tired arm and looking forward once again.

"Tell me your story, *Detective* Pendridge. You do not come from York—or Brittany, do you?"

"I told you," he said, eyeing the manor house in the moonlight. "You didn't believe me. What will change now that I also claim to have met a time traveler?"

"Did you truly tell my father that you were a time traveler and he believed you? I want to know the truth, Michael."

"Why? So you can think less of him for trusting you to me?"

"That, and I never knew my father was so fanciful."

He finally looked at her fully, and when he did, he smiled. It was like the dawn.

"Are you very sleepy?" she asked, gazing up at him in the lantern light.

"No. Why?"

"I know a place. We could go continue our speaking and perhaps watch the sun rise."

What was she doing? She had only been so bold with Preston, whom she'd known most of her life. She'd met Michael yesterday! It was too easy to talk to him. She had to be mindful of what she told him. He was not like Preston and her other friends. Besides being a bit mad in the head, he protected the law. There could never be anything between them…well, first of all, because she was going to marry Preston. Someday. If he didn't marry Amanda. But never mind that. She could not have Michael because he was the enemy. He would put her in a cell if he ever discovered…

"Michael, perhaps we—"

"Okay. Let's go," he said, only hesitating for a moment. He waited for her to turn in the direction of the place she knew, then he followed her. She was going. She was taking him to Belmair

Hill, taking him to the place she used to come to when she was troubled.

"'Tis not far," she said, wondering how far gone she was—never mind him!

"I told your father and John the truth," he continued on the way. "That I received an antique brooch, bequeathed to me by my distant relative, Eleanor Pendridge. I rubbed it and the name Pendragon became clearer on the brooch. I read the name and said it out loud, Pendragon, and then I was here, in England, in the past."

"When do you say you come from?

"The year twenty nineteen."

"You must understand how difficult that is to believe, Michael."

He nodded. "I do. There are moments I don't believe it could be happening either. But it is. You're real."

"Aye, I am."

"You said yourself that I sound different than anyone you've ever heard. My clothes are different. How do you explain the zipper on my jeans? Have you ever seen one before?"

"I admit I have never seen *jeans* before, let alone a zipper. But you could have procured them in some far-off land. Perhaps you come someplace far away from here."

"I do. It's two hundred and ninety-five years away."

She studied him as best she could in the lantern light. He seemed so convinced. If her father believed his mad story for any reason, it was because Michael sounded so sincere.

"Okay, tell me about the world two hundred and ninety-five years from now." She wanted to see how far he would take this.

"Okay, um, there's something called the internet…we have computers and phones, and now, watches, too, that can—"

"What are all those things?" she asked. "You lost your phone."

"Yes, that's right. They are devices that enable you to speak to someone who is far away. You can see them on a screen and talk to them. You can buy things like…I don't know—anything. Everything you can think of, someone is selling it on the internet. With a phone, you can take pictures. They are still images captured on the screen or printed up on glossy paper. You can find a job, find a husband, a one-night-stand, whatever. The world is at our fingertips."

"It sounds fascinating," she said, wide-eyed, suspecting for certain now that he was beyond help and likely had one of the most brilliant minds of anyone she knew. Such a terrible pity. "What is an internest?"

"Internet. *The internet* is like an enormous spiderweb that connects those devices all over the world. It's not something you can touch like a phone or a computer. It works inside those devices, kind of. It's very complicated. Our technology has grown by leaps and bounds. It makes us lazy.

"Some of the other things are lights." He explained what they were. "And plumbing. Oh, man, I miss plumbing most of all."

They arrived at Belmair Hill, or at the bottom of it. It wasn't a steep incline, or an exceptionally high hill. In fact, there was nothing spectacular about it, until the sun came up over the vast horizon. There was nothing around but fields, so there was nothing to mar the view. One could see the light spreading across the earth for hundreds of miles.

She couldn't wait for him to see.

They sat in the thick grass on top of the hill to wait.

"How long have you been coming here?"

"Since I was thirteen. Preston brought me."

"I figured."

Did he sound angry? She decided to find out.

"He wanted to kiss me here once."

"Charlotte, I'm not really inter—once? Why just once?"

She wished she could see his face. He sounded as if he were scowling. "Because I stopped him the first time. I love it here and if our first kiss would have been here and things went sour with us, this place would be ruined for me. I did not want to take the chance and it angered him."

"Well then, I guess kissing you here tonight is out of the question."

Oh, he made her cheeks blaze and her blood boil. The more time she spent with him the worse it was becoming. She had to think with her head, although she never found it so difficult to do in her life! She leaned in, smiling at him.

"Things have more of a chance going sour with you than they do with Preston," she told him with a teasing smile.

"Why?" He didn't smile back. He wasn't angry. He was just earnest.

"I told you. You will eventually cage me, Detective. You will have to. You take your duty very seriously. I think that is also what my father saw in you. But as I told you already, I think you came here to catch me."

"Catch you at what?" he asked, pulling his knees to his chest.

She smiled, but she wasn't sure he could see her. He had put the lantern down when they sat. "Robbing, Investigator. Surely you know I am a thief."

"Surely *you* know that if you're caught and convicted, you could hang."

She didn't know why but the thought of him caring so much made her bones melt a little. "You were paying attention at my father's gathering."

"How else would I know your fate?" he asked. "I don't want you to get caught. I don't want to be the one to catch you. I wish you would swear never to do it again."

What if he found out that Gerald FitzSimmons had acted on her silent orders? That deVille escaped to Hayward House? Could she stop? Would Preston just let her go? No one had ever left him. What about Rosie and the others? Who was Michael Pendridge? No one truly knew. He was most assuredly soft in the head. Nevertheless, he was a lawman. The only one Croydon had at present. No. There was too much at stake. She wouldn't abandon it all for a shadow.

"We shall see what the days bring, Michael." It was all she would promise him.

"I will just have to keep watching over you then," he answered on a low, husky voice.

"Is that what you are doing? Watching *over* me?" she asked wryly, "And why do you sound as if you are not enjoying yourself, when we both know you are."

His eyes opened wider and shone like sapphires in the starlight. He had so mastered his emotions that, for a moment, she couldn't tell if he was amused or angry.

"I am," he gave in gruffly. "And so what? Your father asked me to watch you. I'm sure he meant watch *over* you."

"I'm sure he did not mean the latter," she corrected with an indulgent smile. "There is a difference between the two. My father asked you to spy on me, not to protect me."

Silence reigned for a moment, then he shook his head and smiled. "I never met anyone like you before."

"Is that a good thing?" She bumped her shoulder to his arm.

"Yeah. That's a good thing."

She was close, so she rested her head on his shoulder. He stiffened beneath her, but then warmed up to having her so close.

"Sleepy?" he asked quietly.

"Aye. Michael?"

"Yes?"

"What is a screen? You said people could see each other on a screen."

He put his arm around her and pulled her closer. "Did anything I was saying make sense to you before?"

"A little," she admitted, enjoying how his arm felt around her too much to move away.

"I forget how entirely different our times are," he said.

She agreed though she couldn't find her voice. His body was warm and hard as armor. She felt cared for under his arm and, oddly, it made her want to cry.

"What are the people like?" she asked, hoping to distract her thoughts.

"People will always remain the same, Charlotte. Whatever the era. Maybe in the twenty-first century crime and killing happen on a grander scale because of our technological advancements, but it's the human heart that is so marred. It's the anger, and the hatred, and the hardness that will destroy us."

"You have met many sorry souls being an investigator," she guessed by the deep cynicism in his tone.

"Yeah, and they all had one thing in common," he told her.

They all broke your heart? she wanted to ask him.

"Crime," he told her.

Her belly sank. She realized he thought very little of criminals. What would he think of her when he found out about the things she had done? She had never been frightened before. But there had never been a threat like Detective Pendridge around before.

He was going to catch her.

"Are you cold?" he whispered over her head. "You're trembling."

She tried to slow her breath. She was made of stronger mettle than this. He had not done much to prove that his prowess at catching her was any greater than any other failed attempt made by other men. What was she so worried about? He said he would protect her. That did not mean throw her in a cell.

She let herself relax against him and yawned. He held his breath, feeling her breathe instead. "Tell me more about your world, Michael. Convince me that you are not ill in the head."

He chuckled softly. "I don't know if I can convince you of that, but our music consists of a lot more instruments or synths. There are hundreds of different styles, thousands of different beats. There might be one singer or many. Some are fast, some are slow ballads, and all them can be heard by anyone who has a radio, a computer, phone, you know the rest."

"Oh," she breathed longingly. "I wish I could hear it."

He began humming a tune and hitting his knee for rhythm. It

was a fast tune, but different in tempo than anything she'd ever heard before. He began singing about wanting someone back and seeing her in someone else's arms. Despite the lyrics being on the sad side, excluding the bursts of *oh, oh baby*, the song was playful and catchy.

"I like it," she told him when it was done.

"The little boy who sang it was twelve at the time and grew up to be one of the most famous performers in the world."

"Sing another!"

This time, he chose something slower, softer. His voice swept across her ears and went straight to her heart, slowing it. He had a very pleasant singing voice. She wanted to tell him, but she was too weary.

She cuddled closer and finally felt herself being draped across his strong thighs and her head cradled in the crook of his arm.

She was safe here. She was protected. She was important.

CHAPTER FOURTEEN

MICHAEL LOOKED AROUND in the darkness for Mr. Simeon. Charlotte didn't seem to mind, but Michael knew he sounded like a full-blown, certifiable nut. He knew it. He was sure she knew it, too. He couldn't prove anything he told her about the future. He didn't know why he told her in the first place. He feared she would look at him differently now. He didn't blame her if she did. He wouldn't have believed him if he were her. And yet, her father, whom she didn't get along with, believed him on the first telling. Old John, too.

Mr. Simeon could prove Michael wasn't out of his mind. Where was he? Michael tried to remember everything Simeon had told him. Michael had definitely traveled back in time. He believed it. It was all real. There might be a way to get home. All he had to do was talk about the future enough to maybe threaten the steady course of things. They'd come back for him like they came back for Miss Lancaster. He could tell the judge things. He could tell a whole room of judges things. Did he want to? Was there a reason he got the brooch and came back? What did it all mean? This had to do with King Arthur, but what did Michael have to do with any of it? Was he just unfortunate to get the brooch and find his true love?

Gazing down at her asleep in his lap, his heart melted against his ribs. He would keep her from picking any more pockets if he had to follow her everywhere she went. She'd told him he would put her in a cell. He would make sure he never did.

He wished they had brought some whiskey, but he hadn't even thought of it until now She made him feel lightheaded enough. She made him forget everything, including his duties. He should have questioned their prisoner today. He most likely would have found out much, but he allowed Charlotte to distract him and the bastard got away. Now, here he was sitting atop a hill waiting for the sun to rise, as if it were some huge event. One that Charlotte couldn't stay awake for.

He should be out hunting the perp. Once again, he allowed Charlotte to distract him from his duties.

He was about to wake her and take her home when he was distracted by a wash of golden light. He turned to witness the top arch of the sun dazzle the earth beneath it. Light burst forth in blinding, gold, orange, and crimson shafts. A new day was being born. New chances, new beginnings, new mercies.

He had a gun and he had a bullet, but he hadn't thought about using them on himself. He drank tonight but he would have preferred not to if he knew he'd see Clements. He didn't want to forget his friends. He just wanted peace from them. Maybe here, in seventeen twenty-four he would find that peace.

As he watched the sun make its lazy ascent over the horizon, he thought of all the possibilities that were dawning with the day and he suddenly felt choked up. He wanted to take a step out. Everything would be okay.

He felt a tear fall from his eye and then he felt Charlotte's hand on his arm. She was awake, sitting up—she leaned in and tilted her beautiful face up to his.

Should he kiss her? He wanted to do more than that. He wanted to ravish her.

She slipped her hands over his face and stared into his glassy eyes as the sun rounded to a fiery orb in the sky. He closed his arms around her tighter and dipped his head.

What about ruining this place for her?

She pulled his head down more to reach her eager mouth.

He pressed his lips to hers. She responded with nervousness and shyness, a completely different reaction than what he was used to…before.

Slowly, he cupped her cheek and her nape and took her deeper, molding his mouth to hers, branding her with his kiss. He breathed her, tasted her, and teased her with his tongue, flicking it over her lips, her teeth.

"You kiss very nicely," she said against his neck when she came up for air.

"So do you," he said, biting her chin.

He knew it wasn't a good idea to continue, but he did. He kissed her until she giggled, and then he kissed her neck. She smelled like grass and sunshine, and newness. They didn't kiss long. They both knew what they were doing was foolish. They walked on two different sides of the road. They weren't children who couldn't control their passions. They were both masters of control. They let each other go awkwardly and smiled while Charlotte patted her hair. She was pleasantly shy. He liked it.

"Michael?" she asked later, after the sun had come fully up and she sat beside him. "Why were you crying?"

"I wasn't crying," he corrected her firmly.

"A tear came out of your eye. That is crying."

"One tear, Charlotte. Let's not make more of it than it is."

"All right then," she smiled indulgently. "Why did a tear fall from your eye?"

"I don't know." He shrugged and shook his head. How could he tell her that every morning he was usually holding the barrel of a gun between his teeth? And that this morning, he was glad he'd never put a bullet in the gun?

"Well, I liked it."

"Don't get accustomed to it," he muttered.

He looked at her face. "Charlotte, why are you grinning like a satisfied cat?"

"No reason. Come," she said, rising to her feet. "We should get back before my father suspects something and sends you away."

His good mood returned when he looked up at her and said, "You don't want me to be sent away?"

"Of course not, silly. Is that not obvious? You are entertaining," she added with a spark of humor in her eyes.

He smiled with her. He couldn't help himself. He didn't want to. "So are you."

She quirked a brow at him, as if she wanted to figure something out, then her grin returned, and she held out her hand to help him up. He didn't need it, but he accepted her offering just the same.

He bounded to his feet, close to her. In fact, his body touched hers in certain places. He angled his head and looked into her eyes. The golden light behind Charlotte cast her in what appeared like a halo around her. He felt the urge to laugh. She was no angel. But she was the most beautiful woman he'd ever seen. Even with her dark locks spilling around her shoulders like a tangled cloak, she was ravishing.

He coiled his arm around her waist and pulled her in. "It will be hard to keep my hands off you today."

"Aye," she agreed and pushed off him. "But we must exercise control over our desires. I know 'tis something you can do. I, too, can do it."

"Okay." He let her go. He understood. She didn't want her father to find out. He didn't want to be sent away either. He stepped away and headed toward the house—he hoped—he turned one last time to see the sun resting on the horizon with light, like arms of many shades of gold and red spread out across the vast expanse.

A new day.

"HE SAID TO tell Lord Sutton that Gerald FitzSimmons of

Croydon freed me from the clutches of the new lawman. But I'm sure I heard Lady Charlotte outside of the cell. She called out to FitzSimmons."

Aye, she was a clever girl, and loyal unto death most likely. Sebastian Alexander, Baron of Surrey, rolled his eyes heavenward. Preston didn't deserve her. Sebastian didn't know any man alive who did. He liked to rile her up. She had a fiery temper, a truly fearless nature. She enjoyed doing things her father, the judge, would disapprove of. He smiled thinking of her. One day, he would usurp Preston and become the head of the Horsemen. Perhaps he'd also take Preston's woman.

"What is to be done about this stranger?" deVille asked.

Sebastian didn't know much about him. "He claimed to be a lawman and shot Lord Sutton in the leg."

"I knew he was a danger," deVille whispered and looked around as if the man were here and listening in somehow. Fool.

They would likely have to kill this lawman. Sebastian thought it was too bad. He may have liked this bold, fearless stranger who shot first and asked questions later, especially when it came to Lord Sutton, Preston Bristol III. But deVille was correct. The lawman was too dangerous to befriend or look up to. Whoever had the chance had to kill him.

He told deVille and gave the order to spread the word. The lawman must die. Next was Charlotte. Of course, he wouldn't kill her. He hadn't seen her at Preston's. Surprising, since she was allowing Amanda to see to Sutton's needs, which were many, according to Agnes, one of the scullery maids lucky enough to find herself in Sebastian's bed from time to time.

"Keep your eyes open for Lady Charlotte," he told deVille. "Let me know when you see her."

"Last I saw her, she was with the lawman."

Hmm. According to Preston, she was with the lawman when he was shot. What was she doing with this stranger? Telling him their secrets? Telling him *her* secrets? Was she falling for this man? Perhaps it was time to warn her to keep silent. He would see to it himself.

"Roger!" he called out into the air. "Have my carriage brought around!"

He'd dropped by Judge Whimsey's manor house unannounced before. He and Charlotte were friends. Her father, the duke, knew it. Judge Whimsey didn't mind him. It was Preston the judge didn't like. According to her father, ever since Charlotte met Sutton, she began getting into trouble. Her father believed Preston was the cause of it all. He was partially correct. But there was no proof. And how could there be? Preston was paying off just about everyone—except Judge Whimsey and a few others, and those never saw a side of Preston of which they could grumble. He did not commit the crimes but had others do it for him.

The men paid him what they robbed in exchange for a small percentage and protection if they were caught.

John deVille being proof of Preston's long-reaching arm, even held in a mill in a village, he had been rescued.

By her.

Sebastian grabbed his cloak and hat and left the house. He didn't have to wait for his driver and carriage as they were waiting there for him by his front gate. "Judge Whimsey's," he said, stepping into the carriage. The journey wouldn't be long to the much larger manor house in Croydon. He wasn't home in Surrey, but staying in Preston's lair further west in Sutton. It wasn't far.

Charlotte's father likely hired this lawman to keep his daughter out of trouble. He might be there with her now.

A quarter of an hour later, the carriage pulled up to the front gate of a spacious house. There was a man at the front doors waiting for him.

"Ah, John, my friend!" Sebastian sang, matching the happy spring in his step. "Is there magic at work here? Why, you have not aged a year!"

The old man's face broke into a wide grin. "Lord Surrey, this is unexpected. Do come in."

"Kind of you to offer, John," Sebastian said, stepping inside. "Is Lady Charlotte in?"

"Yes, my lord. She just finished breakfast and is in the sitting room with Detective Pendridge."

Sebastian paused and turned on the heel of his shoe. "The lawman?"

"Aye, my lord," John told him. It was a warning. The old butler knew of Charlotte's goings on.

"Excellent!" Sebastian looked down the hall. He knew where the sitting room was. "No need to announce me, John. I told her I would stop by sometime today. She's expecting me!" Or, she should be. She had abandoned Preston with his wounded leg. Why? He was about to find out.

He walked along the hall getting closer to the room. The door was ajar. She was laughing. He could hear her.

He reached the entrance just as a man spoke, his voice heavy with amusement and desire.

"What's pleasing to me is—" He leaned in and spoke in a softer, quieter voice, something that made Charlotte turn a dozen different shades of scarlet.

Sebastian cleared his throat and had a good look at the lawman, who had been talked about by his men, for the first time. Sebastian would admit the man had a dangerous look to him. He wore white hose and fitted black knee breeches on his long, muscular legs. Though he leaned his arse on the back of a chair, it was clear he was tall, about the same height as Sebastian. He wore a black, padded jacket across his broad shoulders and flat belly. His raven hair was pulled back into a queue, but much of it was loose and falling around his face.

The way Charlotte glowed when she looked at him said much, as did how close she was standing to him, almost cradled between his legs. He was handsome. That much was obvious. She was taken with him.

This could be much worse or better than he thought.

"Lord Surrey!" Charlotte greeted and stepped away from her guest with a shocked looked on her face when she saw him. "What brings you?"

"I was worried about you, my lady," he said sweetly.

"Worried?" she asked, wearing her most well practiced smile.

"Some wonder where you are."

He caught her eyes flicking to the lawman.

"Lord Surrey, let me introduce to you, Detective Michael Pendridge of York."

"Detective?" Sebastian asked, brows raised.

"He's an investigator," she clarified while the *detective* stretched forth his hand.

"Ah!" Sebastian declared. "How very interesting, Detective." He accepted the lawman's handshake and felt the strength in the stranger's arm. "Are you investigating anything or anyone in particular?"

"No, not in particular. Why? Do you have some suggestions?"

Sebastian shook his head. Pendridge was emotionless. Unreadable. What lit the fire? He would find out. "You shot Lord Sutton in the leg."

"That's right."

"May I ask what prompted such a reaction?"

The detective looked between him and Charlotte.

Ah, so it was Charlotte who lit the fire. Preston was competition.

"I don't like having a gun waved at me."

Sebastian chuckled. It was a good enough answer. Besides, he didn't think the detective would answer anything more.

"I'm having a party Saturday night," Sebastian said to him. "Do come to my home in Surry for supper and stay the night. My other guests would love to meet you."

"Who are your other guests?" the detective asked. Odd, his gaze had a way of pinning Sebastian to his spot.

"Oh, some barons, some viscounts—"

"The detective is otherwise engaged Saturday night," Charlotte interrupted, piquing his curiosity. "He cannot go."

"Doing what?" Sebastian asked, wondering how much he could get out of them.

"Keeping Lady Charlotte safe," the detective announced, his dark gaze on her. "I cannot go, so neither can she."

"I see," Sebastian allowed. "Are these the wishes of her father?"

"They are," the lawman answered, switching his gaze back to him.

They both had to be jesting. Charlotte seemed perfectly fine with it all, which was a first for her. She was never fine with anything her father wanted, mainly because he wanted it. Was Detective Pendridge holding her against her will? Wasn't that what deVille thought when he shot at him? Why did they seem so close, so quickly? He wondered what Preston would think of this. If he told him.

"Detective?" he asked, taking a seat and holding out his hand, waiting for a servant to fill it with a cup and some wine. "What do you know of the Horsemen?"

Chapter Fifteen

What was Sebastian doing, Charlotte wondered, glaring at him in her family's sitting room? She glanced at John, hoping he had a way to dismiss the cocky baron. When he shook his head slightly, she sighed. What could she possibly say to sway Michael's attention now?

"Ohhhh!" she cried out clutching her belly.

"What? What is it?" Michael grabbed hold of her and held her while she doubled over.

"It must be something she ate, my lord," Old John offered, hurrying to her.

"Ohhh!" she cried out again. "Oh, I feel terrible. Call for the physician, John. Lord Surrey," she managed, "we will have to cut our visit short. 'Twas good to see you. John, show Lord Surrey out. Detective, please help me to my room."

Michael didn't bother to bid Sebastian good day. Charlotte didn't think he would as he led her out of the sitting room.

Her heart was thrashing. Her blood was racing through her veins. She did feel ill. She felt lightheaded and queasy. What was Sebastian about to tell Michael about the Horsemen? Why was he here? Had Preston sent him? Had it been Preston who had been worried about her? She wished she could have asked Sebastian, but it was best to get him out of the house before he said too much.

"Do you need me to carry you?"

She wanted to look up and smile at Michael. She didn't need him to carry her. She wanted him to. "Perhaps," she allowed in a weak voice.

He swooped down and fit his arms under her knees and under her back. He lifted her as if she weighed nothing. In fact, he told her so.

"You're very light."

"You are very strong," she countered and coiled her arms around his neck.

"Are you feeling better?" he asked after a moment of staring into her eyes and seeing the truth there.

She grimaced and rubbed her belly. "No, I'm afraid not." She didn't want to lie to him but she couldn't let him know that it was all a ruse to get rid of Sebastian. Michael was clever. He would want to know why she wanted Sebastian gone when he began talking about the Horsemen. She wanted no ties to them.

"I will carry you to your bed."

His voice played like a melody across her ears. Before Sebastian had interrupted them, Michael had been telling her how he'd stopped *working out* a few months ago and was letting himself go fat. She'd moved closer to him and boldly reached out to feel his belly. He had not gone fat. He was wonderfully firm. She had wanted to feel more of him. She didn't think he would stop her, though he'd told her he hadn't had time for women and had not been with one in six years. She wondered how he kept their hands off him. She wondered how she would keep *her* hands off him.

"My turn," he had teased and reached for her waist, wrapped tight in her stays. He had laughed and knocked on the stiff stomacher. "How do you breathe?"

"'Tis not about breathing. 'Tis about looking pleasing."

"What's pleasing to me is," he had leaned in to whisper in her ear, in his deep, sensual, sorcerer's voice, "feeling a woman's skin beneath a veil of fabric, nothing thicker—or nothing at all."

"Will you carry me up the stairs then?" she asked him now.

He smiled down at her. "Don't think I can?"

"Well, you have gone so fat." She slipped one hand down his arm and almost sighed. No man's arms she knew felt this hard, this thick with muscle. She would love to see them bare. She closed her eyes for an instant to imagine it. When she opened them again, she realized he was carrying her up the stairs. She remained absolutely still, trying to keep herself as light as possible in his arms. She could feel his heartbeat, fast and furious, his breath pulled a bit more.

She looked into his eyes and lifted a brow at him. He took it as the challenge it was meant to be and hurried up the remainder of the stairs, delivering her to the top.

"Well done, Knight."

He chuckled. "Why do you call me that?"

"Because you behave as if you are one—to me, at least."

He was quiet for a moment, thinking something over in his mind. "Charlotte, do you believe in soul mates…like, people you are meant to be with?"

She thought about her answer before she spoke it. She used to think it was true. That Preston was the man she was destined to be with. "I used to believe in it. But I do not anymore."

"Why not?"

They reached her room and she leaned down to open the door. The bed was the first thing she saw. She had not thought this through. She was in her room, alone with him…and her bed. A lick of fire coursed through her.

"I am feeling better, Michael," she said in a quiet voice. "You can put me down here."

Was it just yesterday that it was so hard to see any emotion in him? He'd laid his hard, stoic exterior aside for her, and what she saw on the inside was so terribly beautiful that it made her forget to breathe. His heart poured out from his fiery eyes. He said nothing but set her down on her feet.

She smiled. It was a shy smile. A *real* shy smile. She felt many of them when she was with him. "Thank you."

He looked at her, studying her, stripping her bare. What did he see? A terrified girl? A strong woman? A crafty thief? She couldn't tell. His guard was up again.

"I'll be outside the door."

"Michael?"

He turned to look at her. Her knees went weak. "I feel better."

"Oh?"

"Aye." What was she going to do here alone in her room all day?

"Then I carried you up the stairs for nothing?"

Her eyebrows shot up. "For nothing? No! I was…I was sick then. No matter what I was feeling, Michael, I appreciate you doing that. I will think of it often," she promised, blushing.

"So will I," he vowed quietly, his gaze fixed on hers as she walked slowly to him.

They were still in her room, but she didn't care. She didn't stop walking when she reached him and pressed her body to his.

Tilting her chin, she let her lips dangle beneath his for an instant, until he took her in his arms and ravished her mouth, her throat, and a bit beyond.

She groaned softly at the scandalous heat flowing through her, making her want to strip naked and then strip him naked, too. No. She couldn't give herself to him. What if she had his child and he had to throw her in prison? Did they allow you to see your child before you were hanged?

Oh, but he kissed her so completely, consuming every part of her. His lips promised pleasures she could not imagine. She wanted to test his promise.

Taking his lower lip between her teeth, she groaned into his mouth. His hands opened and slipped to her bottom. His broad hands pushed her into him while he broke free of her mouth and raked his teeth down her throat.

"Michael…oh, stop."

He released her immediately and stepped back. He didn't ask

her why she wanted to stop. He knew why as well as she.

She caught her breath and they exchanged a smile. "We must practice control."

"For our sakes," he asked "or theirs?"

She didn't know, but they left her room together, resolved to stay strong against the other. As much as they tried not to, they laughed and teased each other on the way to the stairs.

Where the judge waited with his hands on his hips.

"Pendridge, I have been looking for you. Have you found the criminal who escaped you last night?"

"He didn't escape *me*," Michael corrected. "I was here at your party. Next time, I know where to be."

Her father was silent. Charlotte liked it. But the bliss didn't last long.

"There was a robbery on the road to West Wickham last night," her father informed them. In truth, he was speaking to Michael. Not her.

Michael stopped.

"Last night, a highwayman held up the carriage of an elderly dowager," her father went on. "She later perished from the strain to her heart. This is the fifth highwayman robbery in the last few months. I want this to end. If you cannot see to it, I shall find someone who can. Understood?"

"Yes, Sir. Aye," Michael answered, looking sickened by the news.

"And," the judge continued, narrowing his dark eyes on Michael, "what is this I hear that you shot Lord Sutton in the leg?"

"He would not deliver your daughter over to me and was waving his pistol around, so I shot him in the thigh. It gave him a good reason to whine."

Charlotte could see the hint of a smile on her father's face. He was glad Michael had shot Preston. Her father hated Preston. He blamed Preston for teaching her how to be cunning and devious, and a thief. But he was wrong. Preston didn't teach her how to be those things. Her father did.

At first, she did it all for his attention. Then, she did it to hurt him. Now—

"Here." Her father pulled something from a pocket in his justaucorps and flipped it to Michael, who caught it in the air. A bullet. "I will see your stores are full of them."

"Thanks," Michael said.

Her father's smile widened for all to see. He looked at Charlotte and motioned to her and moved his gaze to the detective. *"Thanks."*

"What about me, Father?" she asked while she had him understandably amused by Michael's words.

He raised his brows and gave her a confused look.

"Must he still keep watch over my every move?"

"Of course, Charlotte," he said with the remnant of his smile fading. "'Tis been but two days. Anywhere you want to go, he can go with you."

"Sir?"

"Aye, Detective?" Her father turned to give him an annoyed look, but Michael didn't ask about her. Was he happy to be stuck with her day and night?

"I need a proper jail, and a police force. Men will need to be trained."

"Do what you need," the duke allowed without hesitation. "But we do not usually jail our prisoners. They are hanged."

"I know," Michael told him. "And that needs to change."

"Perhaps," her father surprisingly agreed. "For now though, catch these Horsemen and I will see them hanged for murder."

He was serious, Charlotte thought. As was Michael—as they should be. People were dying. An elderly woman had died. No! This had to stop. But she couldn't give up her friends. She was one of them. One of the worst of them.

She looked at Croydon's knight and wondered what it would be like to be on his side. But it was too late. She was a criminal. He hated criminals.

"Just do what you are being paid to do. Get the rest of the

judges behind you and make even more money. 'Tis up to you. But better off catching them than losing them, aye?"

Michael nodded and her father's footsteps filled the hall.

Charlotte felt terrible for Michael. It was her fault he'd been admonished by her father. It would be her fault if he lost his position as lawman here. If he ever found out what she had done...what was she to do now? She would think about it. Presently, she was grateful that Sebastian was gone and talk of the Horsemen was over. Somehow, she had to get away from Michael today or tonight and speak to Preston about all of this. Things were going to have to change. The Horsemen were going to have to move north, or south, or wherever! She didn't care because if they stayed here, Michael was going to catch them.

"I need to find a building I can make into a jail. Know of any empty buildings besides the working mill?" His expression softened on her.

She nodded.

She led the way, so he didn't see her squeeze her eyes shut as if to fight something from escaping. Would she bring him to Preston and the others this easily?

He put his hand on her shoulder and walked with her, his face tilted to her. "Everything okay?"

And the odd way he spoke—it always made her want to smile. "Aye. I'm just trying to think of ways to help you."

"Oh, you want to help me catch the bad guys?" he asked, following her down the stairs.

"Of course," she said, smiling at him over her shoulder. "Why would I not want to help?"

"Because all thieves stand together," he answered with a shrug of his shoulders. "You won't give up who you know."

He was correct. She liked that he knew things about her, that he noticed her loyalty. "Perhaps I want to stand with you now."

They reached the bottom of the stairs and he stopped and stood in front of her, blocking her path. "After two days, you're ready to stand with me?"

She pushed him out of her way. "Do not mock my affections for you, Detective, or you may never hear them again."

"All right," he said, turning to go with her again. "If you're familiar enough with me to threaten me, I guess you're able to change your mind so quickly on where you stand."

"I have not changed it so quickly," she admitted. "I have done what I have needed to do for Rosie and some others."

"But you have always known it was wrong?" he urged.

"I knew 'twas wrong in the sense of my father telling me 'twas wrong. I'm still not sure the rich should have it all and the poor, nothing. Their children starve, and no one cares."

"There are other ways to raise money for the poor."

"Oh? How?" she asked.

"Have donation drives. You know a lot of wealthy people, I'm sure. Have a raffle of a delicious meal and a date with the lord or lady of the winner's choice. Or tell your friends that you're collecting donations for the poor. See what happens."

"First, what is a raffle? And what is a date? Second, they will laugh me out of their lives."

They left the house with Charlotte learning about what a raffle was. She thought it was a splendid idea and promised to see it done. She knew plenty of young, pretty ladies and handsome lords who might be willing to go on a friendly date with someone who would spend the most on their food. Perhaps she could do it, and she didn't really care if people stopped speaking to her. She'd never cared about what the stately thought. That's why she robbed them.

"Will you come to my raffle dinner?"

"I have nothing to give," he told her. "I haven't been paid yet."

"Offer yourself, silly. For a *date*."

"Will you try to win me?" He laughed softly. Charlotte liked the sound of it. She wished he did it more frequently.

"It depends on the food that is being offered," she teased.

She led him to the stable where they saddled two horses and

sent a stable hand (who wasn't Roldan Simeon) to bring Colin, Liam, William and Gerald to them.

The men were already waiting for instructions, so it didn't take long before they were riding toward the town of Croydon. Michael wanted a jail. She would give him one. There was an old keep on the outskirts of the town. It was big enough to house many men, and perhaps a woman. There were cellars and rooms with bars for doors and shackles on the walls. No one used it anymore. She thought Michael would like it.

He didn't.

"It's a bit barbaric," he complained, holding the back of his neck in his hand.

"What are jails like where you come from?" she asked.

"Clean. Prisoners are treated humanely."

She laughed. "Where—oh!" She leaned up and in and said quietly close to his ear, "You mean in the future?" Before he answered, she looked around and held her index finger to her lips. "Well, this place can be cleaned. The prisoners could clean their cells. It could be part of their punishment." She almost giggled thinking about what Sebastian would do if he had to clean his cell.

"Yeah, and I could run the operations going on upstairs."

She looked heavenward then shook her head. She had no idea what he meant, but she didn't argue.

"What else do you need?" she asked, looking around.

"We need weapons," Colin proposed.

"And more men," William offered.

"And nooses," said Liam.

While the men made lists of what they needed to clean up Croydon, Charlotte felt ill. She wanted to be excited, but these were her friends they were talking about catching and hanging. She eyed Gerald a time or two. He was one of Preston's men. Perhaps she should tell him to go to Preston and let him know what was happening. But no, she needed to be the one to tell him. She needed to know if he was going to try to have Michael killed. What if he was? Michael shot him. His revenge could happen at any time.

Had Sebastian been sent to kill him? Should she tell Michael?

She smiled with them when the conversation called for it. But her mind was on saving them.

How could she save them both?

Chapter Sixteen

THEY MADE WHAT Michael called *home base* in one of the cavernous halls upstairs. It would be a good place to meet once he hired more men. Was he possibly going to build his own police force back here in seventeen twenty-four? Was he going to be in charge of everything? Was he out of his mind? He hated being a cop. It had nearly killed him, but he couldn't stop. Now that he could start over, he didn't want to.

He spread his gaze over the abandoned keep with its cobwebs and splashes of sunlight coming in from the high, narrow windows. Its giant, alcoved hearths and enormous wooden table in two of the halls or rooms or whatever they were, were uselessly big. He wondered who had once lived here.

He couldn't get over the way houses and castle keeps were just abandoned back then…now, he corrected his thoughts. "Is it unsafe?"

"I do not know," Charlotte answered beside him. "It has been here for as long as I can remember." She turned her gaze to the men, and they agreed.

"Who owns it?" he asked.

"The town of Croydon I would imagine," she supplied.

"So…your father," he deduced as if he were playing chess and he just took her king in checkmate.

"That is good news for you, Detective," she pointed out, walking around the large table. "He will no doubt approve of you using it."

"Good," he said, hoping she was right. "Now, the duke said he was sending over more pistols, but I don't know when. We need a few things today."

Colin and William told him of every weapons shop in town. There were three. Good. They would go to them later.

"We'll need a locksmith for keys to the cells and—"

The list went on and on. He was going to be busy today. Perhaps too busy to keep an eye on her.

He didn't want her sneaking off to try to visit snooty Lord Sutton. But he imagined it was all she thought about doing since they were alleged good friends and he'd been shot...by him, her what? Possible future boyfriend? Of course, not *that* far into the future. He would let her go but the roads were too dangerous. Did thieves rob thieves in the eighteenth century? He realized she wasn't new at this. No one got a ring off a man's finger without notice if he...or she, wasn't skilled. But there were other things besides thieves out there. Rapists. Murderers.

Turning to look at her—he raised his eyes from a dusty chair and met her gaze. They both smiled. She was exquisite. He never thought he'd say that about a woman, but she was. When she looked at him with her large, dark eyes and her chestnut hair spilling down her shoulders, he wanted to stare at her forever. He felt entranced, consumed, utterly lost to the fresh, outdoorsy scent of her, the dulcet sound of her, and, oh, the sight of her.

"Tomorrow," he began, knowing for sure that he'd lost his mind, "I'll deliver you to your friend Preston's home in Sutton. I'll stay in the nearest village and await you there, then bring you back home. Okay?"

Her smile widened. "Okay."

Things were happening between them. He didn't want to keep his hands or his mouth off her. She made him feel stupidly happy for no reason at all. He hadn't felt that way since he was a kid, and he liked keeping it behind him. He wasn't a kid anymore. He'd learned that life gives you good days and then kicks you in the gut, cutting off your air, bringing you to your knees. He thought he was safely guarded to never go soft again. How had she managed to get under his skin? A thief, no less! How could he let her?

All he knew was he was glad when her father said he still wanted Michael to keep an eye on her. What a pitiful fool he had become. He almost laughed.

"Are you boys hungry?" she asked them. Of course, they all enthusiastically told her they were. She offered to go to buy some fruit and bread at the market.

"Take Colin with you," he told her.

"Michael, trust me. You have given me no reason to run off."

His expression warmed on her. "For some wine. So he can carry it."

She laughed softly at herself. Was this what she did to other men? With her mouth so perfectly fashioned to smile, he doubted anyone knew how bored she really was. Did her dark eyes dance and look off coyly, half-hidden under a spray of lashes for all men? If so, how could they all not be in love with her?

It wasn't real with anyone else. She was real with him. Wasn't she?

"Colin?" he called out before they left the hall. "Bring me some water."

He didn't want to get drunk and he knew if he started drinking, he would continue. He hadn't thought about quitting. He thought he needed it to get through the day, but he didn't. He needed his life back and he felt as if he were finally finding it again. He was afraid to let go and trust it. Trust her. Everyone lied. She lied, but about how much? So much had changed. The era in which he lived had changed. It was a new day, maybe a new beginning. And if it was, he wanted it with her.

"What do you two know about Charlotte?" He wasn't sure if it was right to ask, but he was sewn together with investigating thread. Asking questions was what he did.

He discovered that Charlotte was well loved by the town's

people. She was very close with Lord Sutton, Preston Bristol III, who was also well loved by many. And how did the rest feel about him? They were afraid of him.

"Why are they afraid of him?" Michael pressed but the men didn't know. He thought Gerald appeared uncomfortable, shifting from foot to foot, his eyes darting from Michael to the entrance of the hall—as if he were about to make a run for it.

Michael kept an observant eye on him.

"What about these Horsemen?" he asked them next. "Know anything about them?"

William was the first to speak. "Other than that there are six of them and—"

"Six?" Michael questioned. "I thought there were four."

"The Bible had four," Liam reminded him. "Croydon has six. The Pale, The Blue, The Red, The Dark, The Kissing—"

"The Kissing Horseman?" Michael repeated, not sure if he wanted to laugh or think about how he would knock out all of the Kissing Horsemen's teeth if he kissed Charlotte.

"And The Gray."

"Hmm, okay. What else?"

"At first, whatever they robbed went toward helping widows and orphans. The poor," Liam told him. He had no idea that his words had made Michael's stomach feel like it caved in. Charlotte said she robbed to give to the poor. Did she know these men?

"But the robberies are becoming more frequent," said William, "and the needy are not getting the help."

She had to be involved with these men somehow. Did he just let her go run and warn them? No. Why would she when he was bringing her to Sutton tomorrow? Should he go back on his word? He never had before. "It's greed, William," he told the young man. He said as little as he could. He felt sick. He knew she was a thief, but if she was involved with the Horsemen...or if she knew them...everything would change.

He fought the urge to push aside every chair, the table itself, out of his way and go find her. But he controlled his desire and harnessed his urge and waited.

"Do we know who any of them are?"

The men shook their heads. "No one knows, and if they do, they are not going to tell you, Sir." Again, William did the talking. "No one will talk about them."

Michael settled his gaze on Gerald across the table. "Fear?"

"Mostly," William agreed.

"What else?"

Liam laughed and leaned back in his chair. "What else is that they are working for the Horsemen."

Michael raised his eyebrows on Gerald. Finally, the young man laughed. "I'm not involved with the Horsemen. I just do not know anything. That does not make me a criminal, does it?"

"No," Michael told him, "it does not." He went to Gerald and patted him on the back. Keep your enemies closer. Right?

What was Charlotte?

And speaking of Charlotte, what was it about her friend, the Baron of Surrey, that Michael was curious about? Everyone else might be afraid to discuss the Horsemen, but Sebastian Alexander wasn't. That had been because he wasn't going to tell Michael anything. He'd been fishing.

Talking about them sure scared the hell out of Charlotte, though, before a word about them escaped his lips.

Sometimes, he wished he didn't have to think out and dissect every lead. And…Charlotte wasn't under suspicion of doing anything more heinous than robbing jewelry from the rich. She wasn't a lead.

And yet, something told him she was his biggest lead.

What if she hadn't wanted the baron to spill any beans about say, maybe, her precious Preston?

"Should Lady Charlotte be taking this long?" he asked.

"Colin is with her," Liam pointed out. "He is the best fighter in town. Do not fear."

Liam was assuming Charlotte was the one needing help. How safe was Colin with Charlotte's friends?

"So, no guesses on who runs the Horsemen?" Michael put to them then waited for any answer. None came.

"There's a code, Sir," William told him.

"Oh?" Michael asked him. "What is it?"

"You do not talk."

The others agreed. Even Gerald spoke up. "That is why the prisoner from last night was set loose. Everyone knows if they talk…to you or any lawman, they will disappear. Or it might be a loved one who goes missing."

Michael listened with a horrified look on his face. "We have to stop this."

"You have to find someone who is brave enough to come forward." Liam told him. "Just working for you puts our lives at risk."

"I'll see that you are all well-armed and paid well," Michael let them know. "But let me tell you this. If I find one of you is a spy for the Horsemen, you'll wish punishment came from their hand instead of mine."

Liam and William nodded. Gerald deflected his gaze. Michael would keep an eye on him.

He looked toward the entrance and grinded his teeth. Where was Charlotte?

He heard the doors downstairs open and then clang shut. "'Tis us," her voice came to his ears like blessed music. "Do not shoot us."

He heard Colin laugh. They weren't hurt. She hadn't run off.

His heart began to beat again. He left the hall and went to the stairs.

"Were you getting worried that I ran away?"

He shook his head. "In truth, I lost track of time."

"In truth?" She grinned as if she saw right through him, and his bald-faced lie was obvious.

Colin had most of the sacks, so Michael helped him first. He could smell the wine sack tossed over his first-in-command's shoulder. He ignored it. He could feel Charlotte's eyes on his back. He didn't ignore that.

"How did you pay for all this?"

"I did not," she replied. "My father will be informed, and he will pay."

Clever, Michael thought with disdain. The duke was keeping tabs on her. She knew it. She wasn't stupid. He looked over his shoulder at her. "Why not buy the other things you need in the same way?"

"I do. But I cannot drain his coffers."

He saw her point, hauled a few sacks over his shoulder, and hurried up the stairs. He called to the others and dumped the sacks, which didn't contain liquid, onto the table. There were apples, a few pears, four loaves of black bread, a loaf of bread with raisins or dates in it, a hunk of butter...or cheese, another hunk of cheese...or butter. They both looked almost exactly alike. Some wrapped packages of dried, salted meat. They weren't sure what kind of meat. But Michael decided when in Rome...

They all sat at the table together and passed the bread and everything else around. Michael wanted the wine, but he wanted to hold on to this feeling of being able to get past his previous life, even more. He wanted to enjoy his time with Charlotte because he really wasn't sure if it was permanent. Did he want it to be? Yes. That's why he was planning to lead a police force. To start over. A new day. He looked at the faces around the table and was suddenly overcome with the feeling of nostalgia.

Arthur had a table. Did it mean something? He didn't care. He had a castle keep. He had men, and he had a woman who was going to keep his life interesting.

"So, tell us about what you did in York, Sir."

Michael gave Colin a cool glance. It was a question that was bound to be asked at some point. Michael had thought about it. "I'm an investigator. I investigate crimes. I wasn't in charge in York, I had a partner. He's...um...still in York."

"Are you going back?" William asked.

Everyone around the table grew quiet, waiting for his answer. Charlotte was waiting as well. "I don't know if I'm going back. I don't—" he paused to clear his throat. "I don't want to, but it may not be up to me."

"Oh, now let us not talk about such melancholy things," Charlotte suggested. "Detective Pendridge does not want to spend the day talking about where he came from. Do you, Detective? Will, why do you not tell us about your dear mother, Gladys Reynolds. She was a friend of Rosie's…"

She didn't want him to talk about his time traveling adventure and sound like a fool to the men. It was thoughtful, but should the men know the truth? He could make better decisions if he knew if he were staying or not.

He glanced at Charlotte. She appeared a bit distracted. Was it because of him? He wanted to smile to reassure her. But he didn't. He couldn't reassure her when he didn't know himself.

"Colin," he said, pushing the rest of his food away and signaling that supper was over. "You and Gerald go recruit some men. Men that you know and tr—"

"Oh, send William instead," Charlotte cut him off with a touch of her hand on his arm. "He is friendly enough and I need Gerald to help me in one of the rooms I was looking in. The shelves are very high, and since he is the tallest—"

Michael held up his hand to stop her and looked at Colin. "Take William with you instead."

He then turned to Gerald. "Gerald, go see to Lady Charlotte's needs," he allowed and watched Gerald as he passed him. He was the taller of the two.

Michael quirked his brow at her then shook his head slightly and escorted Colin and William out of the house, giving them instructions on the kinds of men he was looking for. Something was up with Charlotte and Gerald. He was going to find out.

Left alone in the courtyard after the two men left, he thought about starting over here. Starting fresh, with no past. No ghosts.

"Greetings, Detective," Roldan Simeon's voice broke through

his thoughts and made him jump. "I do hope you're not angry with me for staying away for so long. Apparently, taking Napoleon's hat nearly started a war with one of his allies. Seems he likes his hats. I had to return it back to the exact moment I took it."

Michael would like to grab him and put him in a cell, but he wasn't a criminal…at least, not in this century. "Tell me more about it later. Just don't run away around Lady Charlotte. She thinks I'm crazy."

"Good."

"No. That's not good. I don't want her to think that."

"Ah, right, because she's your true love," Simeon reminded him with a melody in his voice and a grin curling his lips beneath his mustache.

"No, it's not that," Michael said, trying to make light of it. "I have a reputation to uphold if I'm to be taken seriously here. And by the way, what are my chances of staying?"

Simeon walked beside him when he picked up his steps. "True. True. You are an officer of the law. As for staying, Kestrel stayed, so I would assume it's up to you whether you want to go back or not."

"But you don't know for sure?"

"No, I don't," Simeon told him. "You and Kestrel are the first to receive the brooch. I don't know if there will be any more. I only know what I know about you both."

"Come inside. Meet Charlotte and tell me what you know about all this."

They reached the door as it opened. Charlotte stepped out and smiled. She looked at the man standing beside Michael. Simeon hadn't disappeared. Michael breathed a sigh of relief.

"Lady Charlotte," Michael said. "May I introduce Mr. Roldan Simeon, a time traveler."

CHAPTER SEVENTEEN

THEY SAT IN the great hall. Her, Michael, and his friend. Michael had sent the others off to run some errands, so they were alone in the keep. Charlotte had lit more candles, though there was still enough sunlight coming through the windows to see.

Michael had quietly asked her if Gerald was able to help her and how she knew him. He hadn't asked how she knew the other men. She had to be more careful!

So far, she did not know what to think of Mr. Simeon. He was handsome, a man of more years with long, black hair tied at the back and a long mustache and beard. His smile was distracting and contagious, but there was nothing extraordinary about him.

"I don't know if I want the men to know what you're about to discover, Charlotte," Michael said somberly now from his seat beside her.

She nodded, not knowing what else to say and watched him motion to Mr. Simeon. "He can prove that I come from the future."

"No," Mr. Simeon corrected, "I can prove that time travel is possible."

How was Michael ever going to face the truth with a man like Roldan Simeon feeding him lies? "How can you prove that, Mr. Simeon?" she asked with a practiced smile. "Time travel is im—"

He disappeared before her eyes.

"—possible," came the rest in a whisper.

How? She looked at Michael. "What is going on?" She squeaked like a wounded animal when Mr. Simeon appeared again in his chair.

"He just did it, Charlotte."

"Did what?" she asked. Did her teeth just chatter?

"I went to the past," said Mr. Simeon softly. His large, dark eyes grew larger, rounder when he looked at her. "To *your* past. To prove that I can travel."

She opened her mouth to speak but what could she possibly say? He had just disappeared. "And?" she finally managed. Did she want to know?

"You were unwanted," he told her with mercy in his eyes.

"Simeon." Michael warned.

"No. 'Tis all right," Charlotte stopped any further admonishment. "He speaks the truth. But just because he knows something about me does not mean—"

From behind his back, Mr. Simeon produced a small, soft blanket, knitted for her by Rosie, when Charlotte was a babe. She'd had it until she was eleven and then one day, not long after Rosie was thrown out, it disappeared. Charlotte never thought she'd see it again and now here it was as if brand new. "Where did you get this?" she asked him, holding it up to her face and remembering its comforting softness.

"I took it from your pram while your nurse had you out for a stroll. I heard her telling another woman about your mother. Your father, she said, was broken-hearted by his wife's treatment of you. He took you with him to the courts when he could."

That was true. He had taken her on many occasions, but she never liked that side of the law. And began waiting outside for him. That was where she had met Preston.

All at once, she wanted to weep. Her blanket from Rosie, her father—no. This could not be real. "What kind of masterful trick is this, Mr. Simeon?" she demanded, handing him back the blanket.

"It is no trick, dear girl. I was cursed by an old hag to leap through time and never stay too long in one place. It's no way for a bond to grow between two people."

He looked so dejected that, for a moment, Charlotte felt terribly sorry for him. "Is there no way to break the curse?"

"No. But I have enjoyed the days of my life otherwise. I have met almost everyone!" His smile was wide and genuine. All his smiles were. She liked Mr. Simeon. Was he telling the truth? No. It was too farfetched.

But her blanket.

"But no. There is no way to break the curse. At least, I don't know of one as of yet." His grin remained.

"Well, if there is," she told him, "Michael here is a *detective*. I'm sure he can discover the way."

"Thank you for your confidence in me," Michael told her. His deep voice seduced her kneecaps off. Her smile warmed, as did his.

Mr. Simeon cleared his throat. "Did Michael tell you about the brooch?"

She nodded. They could have rehearsed the stories. Who was Michael Pendridge truly? "'Twas bequeathed to him," she told him. "He read the name Pendragon on it and arrived here. Do I have it all?"

"The important stuff," Michael answered, watching her reaction to things. He was skilled at finding deception. She had to use more caution with him. She didn't smile at or with him unless she genuinely felt something.

"The brooch belonged to King Arthur Pendragon," Mr. Simeon told her.

"But those stories are not true. He is just a legend," she argued. This was sounding more like nonsense every moment. He'd deceived her eyes and must have found her blanket somewhere here in the keep.

"He is real, Lady Charlotte," Mr. Simeon assured her. "His knights of the Round Table existed—still exist on a different realm than the one we know."

"You still with us, Charlotte?"

Michael's resonant voice seeped into her flesh and bone, low, like a drum or pulsebeat. She nodded and didn't dare trust herself to look at him without completely losing herself.

"Arthur," Mr. Simeon continued, "used to live in Avalon with his knights and his wife and the sisters."

"The sisters?" Charlotte managed.

"There are nine. They sometimes go by different names. But you may know of one. She is called Morgan. It has recently been verified that it was Morgan who fashioned the brooch. She made it in order to find Arthur if he ever left Avalon—as he had once before when he came here."

"You didn't tell me all of this," Michael brooded at their guest.

"There was no time so I'm telling you now."

"What about Merlin?"

Both men turned to face her. "What did you say?" Mr. Simeon asked.

"Merlin," she repeated. "The wizard. I have read the stories."

"The wizard," Mr. Simeon repeated hollowly. "I...I don't know." He laughed at himself, but slightly. "I had completely forgotten about him. Odd."

He wasn't the same for the next hour. His laughter was subdued and he rarely smiled. But he told them all about Morgan Le Fey's obsession with Arthur. He had heard rumors that if she rose up, she would kill anyone in Arthur's life. There were many other nasty things said about her that need not be repeated presently. She had to be kept from finding him. That was why, it is whispered, Arthur cast another, more powerful enchantment on the brooch.

"What kind of enchantment?" Charlotte asked.

"That the person holding the brooch and saying the name would be sent to his or her one true love."

Her eyes fixed on Michael's. She drew in a deep breath, as if her lungs were starved for air. Had they somehow enchanted her? Is that why Michael didn't want the others around? Why him? Why her? How could they be hundreds of years apart and still be the other's true love? How could an enchantment be so powerful that it could bring two people together who were perhaps born at the wrong time?

"So," she remarked, staring at him, "you were sent here to meet…me?"

He smiled but shielded his gaze behind his dusky lashes. "I don't believe in stuff like this either, trust me. Some old, blackened piece of jewelry isn't going to tell me who I love."

She straightened her shoulder. "Nor me."

"It doesn't matter," Mr. Simeon said. "The question is, are Sir Gawaine and Arthur's knights going to let him stay?"

She smiled and did her best not to laugh. This was all so preposterous. They were talking like mad people. King Arthur and his knights…

"If King Arthur's own magic made Michael come here, I doubt he will change his mind now and send him back," Charlotte said.

"King Arthur has nothing to do with this personally," Mr. Simeon told them. "He cannot be found. Morgan had sent for him and he never showed up. They have not seen him in Avalon in fifty years."

Charlotte didn't care so much about Avalon and its king. She cared about building what Michael wanted here, a jail with *officers*, as he'd called them. She wanted to do what would make him stay. But at what cost? Preston? Michael and Preston didn't belong in the same century. One of them would not survive. The thought of it made her want to weep. Her hands felt shaky.

She had to warn Preston. Would Michael truly take her to Preston's tomorrow?

"I still do not understand how any of this proves that you are from the future," she told Michael. She wished it did prove his story. But as Mr. Simeon had said, it only proved that Mr. Simeon could travel through time.

Which was difficult to believe.

"I'm not one hundred percent convinced you are telling me the truth, Mr. Simeon."

"Very well." He took her blanket in his hand and held up his free index finger. "Be right back."

He disappeared, making her gasp and reach out to feel the air where he had been. She looked at Michael. "Is this real?"

"Yes."

"What if you disappear like that one of these days?" she asked him, more worried than she would admit.

He opened his arms, as if knowing she needed to be in them. She hurried to him and was engulfed in his strong embrace.

Mr. Simeon appeared again a few feet from where he'd been. He smiled slightly when he saw her in Michael's arms, then handed her the blanket.

It was older, tattered, well loved. It looked the way it had just before it disappeared.

"I returned it and then went back for it several years later."

"You truly did," she breathed. 'Tis my blanket." She broke away from Michael and took it and held it to her cheek to let it absorb her tears. "May I keep it?"

"Yes, of course It's yours." Mr. Simeon replied then turned to Michael. "Don't go anywhere."

He vanished and she shook her head, doubting she would ever grow used to that.

He appeared again, and this time he carried a small figure of a man. It was about twelve inches long and wore green clothes. It wore squishy boots and a hard hat on his head.

"My GI Joe!" Michael took it in his hands when Mr. Simeon handed it to him. He looked it over lovingly for a moment and then his eyes shone with tears. "No. It's Geoff's." He looked up at her. "It's one of my brother's toys."

"I took it from the room you and he shared when you were seven," the time traveler told him.

"Thank you," Michael said.

"GI Joe was a toy soldier from the twentieth and twenty-first centuries," Mr. Simeon told her. "This is his uniform, and this," he pointed out, "is his machine-gun."

She took the toy and examined it. The workmanship! The masterful skill! Why, it was a tiny man with perfectly painted eyes and pink lips!

"We played for hours when we were kids."

Her gaze misted when she set it on Michael. This belonged to his dead brother. She'd examined it enough and handed it back. "Very well. You have convinced me."

Mr. Simeon's grin faded. "I must go—"

He was gone before anyone had time to bid him farewell.

"Forgive me for doubting you when he disappeared the first time," she said after a moment, when they realized he wasn't coming back.

"There's nothing to forgive," Michael reassured. "I would have thought you were nuts if things were turned around."

"You told me you had no wife in your century," she quipped, "so I will not ask you the same question, but was there someone you loved you left behind?"

"No. No one."

"No one?" But he was so handsome, so mysterious and dark. Surely women in any century would want him.

He took her hands and sat back down with her at the table. "The police force was my life, Charlotte. My father was a cop, and his father before him. My brother was a cop, too. It's in my blood."

"Aye," she responded softly, not too dejectedly, lest he think she wished it were not so. She looked around at the large table and the chairs on either side of it. He was preparing to build his force and bring the law into Croydon. It was still in his blood. Where would a wife fit in? Not that she wanted to become his or anyone else's wife! But what if Preston never married her and Michael found someone else in the meantime? Oh, the very thought of it sickened her and angered her. Frighteningly, it was the part about Michael, not Preston that fired such emotion in her.

"But it made me very unhappy," he continued. He hadn't been finished.

She remembered him telling her that there was nothing good about his life that he could remember. "Why were you so unhappy, Michael? Because of Clements?"

"Yeah. I think it began with him. Maybe with 9/11. I don't know." His gaze fell to the toy. She wanted to touch him. To make him look at her again.

"What is 9/11?" she asked gently, "'Twas when your brother perished, aye?"

"It is the eleventh day of the ninth month. September 11th. It was a day when some religious terrorists flew some planes—planes are very big metal…carriages that carry passengers from one faraway place to another. They have engines that propel them to fly and wings that keep them balanced in the air. These men flew two planes into two of my city's tallest buildings and killed thousands of people. It began our war with the Middle East."

"Oh, Michael," she cried. "Men do not change. They just have more powerful weapons with which to kill one another. 'Tis very disheartening."

"That's exactly what I became. Disheartened. Things just stayed bad. My next partner was Kelly Harkin. We were friends on and off the job. I was invited to her daughter's second and third birthdays. Kelly was also killed on the job by a child murderer we had been investigating. By this time, I pretty much hated the human race. I had become cynical and negative, expecting the worst in people because most of the people I was around were criminals."

She closed her eyes for a moment, but then opened them again. She was what she was. She would not apologize for it.

"Were there no criminals who committed their offenses for

honorable purposes?"

"You mean like robbing the rich to feed the poor?" he asked. "No. Only in stories. People robbed for themselves, or for drugs—"

Oh, he must have been happy to leave such a place, such a time. She wanted to touch him and draw his attention back to her again and away from the distant memories of his dim past and the world's future.

"You said you did not want to go back," she reminded him.

"I did?" He smiled.

"Aye. When William asked if you were going back. Is it true? Do you not want to? I would not want to go back."

"There isn't much I have to go back to," he told her. "A better gun and a place to put it every morning."

"Then stay here," she said, tugging on his sleeve. His gaze swung to hers and he smiled.

"What do you care if I stay?" he asked with a quirk of his mouth and his brow. "I'm the man you believe will cage you."

He was right! He was right! "I do not want you to be unhappy, Detective. Unlike you, I do not believe this drivel about the brooch bringing people to their true love. I do not need—"

She didn't know what came over him. He didn't seem like the drag a girl in for a kiss kind of guy. But that's just what he did. He pulled her into his arms and onto his lap. He laid her over his bent elbow and slipped his free hand behind her nape to angle her at the perfect degree to take her mouth more fully.

She didn't resist him when he bent and placed his lips to hers and covered her mouth and breathed her breath. She curled her arms around his neck and held him close while his tongue explored her mouth. His kiss was all consuming, turning her soft from the inside out. She moaned softly and he pulled his mouth away. "This will lead to something we're not ready for. There are lots of rooms in this place."

She turned a bright shade of scarlet thinking about being intimate with him. Him ripping off her clothes, carrying her to the bed…

"Aren't there rules about being married first?"

"Aye. And my father will have you hanged if you plant your seed in me and do not wed me."

"Plant my seed?" Michael said, looking down at her. "How romantic."

They heard the doors opening downstairs. Some or all of the men had returned.

Charlotte bolted out of Michael's arms. On her feet, she patted her hair, her skirts. A glance at Michael revealed the humor he found in her concern.

"They're going to know soon enough," he quipped and gave her rump a pinch.

She yelped, leaped forward into the table and then turned to him and gave him a whack on the arm.

He laughed as Colin walked into the hall with four other men. He was smiling with his eyes on Michael. Aye. It wouldn't take them long to realize. To realize what? That the detective was falling in love with her. She bit her lip. Or that she was falling in love with him?

Chapter Eighteen

New York City
Autumn, 2019

CHARLES ARTHUR LANCASTER waited in the small coffee shop on East 98th for Elia, the pretty woman who'd arrived here from the fifteenth century while he was in Egypt last month.

They had met early this morning. This morning, he'd discovered his baby girl, Kestrel, was stuck in the fifteenth century. Well, not stuck per se, as she chose not to come back. She made that decision because only one could return and she would not leave her husband. Good for her. Pendragons did not abandon their husbands or wives. Despite that he missed her terribly and despite what the fiction writers of this realm added to his story, his Guinevere had never been unfaithful with Lancelot, or any of his knights. Arthur, for he was none other than the lost king, had never abandoned Guin. There was no way possible to ever find her without alerting Morgan and putting Guin in danger. He wouldn't do that. After he convalesced from his near mortal wound in Avalon, he'd planned his escape from Morgan and her brooch. Merlin had helped him. Arthur knew what he was giving up. He had no choice.

He missed his old friend. He missed his knights, and especially his Guinevere. He'd loved Cynthia, Kestrel's mother. He loved her and treated her the way she should be loved and treated. When she died, he did not marry again. But he never loved anyone the way he loved his queen. He felt his face grow warm and his eyes burn thinking of her and the children he fathered with her. Micajah and Camelee. He knew he had children before Kes. He just hadn't known who or where they were. But then he met Detective Michael Pendridge, who'd been assigned to Kes' case. Michael had to be Micajah. The names were too similar. The age was right. He had to be! But Arthur couldn't do a damned thing about it. He couldn't tell him. He couldn't risk Morgan finding out anything. He knew having his children in the same century as him would be dangerous for them all. It was why the children had been given up. But now it seemed the brooch was continuing to keep them safe by separating them from him. Would his first-born daughter be next?

And where was Merlin? He wasn't just a great wizard. He was an expert thief. He'd found the brooch in Morgan's castle and stole it and brought it back to Arthur. Together, they wove a powerful enchantment over it to override the first. Instead of seeking Arthur, the brooch united Pendragons with their true loves. He was happy to know—as of yesterday when he read his letter from his daughter—that it worked.

This…Elia returned here in Kestrel's place—with *a crush on him*. What was he to do with her? He didn't want to begin another relationship here on this realm where lifespans are so short. But he couldn't go home. Not with Morgan on the loose.

He had to keep them all away and live alone. If anyone knew where and when he was, it would get back to her. He'd made certain that wouldn't happen by weaving an enchantment over those who knew him in Avalon and in this realm to forget him, and to forget one another. The spell worked perfectly on the others. They all forgot, but Arthur remembered them. He still remembered his past, in Avalon, and then in Britain with his Round Table knights. He just didn't remember what any of them looked like.

The spell had been vital. If his knights found him, Morgan would find him. Her evil knew no bounds. She had cast one of her spells over him so that he would impregnate her and give her a son, Mordred, whom she used to almost kill him.

She wanted him to rule Avalon with her. He'd refused. He didn't want to rule anyplace with her. She was dark and vengeful, a worker of the enemy of God. He wanted to be away from her. He'd told her sisters of her schemes to rule over them and they locked her away for fifty years. But now she was free, and she was using the brooch.

Let those he loved live their anonymous lives without him. He didn't try to find any of them.

He heard the little bell ring over the coffee shop door and looked up to see Elia of York standing at the sunny entrance. She had exchanged her medieval clothes for more modern jeans and a lightweight wool cable knit sweater. Her foster son, Sir Nicholas de Marre, who was also Arthur's new son-in-law in the fifteenth century, sent enough silver and gold coins for her to buy what she needed when she got here.

"Forgive me for being late," she said, coming toward him. "I got a call for an interview for a housekeeping job I applied for. They called five minutes before I was leaving."

He left his chair to pull hers out. She fell into it and kept on talking. "And I forgot how to turn my phone on."

"It is on," he replied with amusement coating his deep voice. "You mean, you forgot how to answer your phone."

"Aye. I mean, yes," she corrected.

He smiled and leaned over the table to pat her hand. "Don't worry. You'll get the hang of this."

She looked around and laughed. "I still cannot believe any of it is real. You would think after a month I would be used to Uber cars and smart phones, alarms blaring and people bumping into my shoulders while I walk. But no." She laughed again, and Arthur thought about how fair she was. She looked to be in her forties, perhaps a decade younger than he. Her hair was gray with streaks of black. She wore it long and braided and dangling down her shoulder and breast.

"What do you like the best about this century?" he asked, feeling her exuberance with her.

"T.V.! I could sit in front of it day and night!"

"Mm hmm." He nodded and motioned to the waitress to bring more coffee.

"Oh, and wash machines! Claire would weep if she saw one!"

"Well, I don't know who Claire is," Arthur said, "but I wouldn't want her to weep if she saw a wash*ing* machine."

"She's the laundress at Scarborough Castle," she continued on as if he hadn't corrected her. "She cared for Nicky before Kes came along."

"She gave up so easily?" he asked, then also asked the waitress for sugar and cream.

"You have not seen the way Nicholas looks at Kestrel. 'Tis as if his next breath depends on hers."

He smiled. He liked hearing that kind of news. "So, you raised Sir Nicholas?"

"Since he was seven," she told him, sipping her coffee black. "And oh my goodness! This!" She held up her cup and he laughed. "This is a potion of some sort. It must be! I take it back. Coffee. Coffee is the best thing. How could Kes give this up?" She took another sip then closed her eyes. She opened them an instant later and gave him a guilty look. "Well, no, I mean, how could she give you up, not coffee. Coffee is just a drink. I—"

"Elianora?"

"Aye? Yes?"

"Are you nervous?"

"Yes." Her wide eyes changed from green to gold. "How can you tell?"

She was delightful. He couldn't help but grin.

"Why ever would you be nervous around me? I'm not going to throw you out on the street."

"I'm hoping to make my own money and get my own place to live."

"Of course. Are you ready to order some breakfast?"

She nodded and ordered what he suggested. Blueberry pancakes with strawberries and bananas and whipped cream, and if she ate meat, two sausages on the side.

When their food came, he watched her eat and thoroughly enjoyed the experience. He liked the way her lips moved, and the way she marveled over the food. He especially liked the sound of her voice when she told him about his daughter. She cared for Kestrel. That meant a lot to him.

"Why don't I take you shopping?" he suggested. "You will need some clothes when you get this job you want." He didn't want his time with her to end, not even for a little while. He hadn't found anyone so easy to speak to since…Guin.

Suddenly, his heart stalled in his chest. Elia could be Guinevere and neither of them would ever know. His blood chilled in his veins. No. No, he couldn't live with that.

He pushed his food away and sat back with his palm spread across his belly.

"What is the matter?" Elia asked.

He scrutinized her and then threw back his head and almost growled with frustration.

"Why did you want to come here?" he asked her.

"I wanted to meet you. Kes spoke of you often."

"You don't give up your life and your son because you want to meet someone," he insisted.

"I had no choice. 'Twas either me or her, and I knew if she left Nicky, he would go mad."

He had to admit, she had a good enough reason. He asked and she told him about Nicholas' family and the day they were attacked in the woods when Nicholas was seven. King Edward had taken him in, and she helped raise him.

"He's fair and generous, honorable and stern," she let him know. "Kes will continue to be very happy with him."

It was what every father wanted to hear—that his daughter was married to a good man, but to know his son-in-law was a knight was more than he could ask for. Kestrel's marriage to a true knight was worth coming here again, living a life here again.

It almost made him forget Guinevere for a moment.

Ah, the thorn in his and Merlin's enchantment. They knew it was best, and they had both agreed. No one remembers. No one recognizes. They would never meet again. It was best.

But when it was all over, Arthur still remembered. He didn't know how or why that part of the spell hadn't worked on him. He remembered. He remembered them all. Their laughter had haunted him for fifty years. Well, all right, not fifty. When Kestrel was born, the voices quieted, laughter faded and was replaced with images and memories of his second wife and daughter.

But he remembered and it was agony remembering and not recognizing them. Elia could be Guin. The waitress could be her. Anyone. It was enough to drive him mad.

"So you're coming here was a sacrifice you made for my daughter."

"And for my Nicky," she corrected.

He smiled.

"And," she blushed. "As I said, for you."

"But why?" He had to know why a fifteenth century woman would give up her life for a futuristic widow. "You didn't know me."

"I felt as if I did. Kes spoke of you often. She said you were a knight to her."

Kestrel saw it in him. Nothing could have made him happier. Would she ever forgive him for not telling her who he was? It would have put her at terrible risk.

"And then when Sir Gawaine came—"

"What does he look like, this, Sir Gawaine?" He'd stayed away from everyone, so he never knew if it was just the remembering part of the spell that didn't work on him.

"He's tall, dark hair, straight nose, somewhat somber eyes—"

Did Gawaine remember him? Or had Morgan reversed the enchantment on him since he was working for her now? More likely if Gawaine was using the brooch to find him, he could have only gotten it from Morgan, and if Gawaine remembered him, he would never be working with Arthur's enemy. So the answer to that question was no. He was hunting for him for Morgan. He wondered if she'd approached all his knights to help her search for their lord. What if this was Guinevere and she had been trying to find him for Morgan when Kestrel had arrived and spoke of him?

"Is everything all right, Mr. Lancaster?"

"Call me Art."

"Not Charles?"

"My friends call me Art."

"Or Arthur?"

Whoever she was, he wasn't ready to tell her that. "Arthur feels very formal. I prefer Art."

He paid the bill plus a generous tip and then helped her out of her chair.

"I just need a pair of boots," she told him. "There is a small shop near the apartment that has a pair I like. And I will pay for them with my own money, Art."

Delicate and bull-headed—just like Guin. No. He had to put Guin away for now. He could do it. He'd done it before.

"Very well. We shall do as you ask, Elianora, and then have a quiet dinner at home."

She smiled and looked at him over her shoulder. "I would like that."

So would he.

"WHAT DO YOU meeeeeeeeean you still cannot find him?" Morgan's screech resonated throughout her castle in the northern hills of Avalon.

"The brooch is not bringing us to him, but others to each other," a man with a deep voice told her.

"What did you do to it, Gawaine? You broke it!" she accused.

Gawaine took a deep breath in, trying to gather himself before he broke. Morgan Le Fey might be beautiful, but she was stark raving mad. Why did he have to spend his days looking for this Arthur Pendragon? One of her many lovers, no doubt. "I did not break it, my queen. 'Twas broken long before I put my hands to it."

"Yes. Yes. It was burned numerous times," she allowed, then sat up straighter on her throne. "He tampered with it. That must be it. Him and Merlin. Can we find Merlin?"

He almost looked heavenward, which would have enraged her.

"How can we find him when you cursed him to roam time? And besides, we don't know who we are searching for. Have you forgotten that?"

"No! I have not forgotten, Gawaine!" Her screaming nearly brought down the walls. "Do you think I am as meagerly made as you? I have forgotten nothing!"

Gawaine closed his eyes. He wanted to be out of here. Let Kay or Sagramore deal with her.

"We need Arthur to break the spell so that I can find my Mordred," she wailed. "Do you think I want to be here all alone? My sisters hate me! I want to find my son!"

Gawaine had no idea what she was talking about. And he no longer cared. He had quests to go on. He was tired of looking for a dead king and the queen's dead son.

"I will do my best, Your Majesty," he promised so that he could leave.

"Your best is not good enough, Gawaine. You have a week. One week. You better find someone in that week. Now get out."

Gawaine wanted to say more. He wasn't going to be able to find anyone. What was he supposed to do? She had threatened to kill him in the past. If he didn't find someone in a week, he was certain she would take his life. He was almost willing to give it up just to stay permanently away from her.

He stormed out of the castle without saying another word to her. What good would it have done anyway?

He decided Merlin might be the easiest to find since Morgan knew she'd cursed him. Gawaine knew a cursed traveler.

Roldan Simeon. He would start there.

CHAPTER NINETEEN

Croydon House
1724

MICHAEL AND CHARLOTTE met in the dining hall for breakfast early the next morning. He was sitting at the head table with her father. Old John stood behind them.

"Good morn to you, Investigator, John, Father. Did you sleep well?"

"Like a baby, and I woke up like one. Hungry." Michael laughed. So did her father.

She wanted to get up from where she was sitting opposite Michael and go sit beside him. She wanted to hold his hand, feel his strong fingers around hers, giving her strength through them. But she sat where her father motioned her to go.

"I was just telling your father about the old keep. He will pay for renovations, as well as pay the men and also pay for whatever we need."

"Father, that is very generous," Charlotte said with surprise lacing her voice.

"Crime will cease here, Charlotte," the duke vowed to her as her softly boiled egg and bacon, along with toasted bread, was set down before her. "I will see that every criminal is caught and brought to justice. Especially murderers."

She nodded. "I believe you have found the right man in Detective Pendridge."

Michael smiled at her. She had to keep her head on today. Last night, she was mad, just as he was. She remembered some of the things she'd said and blushed to her roots at her boldness.

They'd kissed by her door for hours. He was patient with her and visibly happy to hear when she admitted she hadn't kissed many men.

They had spoken a little about Preston, but she stopped before he began to brood. Michael didn't like hearing about him. He was jealous. She smiled thinking of it but, in truth, she was worried sick. Whatever would she do about her childhood friend? Was Preston in love with her? And was she with him? She'd never questioned it before because there hadn't been anyone in her life to make her question anything. But Michael made her stop and think about the time she was wasting with Preston. She wasn't getting any younger. She'd thought Preston would marry her when Lord Adere had asked for her hand. But he had done nothing. He had been willing to let another man take her. At times, he seemed more interested in how much money she could make him than in her. And Amanda. What were his intentions toward Amanda? She had to know, and she would find out today.

"What are your plans for today?" her father asked as if reading her thoughts. She looked up from her bowl. He was speaking to Michael. Not her.

"I'm escorting your daughter to Sutton so she can visit with the baron," Michael answered.

"Viscount," Charlotte corrected.

He squinted his eyes on her just a bit. Enough for her to understand that he didn't like her correction because he didn't give a damn about Preston's title. She tilted her mouth up at one end. She liked the small flares of his temper that his eyes could not conceal from her.

"Viscount," he muttered to her father. "And then, unless we are attacked again on the road—"

"No," her father interrupted. "I do not want Charlotte with Preston Bristol. The visit is no longer part of your plan." He lifted his cup to his mouth and drank.

"'Tis part of my plan and I'm going," Charlotte told him, setting down her knife and fork.

"No. You are not," he argued.

"My lord," Michael appealed, "we both know she'll go whether I escort her or not. I want to protect her. I can't do that if she runs off when I'm not with her."

Her father stared at her. Michael was correct. She would go with or without him.

"I'll keep her safe in the forest," he promised.

"All right then," her father relented, giving Michael a hard stare, and then aiming it at her. "Do not let trouble find you, Daughter."

She nodded. She didn't tell him that Michael was going to leave her alone with Preston and wait for her in a nearby village. Michael didn't tell him either.

They set out a short time later, packing midday meals to eat upon her return.

"Thank you for not telling my father about leaving me alone with Preston."

"Are you certain you're safe with him?"

"Preston? Of course. He has been my friend for a long time. Do not worry."

"Does your mother not sit at your table?" he asked a little later, on their way to Sutton.

"Hardly," she told him, keeping her horse at a slow pace with his. "She was not around much. Rosie used to stand behind me as Old John stands behind my father. She took care of me. She raised me until I was eleven."

"I would like to meet her," he said with a smile.

"Michael?" Perhaps she was mad. She had the urge to laugh. "Let us go visit Rosie instead of Preston."

His smile widened. "Are you sure?"

She nodded. She was very sure. Preston would be fine. Rosie was another matter.

She told Michael where to go while butterflies awakened inside her at the thought, even the faintest one, of Michael wanting to meet Rosie. "She will like you."

"How do you know?" he asked playfully.

"You are handsome and tall, strong and well-mannered—and you are not Preston."

"No one in your life seems to like him," he pointed out, as if she did not already know. "Why is that—besides the obvious, I mean?"

She began to speak and then stopped half a dozen times. She didn't want to tell him too much about Preston. She still wanted to protect him if she could. She couldn't bear to see him in a cell.

"They blame him for much he did not do?"

"And what *has* he done?"

"Can you cease being a detective for a few hours?" she asked. She flicked her reins and picked up her horse's pace.

He rode up beside her and kept his pace steady with hers. "I don't think so but, today, for you, I'll try."

She felt her blood go warm. He was honest, and he sacrificed for her. "You have my thanks."

He cut her a warm side-glance and then rode off.

She raced to catch up, but he laughed at her attempts, pushing his horse to bound over rocks and race as if it were running against the wind.

It felt wonderful to let her horse open up and run. She loved the wind snapping her hair behind her, making her squint to see and fight to breathe.

She gave a shout of victory when she passed his horse and won the race. They both laughed, out of breath, and dismounted to walk their horses slowly.

"Where did you learn to ride so well?" she asked him.

"My grandfather had a stable upstate. We used to visit every summer when I was a kid. Geoff was a better rider than I was. But I loved it. I've missed it."

"You said you were adopted—"

"Yeah. By the Davenports. They were good people. I loved them very much. To me, they will always be my parents."

"Why do you use Pendridge as your name?"

He shrugged. "They never changed it. I never asked my father why he didn't. It always made me feel like I didn't belong there. Deep down inside, you know?"

She nodded and swiped a tear from her eye. They had much in common. Perhaps he was her true love.

"What else do you miss?" she asked as they walked.

"I will miss my father eventually. He moved out to the west coast—New York is on the east coast—so I don't see him too often. After my brother died, things between us changed."

"Where is your mother?"

"She died of a heart attack twelve years ago."

"That is very sad," she told him, moved by his story. "Do you have other brothers?" When he shook his head, she continued, "One would think he would cherish you more deeply now that you are his only living son."

"Not if he never considered me that to begin with. Besides, my brother died a hero. He ran into the burning buildings and was inside trying to save others when the tower collapsed. He'll always be a hero. I can never compete with that."

"You should not have to, Michael."

"Yeah. You're right. But even knowing it, I still wanted to prove myself. Until my third and final partner was caught taking bribes. It was assumed that I was doing it as well."

"Were you?"

His flashing blue eyes lit on her for a moment. "No."

She believed him.

His father obviously did not.

"My eleventh birthday was approaching," she began, wanting to say something to him to soothe him, but not knowing what. She thought sharing a part of her, as he had done, was a good offering. "John and Rosie and the others had planned a large celebration. My parents both promised to come. Of course, no one expected Lizette to show up to something so trivial as someone else's celebration. But I had fallen over a cliff, three months before. A cliff that, thankfully, ended underwater. I nearly perished, but I stayed awake, and with a broken leg and two broken ribs, I managed to swim to shore. I made it home, where I remained abed for three months. It was the worst time in my life. I hated being dependent and helpless. My parents knew I had had a difficult time. My father had spared no expense for my birthday celebration. He bought me the bracelet that I will never wear."

"Why won't you ever wear it?"

"Because it came with a promise he never kept."

He reached for her hand and entwined his fingers through hers. Then he brought her knuckles up to his lips and kissed her softly. "What was the promise, Charlotte?"

"That things would be new with us. We would start over and he would be the father I needed. I knew 'twas all vain talk, for he did not show up to my celebration. I waited all day for him. I waited while all the foolish fancies he had birthed withered and died before my eyes. I ran away after that, but not for long. I would have missed Rosie and John and Anna too much."

"You will have your own family someday," he reassured. "All the fancies you dreamed of can be real."

"I have heard this before from Preston," she told him.

"Did he promise to give it to you?" She nodded and he scowled and mocked his adversary. "What is he waiting for? Someone to come and steal you away?

She laughed and slid her playful gaze to his. "Perhaps. Will that someone be you?"

"Yes," he told her brazenly and without hesitation. "It will be me."

Her eyes opened wide with surprise. "Detective, how do you know what I want?"

He moved closer, so close that their bodies touched. He snaked his hands around her waist and drew her in gently. "You want me. Am I wrong?" he asked letting his lips hover over hers.

"No. You are not wrong." How had she come to love being in his arms? She hadn't been there often, but it was as if she were coming home. Home…to a husband and a babe. A family. He held her as if he cherished her and hated to let her go.

His kiss was deep and long, curious and hungry. His lips felt as plump and pouty as they looked when she sucked his bottom lip between her teeth. Preston never hauled her into his arms before. He never kissed her so passionately.

Michael desired her. She could feel it in his salacious kiss. She could see it when he looked at her, which she found him doing often. She wanted to kiss more of him, his arms, his belly…

He groaned into her mouth and she felt as if she was being set aflame. She could feel his desire growing harder and boldly, instinctively rubbed herself against him.

"All right," he said, breaking their kiss. "We need to stop before I can't."

She smiled, liking that she could bring him to such pleasure that he would abandon his control. But liking more that he would not force her to do what could possibly ruin her if she ended up carrying his child and he was taken back to his home in the twenty-first century.

She still found it difficult to believe his story about time traveling—or her own eyes when Mr. Simeon appeared and disappeared and brought her back her blanket and a toy from the future. But it had to be real. What else could it be? Presently, she didn't care, except that she didn't want to fall madly in love with him if he was leaving.

"Michael," she asked, staring up into his starlit-blue eyes "what if you are given the choice to stay here or return to your future? What will you choose?"

He didn't answer her. Not for a few moments, at least—and that was enough.

She straightened her spine, patted her locks, and moved away from him.

"Charlotte," he called out to stop her as she walked off with her horse. "Hang on, let me—"

"There is no need, Michael." She stopped and turned to face him. "You fear that speaking the truth of your heart will hurt me, so you avoid it. 'Tis kind, but your pity will do me no good."

"Will this do you any good?" He appeared beside her, pulling his horse by the reins with one hand and holding out the other to her. In his open palm was the ruby ring she'd lifted the morning she'd met him.

"You had it all this time?" she asked, reaching for it.

"It was in the back pocket of my jeans." The same black jeans he was wearing now, and that he hadn't worn since changing into eighteenth century hose. "I never gave it to the constable."

Her eyes danced at the sight of the glittering red stone. "Bromley is not far. We could go to the town and trade this for food."

He smiled at her. "Let's go."

She chose not to think about his hesitation in answering her question. Not now. They had the ruby ring! He could have kept it and said nothing to her, but he gave it up to her. He agreed to trade it for food.

So, he was exactly the sort of man she wanted as a husband; compassionate, considerate, strong, handsome—the list went on. So what? He didn't know what he wanted, and she didn't want to be waiting around the way she'd done for Preston.

They rode on toward Bromley without exchanging much talk. He said a few words, but nothing substantial. He didn't try to explain why he'd hesitated and, at this point, it would not have mattered. At least, with him, Charlotte knew where she stood.

The vendors in the town were all willing to trade food for the ring. The only question now was which vendor would give them the most? None of them asked any questions about where the ring came from or who it belonged to.

Michael haggled for the best offer, which was more than what she'd ever received for anything she'd brought them. It angered her that the vendors would offer him more, but she was thankful Rosie and her family would be getting more. In fact, Michael was able to acquire at least a sennight's worth of food and still had coin left over to purchase a cart. Charlotte was ecstatic.

"You are very good at bartering," she remarked after they tied their horses to their new cart and rode out of Bromley.

"When you're a New York City detective," he answered, glancing at her sitting beside him on the cart's small bench, "you learn how to talk to people to get what you want."

"Oh?" she put to him with a half-smile and a raised brow. "Do you use your wiles on me?"

"As much as you use yours on me." He winked at her and then looked forward as they rode.

"Why, I hardly use my wiles on you at all, Michael."

"So then, it's your natural charm that's been knocking me on my ass lately."

She nodded, enjoying the way he spoke, and smiled. "As it has been yours knocking me on mine."

"Your what?" he pressed playfully.

"My *ass*." Almost instantly, she lifted her hand to cover her mouth.

He laughed and then so did she. When he put his arm around her, following a slight breeze, she melted against him. She was still stung that he would likely choose to go back if the option became able. It saddened her.

Thankfully, Rosie's small village was just outside the town and, within minutes, the group of thatched-roof huts came into view.

"It's like going back even farther in time, Michael remarked. "This place looks medieval."

"They have nothing," Charlotte told him and sat up straighter, eager to see her friend.

They rode the cart to one of the four small, thatched-roof cottages along the road out of the large town. Charlotte bounded from the cart and found her friend in the sunny backyard hanging her bed linens out to dry.

There were three rows of thin sheets billowing out around her, but Rosie, with her deep auburn hair and her ever wind-burned cheeks, saw her and pushed her way forward.

"Charlotte, I feared you had stopped coming and I would not see you again."

"That will not happen, my dearest," Charlotte promised, holding her close. "And look at how much we brought you this time."

She moved away and let Rosie see around to the front of the house where the cart, piled with sacks of grain, rice, and vegetables, just to name a few things, sat waiting. There were smaller bundles of fruit, and dried meat, and all manner of small boxes.

"And that is not all!" Charlotte nearly burst with excitement telling her. She was so wrapped up in it that she forget to introduce Detective Pendridge to Rosie. "The cart is yours!"

"How?" Rosie nearly shouted, and then she did call out to her husband. "Who is it that you travel with?"

Charlotte laughed into her hand. "Oh, forgive me. This is Michael Pendridge, he is a paid investigator, hired by my father to make Croydon safer."

"Greetings and welcome to our home," Rosie said with a friendly grin that revealed three missing teeth. She gave a pat to the hair gathered at the top of her head and covered by a caul.

"What is this?" came a man's voice. "Ah, Charlotte!" called Rosie's merry husband, Warren, as he entered the backyard. He pointed to his wife. "She has been waiting for you."

Charlotte knew it wasn't just for food. Rosie loved her as a mother loved her daughter. "Well, I'm here, Warren," she addressed him, a man she didn't think could be any more perfect for her Rosie. "Did you see the cart packed with food in front?"

They all went to see and unpack. Rosie cried and invited her three neighbors over for supper this evening. Warren cried when Michael told him that he could keep the cart.

The men were together doing something outside, and Charlotte and Rosie were cutting carrots and kneading bread in the kitchen, which was also the sitting room.

"What about Preston?" Rosie asked.

"Michael makes me forget Preston," Charlotte confessed to her. "Michael makes me forget everything but him. All my thoughts, day in and day out, are about him! I just met him, Rosie, and you know I don't give my feelings away so easily."

"I haven't known you to show interest in anyone your whole life except for Preston, Child."

"Exactly, but Michael has come into my life like a consuming fire. My father hired him to keep an eye on me and it has been infuriating. But I find Michael so appealing, so amusing…and he is passionate, Rosie." She felt a rush of heat course through her and felt her face go red.

Rosie laughed. "Aw, then he has kissed you."

"Aye, and 'twas wonderful," Charlotte said with a sigh and flung her hands to her chest. "But…"

"What is it, my girl?" Rosie asked in a soothing voice.

"He—" Oh, she couldn't tell Rosie that he came from the future. Without Mr. Simeon here to pop in and out, Rosie would never believe her. "His employer in York may call on him again. It would be his choice to stay here or go back to his old life. I asked him today if he would go back and he couldn't answer."

"I see."

"I don't know where he stands in his feelings for me. Why should he have any feelings at all? It's been a few days! He's very detached to begin with. He's—"

"He who? Me?" Michael appeared at the doorway. It wasn't fair how just the sight of him made her feel as if she couldn't breathe her next breath unless she were looking at him. He bent below the lintel and entered the cottage. "Here's where I stand in my feelings for you, Lady Charlotte."

She couldn't keep from smiling at him. She looked at Rosie and blushed again. The older woman smiled at her, and then at

Michael.

"I haven't given my heart to anyone in a very long time," he told Charlotte. "I don't know the first thing about dating anymore—in any era." He flicked his sapphire gaze to Rosie and laughed at himself before returning his attention to Charlotte. He sighed and his smile faded a bit. "I've felt stale for a long time. Everything inside," he pointed to his torso and his head, "had become old and musty. And then you banged into me on your way from pi—" his gaze darted to Rosie and he cast Charlotte an apologetic look.

"She knows," Charlotte told him. She'd told Rosie everything. Rosie knew what having a family meant to Charlotte, but it was more than that. She wanted a loving husband. Someone who couldn't live without her. She wasn't sure if that man was Preston. Of course, he hadn't come for her because he'd been shot in the leg. She was glad he hadn't come.

"She was difficult to ignore," Michael told Rosie.

"She always has been," her foster mother replied with a warm smile aimed at Charlotte.

Aye. She had to make herself difficult to ignore or they would forget her altogether.

"I feel as if I've woken up," Michael said, taking her hand and bringing it to his lips. "You're doing it, Charlotte. You're waking me up. I think about you all the time." He shook his head and laughed at himself. "Even when I'm with you. It's crazy."

"I think about you all the time, too," she confessed and then felt like weeping.

He wouldn't forget her.

"You're making me want things I haven't considered before, like a wife and a family. I just need to absorb it all without the prospect of being pulled back at any moment eating up my thoughts."

Charlotte couldn't speak for a moment. She thought if she opened her mouth, it would open the floodgates and her tears would rush forth from her eyes.

"Well," Rosie said, filling the silence and preparing the rest of their supper, "I think that answers your questions on where he stands, Charlotte."

"Aye, it has," Charlotte answered and took his hand. But how safe would his feelings keep her when he found out she was a Horseman? She would lose him and that would be worse than never loving him in the first place. Not that she loved him. Did she?

CHAPTER TWENTY

CHARLOTTE WATCHED MICHAEL laugh with Rosie and Warren and their friends while they all sat around a fire in the yard and ate supper. Rosie used one of the hare carcasses Michael and Charlotte bought her and made her delicious rabbit stew with fresh, warm black bread slathered in honey from Bromley. Warren had some homemade ale in his shed, but Michael didn't drink any.

When Charlotte questioned him about it, he told her that drinking was a problem for him in the past. He wanted a different life here.

He planned on staying. She wanted to rejoice, but his heart would change for her soon. She didn't want it to but there was nothing to be done. He might actually be her true love. He could lock her away until they hung her. She couldn't think of it. Not today.

She was glad Rosie and her friends liked Michael. She was glad he'd confessed his heart in front of Rosie and saved her the trouble of repeating it and not getting each perfect word correct. She liked the sound of his laughter. It was deep and authentic, as if it came from his belly. It made others want to laugh along with him. She noticed that his laughter came more easily in the last few days.

Since he came here.

Sadly, too late to stop it, she realized she was, indeed, falling in love with him while he laughed and ate with her friends. How could her heart betray Preston like this? She looked around at all the food. There was enough for the neighbors, Robbie and Alice Brinton and James and his wife Rebecca Houghton and more. Michael had done this. The thing she had always wanted Preston to do. Feed the less fortunate with her. She couldn't imagine sharing such a desire with someone she loved. She couldn't imagine how much they could get done together. She certainly could and would stop robbing if there was no reason to do it. She was older. It wasn't the kind of attention she wanted from her father. She'd known it for a long time. She did what she did for attention from Preston now. Not her father.

Michael caught her eyes and smiled at her over the flames. She smiled back. Every part of it was genuine. She hadn't trusted anyone in so long that she was still afraid to make the leap. But she trusted him to catch her.

He made his way over and nudged her with his shoulder. "You're quiet. Pensive," he said for her ears only.

"Just watching you."

"And thinking."

Her smile widened. "About you. What else?"

He chuckled and buried his hand in his hair to pull it away from his face. "Well, now you have to tell me what you were thinking about me."

"Very well," she gave in with a giggle. "I was thinking how I love feeding my friends with you."

"I am enjoying this with you as well," he said in his sorcerer's voice. "We can do it more often."

"We can?" she asked wide-eyed and excited. "Where would we get the money?"

"I told you. Charitable events. Your father could have one of his gatherings and invite all his friends. They can donate. They all look like they have money."

"What if they don't want to be charitable?" Charlotte asked him. "I don't know about some of them caring about the less fortunate the way we do."

"We'll figure it all out, love. We…"

She didn't hear the rest. Did he just call her love? Was he falling in love with her, too? Oh, this was happening too fast. A few hours ago, Preston was the man she was still waiting for. Now, she only wanted Michael. Was her heart so fickle to love a man yesterday and a different one today?

No. She had stopped loving Preston long ago. There was no passion between them. He only wanted what she could rob for him and for what kind of trouble her father could get him out of. Coming to think of it now, her father had done much for Preston, for her sake. He hated the cocky viscount, but he had whichever justice of the peace was involved drop all charges. For her.

What would Michael think of that if he knew?

She thought about how disillusioned he had become with his world. She didn't want that to happen here. The longer he stayed, the worse it would be for him if he didn't know the truth about some things. She had to tell him. Tell him everything, and then if these magical people came to bring him back, he could make a better decision as to if he wanted to stay or not.

"Michael?"

He turned from clapping for Rosie and Warren when they got up and began dancing to a merry tune sung by Robbie.

"'Tis not important," she told him, joining him in the clapping. He was so happy tonight. She wouldn't take it from him. She would tell him when they returned home.

She refused to think about anything else and, instead, enjoy the happy time with the people she loved.

She danced when Rosie pulled her up and laughed at Michael's protests when she pulled him up next.

They danced together and then switched partners with Rosie and Warren. When the other women insisted on dancing with Michael, Charlotte knew the ladies were a bit drunk. Michael was patient and courteous with them all, making her proud to show him off to Rosie.

They ate and laughed and danced some more. Michael even sang a ballad about them being champions, which they all learned quickly and sang along.

They finally put out the fire well into the night. Rosie wouldn't hear of them traveling home at such a late hour and invited them to stay in the empty cottage of their other neighbor, Enid Albertson. Enid, a widow, died last year from a malady of her stomach. Most likely caused by hunger. Rosie brought them fresh linens, washed this morn, for the bed. The small, single bed.

"I can sleep on the floor," Michael offered after Rosie made the bed and left them alone.

Charlotte nodded, not really wanting him to sleep there, but loving him for honoring her.

"But tomorrow," he said, pulling off his jacket and justaucorps, "I will speak to your father about making you my wife. You have until then to decide if you want me or not." He turned away to throw his clothes over a small chair.

His wife. He was ready to give her everything she wanted. Should she tell him how he made her feel? Or hide it and deny him such power over her? "Michael?" She stepped forward while he stripped of his black shirt next and tossed it aside.

Her eyes beheld him colored with images of everything from the Lord Jesus and crosses, to crisscrossed guns, a snake, and two long, square vertical towers with a stairway coming from them, leading up his side to his heart. She wondered if she was brave enough to climb up. "I already know what I want," she told him, touching his arm. He turned to look at her. "I want you."

He took her in his bare arms. She ran her hands up and down the corded sinew in his forearms, the interplay of muscles in his back. "You frighten me, man of the future," she whispered across his painted chest. "Your determination to fix what is wrong here is admirable. But I am wrong, too, Michael. I have done many things—"

"Now you will no longer have any need to do them, right?"

"Right," she whispered with a smile and tilted her face up to receive his kiss. She would tell him the rest another day, when his mouth wasn't so hungry yet controlled for her.

What if she took off her clothes? What would their skin feel like pressed together? But he wasn't her husband yet, though it was his intention and, to many churches, a betrothal was as good as a marriage.

Michael's mouth was like a hot brand on her skin. When he traced a path over her chin and down her neck, his dark scruff tickled and scratched. His tongue set her on fire, making her want to rake her teeth over his skin, his muscles.

When he scooped her up in his arms, she didn't fight him but coiled her arms around his neck, even for the moment it took to carry her to the bed.

He set her down on the fresh-smelling bed and backed away to finish undressing. He kicked off his own boots, glad to have them over the pinching shoes in his room. He looked eager to be near her and climbed into bed next to her in his jeans. Close to her.

This was it. She was giving herself up to Michael. An investigator from the future sent here for some purpose, perhaps to find his true love, as Mr. Simeon said. She didn't care about any of it now. She only cared about this moment with him in it.

"Michael?" she asked shyly "What are the women in the twenty-first century like?"

"They are not like you," he told her softly, tenderly, lifting his fingers to her hair.

"Is that a good thing or bad?"

"It's a good thing. They fit into their time. You don't." He touched his hand to his healing nose. "My nose can attest."

She laughed and then groaned when he buried his face in her neck. She sat up and pulled at her laces of her gown. The stays came undone with a loud breath from her. There were some laces in the back that Michael sat up and pulled with his teeth. More of her came loose, as if answering the call of his touch.

She took a deep breath and pulled herself out of all her layers.

She lay back down and smiled joyfully when he spread himself over her and pressed his hot mouth against her throat.

She felt the hard desire between his legs. He was abundant, as she suspected. The weight of him against her legs made her want to instinctively sit on him.

But surely, he would stretch her to bursting.

She'd never gone this far with Preston or anyone else. Never had she surrendered beneath the weight of a man. Or opened her legs so wantonly. Inviting, begging him to fill her with himself.

She had no idea what she was asking for. But she held on to his shoulders and rubbed herself against his jeans and the thick lance bursting to be free.

He moaned like a wounded bear and moved away from her.

He slipped his hand between them and freed himself from the confines of his pants.

She gasped feeling his hot flesh on her. She felt herself became wetter. Her body was preparing itself for him. Rosie had told her what she knew about being intimate, which wasn't much. Her friends had taught her more. Still, doing it was something altogether different.

She ran her fingers through his hair and directed his face over her breasts, where he sucked until she almost begged him to suck somewhere else! She stayed open to him when he played with her tightening nub. He controlled her, titillating her with his fingers, his mouth, his tongue.

She cried out into his mouth as he guided himself to her opening and then pushed. He came almost instantly, soaking her and making it easier to get inside her.

With all the touching and rubbing, Charlotte began to feel a sizzling thread of pleasure like nothing she'd ever felt before. It was coming from her muscles convulsing around him, or trying to. He was pushing in. She opened her legs wider and cupped her hands around his bum.

He came again and slipped into her to the hilt, pushing her open until she thought she would cry out. But pain soon turned to pleasure, and she drowned in the tides of it.

He laughed and almost filled her for a third time when they had to hold their hands over each other's mouths so Rosie and the others wouldn't hear them from their cottages.

"'Tis like nothing I'd ever imagined!" Charlotte said between short breaths as he separated them and fell beside her on the bed.

"I'm glad you liked it," he whispered hoarsely. "It will last longer in the future."

She liked the sound of him next to her in bed, after…she blushed at her own thoughts and memories already emblazoned on her mind.

"There are many other ways to do it," he told her.

She knew of some. She'd had to listen to Sebastian and Preston's other friends enough times when she rode with them.

She'd wanted to become a Horseman. She'd begged Preston to let her and, finally, he'd agreed. She became one of them. She was The Dark Horseman, holding up carriages with them for months before Preston let her lead a hold up. It was a disaster. The Earl of Chester had been killed. She'd watched Sebastian kill him because the earl had pulled down her kerchief and saw her face, saw who she was.

"What is it?" Michael rose up on one elbow and wiped his thumb across a tear falling from her eye.

"I was thinking of my past."

"You will miss it?"

She shook her head and rose up on her elbow to face him with more tears rolling down her face "No. I regret much of it. Save for being able to help Rosie and some others, I'm sorry for it. I have not been able to tell anyone my feelings, Michael. I was a fool. I—"

A loud rapping came on the door.

Michael hurried out of bed and reached for his jeans. "Yeah?" he answered through the door, pulling his pants up.

"Michael!" Rosie screamed on the other side. "We are being attacked!"

Upon hearing this, Michael flung open the door and Charlotte leaped out of bed, already halfway dressed.

He looked outside the door, then pulled Rosie inside. "Stay here! Both of you!" He grabbed for his pistol, loaded and ready to fire. One shot. He'd better make it good.

He hurried outside, barefoot and bare-chested. Someone's hut was on fire. The people he'd had supper with tonight were running for their lives.

He had to get them to safety. He sprinted toward them. Someone shot at him. He ducked and ran serpentine the rest of the way. He found Robbie and Alice and raced to get to Rebecca. Her husband, James, was trying to fight against two figures. There was no sign of Rosie's husband, Warren.

Michael had no more time to search for him. James needed his help. Michael didn't think about how he would fight guys with swords, he just ran into the fray. His pistol was still good for smashing into the back of someone's head. Which is what he did to the first one he came to. The second guy had a bit more time to prepare now and lifted his sword high when Michael turned on him. Michael shot him in the belly and then took his pistol and bullets. He did the same with his first victim.

He went to James and made sure he was all right.

"Our home!" James cried, keeping his focus on the flames.

"Hey!" Michael gave him a little shake. "Your wife is alive. Keep her safe!"

He left him and went in search of Warren. He heard a sound to his right and spun around, ready to kill.

When he saw Charlotte in the firelight, he scowled. "Go back to the house. They're shooting!"

"I will not leave you out here!"

"Go! I won't have you killed!"

Someone rushed by. A shadow. But it was difficult to see with smoke rising and only flames and moonlight by which to see. For one instant, the shadow came into view as clouds and smoke both passed by. The man slowed and looked at Charlotte. He wore a kerchief over his face, but Michael recognized him. It was the man who had escaped the mill. Why did his gaze settle on Charlotte as if he knew her? He hadn't looked at her that way the first time they'd met. Unless they were hiding the fact that they knew each other.

Did she have anything to do with him escaping the mill? She had been late to supper. He wanted to clutch his belly. No. This was all just a trick of the light. The man hadn't looked at her. She didn't know him or aid him. He was behaving like a madman.

Still… "Go back to the house, Charlotte," Michael said, keeping his eyes on the shadow as the man hurried away.

She went without another word. Michael didn't go after the assailant but rushed to Rosie and Warren's cottage. It was just starting to burn, a gift from the man who'd escaped.

Someone appeared beside him with a bucket of well water and threw it at the flames. Charlotte. He should have known she wouldn't obey a command. Rosie and her friends appeared next, each doing what they could to keep Rosie's house from burning down.

In the end, they saved part of her house. They couldn't save Warren when they found him later burned near James' house. He probably saw the strangers trying to start the fire. They caught him and killed him and let his body burn.

Charlotte refused to leave her friend's side, and that meant Michael wasn't leaving either. He did ride to Bromley that morning and hired a messenger to inform the duke that he had the bird. That it was safe.

If he sent men, good. But Michael wouldn't force Charlotte to leave. The men could stay and fight if anyone returned.

And maybe help rebuild some huts into houses.

CHAPTER TWENTY-ONE

CHARLOTTE WOULD NEVER forgive herself. She deserved to be hanged for her crimes. First, she'd panicked during her first carriage robbery and was the cause of the Earl of Chester's death. She'd been horrified and guilty over it for months. Hoping Michael would catch her, too afraid and ashamed to confess. And now this. She'd made certain John deVille escaped Michael's prison at the mill. It was her fault he was running free, killing her friends! Did Preston know about this? He would never have ordered the death of the people here. He knew what Rosie meant to her. But why did deVille come here of all places? Why this tiny village of four huts and people so poor they couldn't eat some days? She had to find out if Preston knew about it. She had to know. If he did, she would never forgive him. And why did the fool have to look at her as if he knew her? She was almost certain Michael saw. It was a look of recognition, a look of surprise. She'd been torn between running and hiding or clawing out deVille's eyes.

Oh, she just couldn't think about it too long. She had to be strong for dear Rosie now. But she was falling apart inside. Her façade was crumbling. She wanted Michael to hold her. She wanted...no, she needed more of the intimacy they had shared last night. But he seemed distant this morning. Of course, it could be that he, too, was heartsick for Rosie. Or, he suspected something. He didn't question her about deVille. What should she do? It was all too much. She was going to burst.

She heard one of the women crying outside. James and Robbie were burying Warren.

She couldn't bear the weight of it. She looked over at Rosie, sleeping in her bed. What was taking Michael so long? She needed his reassuring embrace. He'd promised to marry her. He'd taken her body. He'd made her fall in love with him. He'd made her want to change her life around. Michael. Just thinking of him made her happy. Who would have thought she could feel this way about a man of the law?

She heard a bit of a commotion outside. Rebecca peeked her head inside the front door. "Michael has returned."

Charlotte's heart began to race. She stood up, ready to leave and go to him when Rosie's voice speaking her name stopped her. "Do not return home yet."

Charlotte hurried to her side. "I have no plans on leaving you. I will stay as long as you need me."

Rosie smiled at her and Charlotte's heart broke. After all the years of trying to help her and give her what she needed, she ended up taking away what was most important to Rosie. It made her want to sob.

The door opened and Michael's frame filled the sunlit entrance. For a moment, while he stood there, Charlotte couldn't see his face. Then he stepped into the hut and looked at her. She smiled. His response was strained.

"Did all go well?" she asked him.

"Yeah."

He came closer and stood over the bed, looking down at Rosie and took her hand. "You have my promise that I will make this right."

"Aye," Charlotte let her know. "We will help you."

She felt a little better already. He would help. She loved him for his promise. She didn't think about telling him the truth. Not yet. She needed some comfort from him. The truth could wait.

"Charlotte?" He set his gaze on her as he straightened, "May I speak with you outside?"

"Of course." She wanted to be alone with him, too. She practically pushed him out the door.

When they stepped out, she wasted no time to throw herself into his arms. She held on to him and closed her eyes, praying that he did not reject her. His strong arms came around her and he held her tight. They embraced for a moment or two, neither one in any rush to let go. He seemed to know what she needed, and she soaked it in like a flower soaking in the sunlight.

"I spoke to two vendors in town," he told her, standing straight so he could look at her, but still holding her. "I told them what happened, and they've agreed to gather supplies and have them brought over, just some extra food and spices and stuff."

She smiled at him and tried to remember what her days were like without him in them. A sennight hadn't even passed and yet he felt like he'd been in her life all her days.

"I also spoke to a few brickmakers and carpenters. They will help us rebuild homes for Rosie and the others. I'm going to train some handpicked men at home and send them to Bromley to keep the law."

"You are planning a life here," she said softly and with a warm smile, reaching up to touch his temple.

"Yes, I told you. With you."

"And children?"

"If you want."

"I want four."

He gave her a doubtful look. "It hurts you know."

She let out a little laugh. "So I have been told."

He shrugged and she trembled a little in his arms. "Then we'll have four."

Something rolled over her like a wave of mud, cold and suffocating. For a moment, she couldn't breathe. She didn't want to breathe anymore. She broke away.

"What's wrong, Charlotte?"

"This is too good," she answered on the edge of hysteria.

"You are the answer to my prayers, Michael."

His beautiful face broke out into a grin. "What's wrong with that?"

"God does not hear my prayers."

His grin faded and he came forward to her. "He hears all your prayers, Charlotte. If you think about it, He's probably answered many of them, but not the big ones, like the ones for your parents, or maybe even Preston Bristol III. Come on," he motioned to himself with his hand. "He knows what's good for you, eh? Me."

He made butterflies come alive and dance inside her. She wanted to giggle but wrapped her arms tighter around him instead. "Promise to always want me, Michael," she said into his chest. "Promise me you will love me without condition."

"I promise," he whispered and ran his hand down the back of her head. She tilted her face to his. "I promise, Charlotte. I know you have some secrets. Keep them as long as you don't trust me enough not to."

His words were like knives in her heart. Did she trust him enough to tell him that Preston was the head of all the crime in Sutton, Croydon, and anywhere else he could send his men? That she was The Dark Horseman, accused of killing an earl? That her father worked underhandedly with justices of the peace to drop all charges against Preston because of her? Did she trust Michael enough to not have everyone in her life, including her, sent to the noose? No. In truth, she did not. Why would he spare Preston or her father from justice? A thought occurred to her. Could Michael be bribed if enough was offered? No! She remembered his reaction when she asked him if he, like his work partner, had taken bribes. Michael was honest and honorable, if not hardened and detached.

Soon, their embrace was interrupted by the service for Warren.

Charlotte wasn't sure how much longer she could hold herself together. But for now, she encouraged Rosie with soft, heartfelt promises and supported her when she stepped outside.

When the priest from the next village said his last prayer and Charlotte turned to go with Rosie, she spotted Colin and William arriving on their horses.

"I sent word to them," said Michael, coming up beside her. "I need to know who that man was last night. I'm going to find him, and anyone involved with him, and make certain justice is done."

Charlotte's belly burned. She felt faint. John deVille would certainly tell Michael everything about her. "Michael," she said stopping him. No! She couldn't tell him anything about deVille with Rosie standing with her. She couldn't let Rosie know she was responsible for this. She wasn't ready for that yet. "I wish to speak to you, please."

Colin was off his horse first and reached him in seconds.

"Rosie," the young man said first and bowed his head in respect for who she'd lost. "Rest assured, we will find the ones who did this." He turned to Michael. "There was another robbery on the road last night."

"Where?" Michael growled. Was the village a diversion?

"Outside Cheam. One of the Horsemen held up Lord Crawley, John Eddren, who traveled with his young wife. The Horseman made off with the lady's jewelry and Lord Crawley's signet ring and some money."

"How do you know it was one of the Horsemen? Was anyone killed?"

"No, and we know because before he left, he kissed the lord's wife."

"The Kissing Horsemen," Michael muttered. "How ridiculous."

Sebastian. Charlotte knew it was Sebastian. He'd been planning the hold-up for a while. She didn't tell Michael and hated herself for it. But she knew she would have hated herself even more if she turned on the people who had always been there for her.

"There is something else," Colin told him. "But I would prefer to speak to you alone about it."

Michael nodded and excused himself from her and Rosie.

Charlotte's heart raced. She almost couldn't call up the strength to keep moving but, somehow, she did.

She smiled at her betrothed, perhaps for the last time. If Rosie didn't need her, she would get on her horse and run away. But no. She was not a child anymore. Running away was not the answer. No matter what Colin told Michael—and she had the dreaded feeling that it was about her—she would try to trust that Michael would keep his word to her and love her despite what he learned.

It didn't take long for him to return. She'd just settled Rosie into a chair that looked about as comfortable as sitting on rocks when the front door opened.

"Charlotte." He filled the doorway and blocked the sun. His voice was low, deep, angry.

She turned and, without a word, gently pushed past him and stepped into the sun.

He closed the door and took her by the hand. "I want to talk to you alone." It was almost a bear's growl.

"About what?"

"About Gerald FitzSimmons."

She swallowed. Gerald talked! That worm! He must have told Colin or William and here they were to warn him. "Are you going to shout?"

"I might." More growling as he dragged her away.

"Before you say anything, I would like to speak." She had plenty to say. Things she needed to say.

"You won't charm me," he vowed, reaching the tree line of the woods where John deVille had fled last night.

"I do not intend to charm you," she let him know, yanking her arm away. "I just want to tell you things I should have told you before."

"Oh? Like you acknowledging that you told Gerald he had to set my prisoner free, right? Thieves stick together. I know all the clichés."

He looked and sounded so disgusted by her that she wanted to look away, but his gaze held hers still. "Aye, that is what I did, and I must live with the knowledge that my dearest Rosie..." a short sob escaped her, "is now a widow because of me."

His hard expression didn't change. Then again, she did notice the slightest crease in his brow. He fought not to pity her.

"Why did you do it?"

"You already know. I'm sure Gerald told them."

"Why don't you tell me?"

"There's a code, Michael. I don't want to be the one to break it. If a thief is in trouble, we help."

"Whose code is it?" he put to her. "Preston's?"

"It existed long before Preston."

"Is he involved in all this? Is that why your father doesn't like him? Because he's a thief, too. Maybe he taught you."

"Michael, I—"

"Is he the leader, Charlotte? The one everyone is so afraid of?"

It was much harder to betray Preston than she thought. "I won't—"

His eyes opened wider and sparked like deep topaz instead of blue. What? How? But instead of being afraid of him, her blood seared hot through her veins. "Did you really expect me to go against the one I had been loyal to almost all my life? I didn't have a friend until I was eleven, Michael. No one my own age or close until I met him. He wanted us to look out for each other and that was what I did. What I thought was the right thing to do. I was wrong."

"So you defied my wishes, my *duty* and returned to the mill that night. Yeah, I know the whole story."

"You know also what happened last night," she said, tightening her jaw to keep from crying. "You know now that regardless of everything else, 'tis my fault Warren is dead. I can never forgive myself for that. Do you understand, Michael? It will destroy me. 'Tis already doing so."

"You can't let it," he told her woodenly. "You can't live with regrets."

"Is that what you do?"

"I did. I plan on starting fresh here."

"With me?"

He stepped away from her as if she carried a sickness. "That was the plan, Charlotte. But things must change. Are you in love with Preston?"

She almost blurted out no, she wasn't, but she didn't take her heart lightly. Michael and Preston deserved for her to examine what she felt. Thankfully, she had been doing that slowly with Preston for the last few months and he was coming up short.

"In truth, I only know one thing for certain, Michael. I have fallen in love with you."

She'd never poured herself out to anyone, not even to Preston or Rosie. Not really. She always kept part of herself back because if one's parents could not be trusted, how could anyone else be?

But she'd shared her body with Michael—and she hoped to do so again. If she was going to share her life with him—and she hoped she was, she wanted to share her heart with him, as well.

"It doesn't matter what you do," he told her in a quieter, somewhat shakier voice. "I look at you and I wish I could thank Mr. Green for giving me that brooch."

Tears welled up in her eyes. He was more than she deserved. She smiled and breathed again.

"Is there anything else I should know?" he asked, smiling with her and taking her hand.

She couldn't tell him about being a Horseman. She couldn't! Not now when he was smiling at her and the wind was blowing his hair across his face against a backdrop of azure sky. She would never ride as a highwayman again. She would give it all up and spend her days raising money for others, not stealing it. And having his babes.

She was too ashamed of her gravest sin to confess it. And she hated herself for being a coward.

"No," she told him. "There is nothing else."

SEBASTIAN ALEXANDER, BARON of Surrey, sat in the sunniest spot of Preston's private solar and sipped his wine. He crossed his hosed legs and examined the smudge of dirt on his shoe while John deVille gave an account of what happened last eve in the small village where Charlotte's friend, Rosie, lived.

"You ordered them to burn it down?" Sebastian asked Preston nonchalantly. He was glad Charlotte would hear of his robbery last night and realize he was too far away to have anything to do with killing her friends.

Sebastian had grown up with an abusive father. The rat scum wasn't even his real father. When Sebastian finally had had enough beatings, he killed him. He'd done many bad things, but he didn't betray his friends.

"Aye. And now you see why," Preston railed. "She was with him yet again—after what he did to me! I should kill you, deVille," he said turning to him. "For letting her and her investigator live!"

"You called for Charlotte's death?" Sebastian asked, not hiding his surprise.

"Aye! John! Ride back to that village and finish her. She has given her allegiance to someone else. She may have told him everything." He turned his pale face to Sebastian. "I'm not a monster. I will cry for her."

"Amanda!" he shouted next. "Where in the bloody hell are you with my tea!"

"Tell me, deVille," Sebastian said, sparing the man a glance as he was leaving. "Where was Lady Charlotte while you were killing her friend's husband?"

"I do not know, my lord. I saw her after I returned from one of the other houses. She was standing with the investigator. He was bare-chested and barefooted. And he had blood on him. He is most likely the one who killed my men."

"Why do you suppose he didn't kill you?"

"I…I do not know—"

"Why would a man who shot our esteemed viscount," he turned to offer Preston an indulgent smile, "and killed three men on his own last night, let you live? Why, *you* said earlier that 'twas as if he were on a rampage. Yet, he didn't harm a hair on your head. Why do you suppose that is?"

"I don't know, my lord. "Perhaps he—"

"Did you not spend time with him in your prison cell?" Sebastian asked him and slipped his gaze to Preston. He watched him grow infuriated.

"You are working for him and spying on me!"

"No!" deVille cried out "I don't know why he let me live!"

Preston didn't wait to hear anything more. He called in his guards and ordered that deVille be taken outside and shot.

He left, kicking and screaming and glaring at Sebastian. Hmm, the baron thought, deVille didn't seem to mind the thought of killing Charlotte. Now he couldn't.

Sebastian put down his cup of wine and rose to his feet.

"Where are you going?" Preston demanded.

Preston would never admit it, but he was in love with Charlotte and her being with Michael Pendridge was driving him mad. Though he thought nothing of his own unfaithfulness with Miss Amanda Beasley and several others.

Personally, Sebastian didn't care what Preston did; if he lived or died. He'd started the Horsemen with Preston, but the viscount received all the glory from the men. He treated Sebastian like a favored pet instead of his equal. But favored pets, like him and Charlotte, knew how to get what they wanted from him.

"Sebastian!" Preston demanded. "Where are you going?"

"For a walk…to ponder you ordering the death of Lady Charlotte."

"Sebastian." His voice was softer now, curious with a menacing spark in its depths. "Did you plant seeds in my head that deVille was disloyal so that I would have him killed and Charlotte would be saved?"

"Preston," he said with the same patient smile he would offer a lackwit. "Are you that easy to play upon?"

Preston laughed, a choked-out sound. "Your wiles will not work on me, Surrey."

Like magic.

He would never admit that Sebastian had compelled him to do anything. His pride couldn't let him. He would drop the matter of deVille.

A shot rang out from outside. deVille was dead. Sebastian had to bite his lip not to smile. Charlotte was safe for now. None of the other men knew exactly where she was. It wouldn't take the next one Preston sent long to find her.

"Pres," he said as he walked to the door, "are you sure you want Charlotte killed? Who will be left to love you if she's gone?"

"But I'm losing her now to him," he cried. "She hasn't come to visit me once!"

"Then he is the one who needs killing, Pres. Not Charlotte."

Preston gathered himself together and ground out his words on a wrathful groan. "Then go kill him, Bastian."

Chapter Twenty-Two

MICHAEL VOWED TO love and honor and cherish Charlotte until death parted them. He didn't mean it. Death wouldn't part them. If he died first, his spirit would stay with her. If she died first, he would go to her. He heard the priest in the background reciting Scripture, asking Charlotte the same question.

They were in Croydon, at the manor house. He was marrying a woman he met a few days ago, who had lied to him and let a criminal, who later killed the husband of the woman who was more of a mother to her than her own, go free. Michael knew Charlotte suffered for it. Her heart was broken. She even wept when she apologized to Colin because he'd been hurt. What she had done was wrong, but she was sorry, and Michael understood why she did it.

Rosie and the others were with them while they spoke their vows. They were invited to stay in rooms throughout the large house until their homes were rebuilt. Rosie agreed, happy to be around Charlotte again. Her father had gone along with it, since Charlotte threatened to live in the woods with them if he didn't. Charlotte didn't give a damn what her mother thought of the arrangement. Neither, it seemed, did the duke, her father. He'd also gone along with their marriage, since Michael was better than Preston Bristol III, and he knew any protests he had would go unheard by his daughter.

The priest said he could kiss her. Did he dare do it with everyone standing around watching? He was afraid his legs would fail him, or he would throw up.

Had he gone mad somewhere along the way down this rabbit hole? What was he doing getting married? Especially to a troublesome woman?

But he couldn't look at her without falling in love with her all over again, every time.

This was what he wanted. Her.

He reached for her and cupped her face in his hands then bent to kiss her. When her arms came up around him, he responded—

The priest cleared his throat. People laughed. Michael broke away and laughed with her.

"You are now husband and wife," the priest informed them.

Michael couldn't wait for tonight. To have her alone and just...get to know her in every single way possible.

But first would come the celebration. Allegedly, everything was planned out by John, the butler. Some of the women who lived here helped and according to all, her father helped as well and paid for everything.

Her mother stayed away.

"Well," her father said, coming to stand with them when the ceremony ended, "my daughter is a Pendragon. Tell me," he said, turning to Michael. "About your father."

"Albert Davenport was a good man. He—"

"Davenport?" Her father paled. "But your name is Pendridge."

"I was adopted when I was six months old. My name, I was told, was already given to me. Micajah Pendridge."

"Micajah?" Charlotte asked, repeating it over. "'Tis very beautiful. Like you."

Michael grinned like a fool. He didn't care. Let someone mention it.

The duke set his dark eyes on him and said with all seriousness, "You are a Pendragon, Son." He sounded as if it were the most important thing he had to say. He'd said it once before. After Michael had told him everything. *You are a Pendragon.*

"Now that you are married to my daughter, there are things I need to discuss with you in private."

"Not tonight, Father," Charlotte said. "No serious discussions until tomorrow."

She pulled Michael away and headed for Rosie. Michael would rather head for the stairs and their room, but they had all been through so much trauma in the last few days, Charlotte needed to spend time with her friends. He smiled and waited patiently while some of them gathered with the duke's men and discussed how the new houses in the village would be built.

"Rosie is excited about her new house," Charlotte told him when they made their way off to be alone again. "Thank you for doing this for her."

"She deserves to have a place to live where she's happy."

"Aye," his beautiful wife agreed. "She does."

He leaned down and said softly against her ear, "When is it customary in the eighteenth century to leave the party and go to our room on our wedding night? I'm impatient for you."

"I, too, am impatient for you," she let him know with a slight flush. "If we are to leave, you must announce it."

"Really?" he asked with a pained look on his face. "Why does everything need to be announced in this day and age anyway?"

She covered her mouth with her hand and chuckled as he cleared his throat. "Attention everyone." What now? He couldn't thank them for coming. They all lived here. He knew the instant he said they were leaving people would know why. His gaze caught her father's. He looked away quickly. "Charlotte and I are tired and we're going to—"

A cheer went up. Michael cringed. He pulled her by the hand out of the large hall and stopped to laugh as they reached the stairs. "I'd rather announce the beginning of a new plague than ever do that again."

"I would rather have the plague than remember my father's

face when you announced it."

When he swept her up off her feet and cradled her in his arms, she squealed with laughter and coiled her arms around his neck.

They would sleep in his room since it was larger. All her father's belongings had been cleaned out by John and the others. Now it was bare, but soon Charlotte would add herself to it and make it livable for them. She'd invited him to help, and he promised to make time to do so.

The bed was made with fresh linens but the soft woolen blankets he'd been using were still there. Still inviting. He carried her to the bed and fell with her to the mattress. They kissed as they fell, excited and eager for each other. They tugged at each other's clothes, wanting to begin, to see, to touch each other's body.

She tore at his jacket and léine, pulling him free of constraint. He tugged at her stays, not really understanding how to release her from them. When she pressed her mouth to his bare shoulder, he unlaced her skirts from behind her back and then pulled them from her body. She was left in her hose, underpants, and her stays. He never wanted anyone so badly in his life. He wanted to cleave to her and protect her. "Would you rather be my lover and the mother of my children than a thief?" he asked, scraping his teeth over the milky white rounds of her breasts being pushed up in a bone corset.

"Aye," she answered silkily. "Will you convert me?"

He groaned and pressed his hardened body against her legs. "Yes. As often as we can."

They laughed and kissed and explored as they stripped each other completely bare, leaving nothing but tattoos, scars, and beauty marks.

He was ravenous and licked and nibbled her inner thigh. First one, and then the other. When he buried his face between them, she scooted back, startled, with laughter in her eyes and shyness in her smile. He watched her while he spread her wide and dipped his tongue into her then suckled her fiery nub.

He waited until droplets of inviting nectar fell from her, then he hoisted himself up on his knees and came down again, sinking deep into her. She was hot and tight. The feel of her made him want to explode. He slowed down, taking her gently, remembering that she was new at this.

He stretched her under him and moved up her body. He took her hands and held them over her head. He had to stop twice to keep himself from coming.

"Charlotte, you don't know how you saved me," he told her tenderly, kissing her chin, her neck. "I was ready to give up my life and then I met you."

She clung to him as he pushed inside her, entering deeper He wasn't sure how hard to push. She'd just lost her virginity and he didn't want to hurt her. He moved slowly, taking his time with her, relishing every moment. He kissed her breasts and suckled each taut nipple, all the while sinking deep then slowly retreating. He felt the cascading rush of pleasure wash over him as she released herself with rapturous cries.

⟫⟪

CHARLOTTE COULDN'T STOP it. She didn't want to. Her body was reacting to his, squeezing him tight, tighter. She roved her palms over the trembling muscles in his arms, her gaze over beautiful images and swirls that accentuated his physique.

Instinctually, she wrapped her legs around his, and then flipped him over.

Sitting atop him was like nothing she'd ever imagined. He filled her to the hilt and went still, wanting to keep her there forever.

But she moved. Oh, she moved atop him. At first it pained her, stretching her open wider. But she pushed down and pulled up until he gritted his teeth and threw back his head. She watched him. She felt him filling her to overflowing. She would never share this kind of abandon with anyone else. "I love you," she whispered, falling upon him when it was over.

They dozed and woke up twice more to make love. She was certain she was going to hurt in the morning, but she didn't care. This was her night. This was Michael's night. They would have what they wanted.

"Tell me more about the twenty-first century?"

"Everyone is in a mad hurry to go places or to get things done. It's a time of instant gratification. There are millions of people."

"Where do they all live?"

"Everywhere," he told her. "In the city where I live, people live in buildings." He described them and she sat up.

"You have images of two *buildings* on you!"

He shook his head at himself. Here was proof that he was telling the truth. He explained that they were the towers of the World Trade Center. He told her they were the towers of 9/11, where so many, including Geoff, had died. The date of the tragedy was tattooed on him. September 11, 2001. But she already believed him. Michael was honest.

It sounded like a very violent world. Everyone seemed as if they were smarter, creating things like cars and planes, ships that traveled to space, phones. There was so much, but what good was it all if everyone was killing each other? She was happy Michael came here. But was he any safer with Preston around?

They slept for the night in each other's arms. Charlotte felt safe there. She felt loved and cared for. She fell asleep thinking how strange it was that one man could provide everything she needed.

Only one thing spoiled her dreams. Preston. She had to tell him she was married! She also had to tell him that she was quitting the life he followed. She was going to follow her husband and do things the right way. Preston would hate her for it. He would hate Michael and, most likely, would send someone to kill him.

He would also hate her because of what she'd told her husband. Though she admitted nothing, Michael was no fool.

They woke early the next morning and met her father in the dining hall. Rosie and the others chose to go back to the village with provisions for another sennight.

"I supplied your keep with weapons last night," her father said, sitting to his left. "I need to ensure your safety now that you're married to my daughter."

"Thank you for your concern," Michael told him, happy to finally get the weapons. "Even if it is only for Charlotte's sake."

"Aye," she agreed, sitting at his right. "And thank you for putting my friends up for the night, Father."

He smiled at her. "Of course."

"You'll have as many men as you need to rebuild and all the supplies," her father told Michael. "I just want you back at the keep, training men to go out there and fight these masked bastards." He meant the Horsemen.

"That's my intention, my lord."

Her father smiled at him and patted his back again. "Sutton has written to me twice demanding that you be arrested for shooting him in the leg. What do you think, Detective? Should you arrest yourself, since I did put you in charge of everything?"

Michael thought about it for a moment and then shook his head. "No, I was innocent."

They both chuckled and the weight of what was about to change hit Charlotte. Michael and Preston were going to go to war. One might not come out alive. The backs of her eyes burned but she held back her tears. She loved Preston, but she would do whatever needed to be done to keep Michael safe.

"Father," she began. Things seemed to be cordial enough between them to finally ask what she wanted to know. "Why did you believe Michael when he first came to you, instead of throwing him out? A man comes to you out of nowhere, claims to come from the future, and you believe him. And not only do you believe him, you set him as a watch over everything, including you daughter. I must admit, it has made me feel terrible. Why? Why did you believe him?"

Her father looked at them both as if he were trying to decide something. He apparently did because he blew out a heavy breath, one he seemed to be holding for quite some time and turned to Michael.

"Three weeks ago, I received a letter from a man who claimed to be living in the twenty-first century. He told me who you were and to expect you. You would not know how you arrived here. But 'twas by his hand, he claimed—to end your loneliness. He told me you were a *detective* and would make a fine 'officer of the law'. He advised me to listen to you."

Hold on, Michael thought, putting down his cup. To ease my loneliness? What? Who was behind this?

"He said you would help Charlotte," the duke continued. "No one knew that she was in trouble. I cover up everything for her. He told me you would help my daughter as you tried to help his recently."

Michael had the urge to laugh. He might not stop until he went mad—if he hadn't gone there already. This was getting crazier all the time. "The letter was from Charles Lancaster?"

"That is what some call him, I imagine," her father told him and looked around cautiously. "No one must hear. No one must find out."

CHAPTER TWENTY-THREE

"FIND OUT WHAT? What do others call him?" Michael asked. He could feel Charlotte's eyes on him. He felt as if something life-altering were about to take place. Something even more life altering than traveling back in time. He took Charlotte's hand under the table. He felt calmer with her near. What did Charles Lancaster have to do with anything?

"I only know how he signed the letter and he bid me to tell you never, *never* mention this to anyone. It could mean everyone's lives."

"How did he sign it?" Michael asked. His heart was pounding in his ears. Why? Why did he feel sick…dizzy…

"He signed it exactly as Arthur Pendragon, King of Briton, King of Avalon, father of Micajah Pendragon."

"My—no." No way! He began to rise from his seat but Charlotte's hand tethered him to sanity. Now, he was supposed to be King Arthur's son? He laughed. He had to. This had to be a dream. He was in a coma. He was dead. Something, but this couldn't really be happening to him. He couldn't be King Arthur's son! He shook his head. Why couldn't he be? He didn't know his true parents, only that they gave him his name. They were Pendridges. Pendragons.

"John, get him some wine!" he heard Charlotte cry.

"No." He shook his head. "No wine. I'm all right."

It was a grand delusion, this. King Arthur's son, eh? He

looked deep into his wife's eyes as she leaned into him. "Charlotte, you aren't real. You're the perfect woman in my imagination."

She glared at her father. "What you're telling him is madness."

"Why didn't you tell me before?" Michael asked him.

The duke shook his head. "I have said too much already. You asked me why I believed you and now you know."

"Detective?"

Michael and Charlotte turned to look behind them and saw Mr. Roldan Simeon, the time traveler, stepping into the hall with poor Old John looking around behind him.

"Who are you?' the duke demanded, standing. "How did you get in? John!"

"'Tis all right, Father," Charlotte calmed him. "He is a friend of Michael's."

"And, I would hope yours, as well," Mr. Simeon said with a wide smile to Charlotte.

"I would hope so as well," she agreed and invited him to sit for some breakfast.

He thanked her, bowed to the duke when Charlotte introduced them, then asked to speak privately to Michael.

"Charlotte and I were married yesterday, Simeon. You can speak in front of her. Come, we will go outside."

He excused them to the duke and led the way to the front doors.

"Are you ill?" the time traveler asked him.

"Yes, Simeon. Tell me the truth. Am I dying? Was I hit by a car? Shot by someone with a grudge?"

"No, as I told you," Simeon said, "this is real."

"Am I Arthur's son?"

Simeon laughed. Charlotte went pale and shook her head at him. He remembered her father saying never to tell anyone else. That included Roldan Simeon.

"Who told you such a thing?" Simeon asked and then looked

around for anyone else. "Arthur's son?" he repeated. "As far as I know, King Arthur's sons are all dead. All except..." He gave Michael a grave look. "Mordred."

Michael laughed. "Okay, now I'm Mordred?"

"If Arthur didn't die in Avalon, then mayhap Mordred didn't either."

It was too preposterous to consider. Michael knew a little about Mordred from books. He was the one who dealt King Arthur the fatal blow, but not before Arthur killed him.

"Charlotte!" Another man's voice called out as he stepped into the house, shattering the images in Michael's head of a battlefield and men lying dead on it. "Did I miss the festivities?"

Lord Sebastian Alexander, Baron of Surrey, asked, entering the hall. Great. Michael stood up straighter. Did he like Alexander? He couldn't tell yet. He didn't dislike him.

Michael did notice Simeon's reaction to the baron though. The time traveler didn't have time to disappear without being seen, and it looked as if he couldn't have done anything even if he wanted to. He was struck mute at the sight of the young baron. He stared at him, unblinking, jaw tight.

"Simeon, what is it?" Michael whispered while the baron went to Charlotte.

"I was wrong," Simeon told him softly before Lord Surrey reached them. "You're not Mordred. He is."

Michael needed a minute. He felt as if he was losing his mind. King Arthur? Mordred? It was all so crazy. Then again, he'd traveled back in time to seventeen twenty-four. Wasn't that crazy enough?

"The gardener informed me outside," Surrey said, his smile fading on Charlotte, "that you and Pendridge were married yesterday."

"That's right," Michael answered him. "We would have invited you, but it happened quickly."

Surrey blinked. It was difficult to tell what he was thinking as he remained impassive. Then he asked, "Why did it happen quickly? Is Charlotte—"

"In love?" Charlotte finished what he had not been insinuating "Aye, I am."

"So soon?" he put to her with skepticism marring his brow.

Michael noted though, that the baron's gaze softened just a bit toward her.

She nodded then laughed, the dulcet sound of her filling Michael's ears, and the baron's. "I know it sounds mad, but our love is the sanest thing I've talked about all morning."

Surrey slipped his gaze to Michael. "Oh, you share her feelings?"

"Yes, very much."

"That is good news," the baron said, sounding sincere enough. "It changes things now, though, doesn't it? I must ask," he said turning to Charlotte again with a widening smirk, "were you intending to tell Preston?"

"I will tell him when I see him," she replied. "And don't look so gleeful. You are supposed to be his friend."

"So are you, and yet, here we both are." He grimaced and scratched his chest, the place above his heart. He looked at Simeon and, for an instant, Michael would have sworn his eyes changed to pale topaz-green, like a spark of fire.

"Who are you?" he asked with a tilt of his head and a thread of menace in his voice.

"The question is," Simeon countered, "why do I know who you are?"

"Many know me. I'm the Baron of Surrey." But that wasn't what Simeon meant. Surrey didn't know that he was Mordred. If he was truly Mordred. Michael wanted to rub his hands down his face and sigh.

"Aye, pardon me," Simeon amended diplomatically. "I'm not feeling myself. I'm Roldan Simeon, a trader. I'm told I have a familiar face. Many think they know me—"

"Mmhmm," Surrey mumbled, quickly losing interest. He turned back to Charlotte with a wide smile. "Well, I'm quite happy for you, Char. As a gift, let me be the first to tell you that John deVille, the man responsible for your friend's death, has met with his own unfortunate demise."

"What's that supposed to mean?" Michael pushed forward. "If you killed him—"

"Oh, I didn't kill him, Investigator. But I made certain the order he had been given to kill Charlotte was not carried out."

Michael felt his blood boil. He forgot about King Arthur and being his son, and everything else. "Who gave the order?"

"She knows," Surrey said, setting his gaze on Charlotte.

"No. You are lying," she insisted. "Preston would never—"

The baron smiled and shrugged his shoulders. "Believe what you wish." He turned to leave but stopped in front of Michael. "There is a law unto itself here. 'Tis called Preston Bristol III, if you did not already know. You would do best to go back to where you came from. When he hears of this marriage, he will stop at nothing to kill you. As a matter of fact, he already sent me to do just that because she is spending time with you. The only reason I don't do it is because, for some reason, I like you, Pendridge, and I like her." He pointed to Charlotte. "She's my friend."

Instead of thanking him for the information and for not killing him, Michael pulled him in by the wrist and twisted his arm behind his back. "And that's why I won't break your arm," Michael said close to his ear. Then, louder, he added, "Ah, my first guest at the keep."

"He will send someone else," Surrey warned.

"You'll tell me all about it when we get to town," Michael told him then turned to Charlotte. "Tell your father everything. Tell him—"

"John will tell him. I'm coming with you!" Charlotte insisted, following them.

"No, Char—"

"Sebastian is my friend, Michael. He came here to warn us."

"She's correct, Michael. I came here to warn you," the baron drawled.

"He came to kill you, Michael!" Simeon called out, stopping them.

"I already confessed to that, old man," the baron defended. "Who in the blazes are you again?"

Michael's investigator mind immediately latched on to the baron calling Simeon an old man. Sure, he was older than they were, but he was no Old John.

With a shrug, Michael dragged him to the door. He was thinking crazy. Could anyone blame him? If any of this was real, and he held Mordred, who, according to some great literature, was the son of Arthur and Morgan Le Fey, he didn't want Surrey realizing who he really was right now.

"Did you come alone?" Michael asked the baron, not wanting any surprises when he opened the door.

"Of course I did. Do you think I need an army to take you down? If I hadn't changed my mind, that is?"

"If you're lying, I'll kill you."

He was telling the truth. Outside was clear. They made their way with caution to the stable. Michael didn't let Sebastian mount until the stable hands saddled his and Charlotte's horses.

"Why haven't you arrested Preston by now?"

"On what charges?" Michael asked him.

"Whatever she has told you."

They both looked at Charlotte, riding a few feet ahead. "She has told me nothing," Michael said and brooded the entire way to the keep.

The fact that Charlotte had not betrayed her friends kept the baron smiling for the rest of the way.

Michael understood her loyalty. He was a cop. He'd never snitch. Still, he hated that she wouldn't tell him. He wouldn't force her, or arrest her for withholding information, but he wasn't happy.

He slipped his gaze to her while they rode. She looked away. So that was how it was going to be then? She would stand with her criminal friends while he spent his time trying to clean up Croydon and the roads.

He didn't speak to her when they reached the keep or when they went inside and met up with Colin and Will and some of the other men who had joined his force.

Could he really start over here?

He brought Surrey downstairs to the cellars and lit a bunch of candles. Then he brought the baron to one of the barred cells. "Get in," he told his prisoner.

Surrey obeyed and walked to the wall, expecting to be shackled. Michael shut the bars. He made a mental note to have all the shackles removed.

"Tell me about the Horsemen," Michael said from the other side. Charlotte stood nearby, listening. Michael was sure he could hear her breathing fast and labored.

"What do I get out of this?" Surrey asked. "I could get shot for telling you anything."

"Oh? Who will shoot you?"

Surrey laughed. "I told you, Investigator. Were you not listening? There is a law unto itself here."

"Preston," Michael said. "He's the head of this entire thing?"

The baron nodded but said nothing. "His people are everywhere."

Michael flicked his gaze to his wife, and then moved in closer to the bars. "I'm going to roll over his people like a bulldozer. Whoever doesn't want to work with me will likely hang."

"Work with you..." the baron said carefully. "What would that entail?"

"Giving me information. Testifying against him in a courtroom. His reign would end."

"He would hang." Both men looked at Charlotte.

"Is that what you want, Sebastian?" she asked.

"No, dearest," he told her. "But I don't want anyone else to hang with him."

Were her lips trembling? Michael looked around for more

candles or lanterns or whatever else they used for light these days. There was nothing.

"He's going to find out you spoke to Michael and he's going to kill you."

"Now, how will he find out?" the baron asked her. "Will you tell him, Char?"

"I will not have to," she retorted. "You said you were sent to kill Michael. When he finds out Michael isn't dead, he'll put the pieces together."

"Are you saying I should kill Michael?"

She slapped her thighs and he laughed, finished with teasing her.

"All right, all right."

"'Tis no laughing matter, Bastian," she scolded.

Listening to them, Michael was reminded of family members, brothers teasing their sisters. He thought he finally understood that she was more involved than she had told him, and she likely wouldn't be much help putting her "family" in jail.

"You will have to keep me locked up," Surrey volunteered, "until Preston is no longer a threat."

"Protection is not free, Surrey," Michael told him.

"Hmm. Preston is the head of the Horsemen. He's the head of all crime in this area. How's that?"

Michael ground his teeth together. That haughty little worm had people crapping their breeches and hose. How? "What kinds of tactics does he use to enforce his threats?"

Surrey shifted his gaze to Charlotte. Yes. Michael turned to look at her, too, but without the regret and tenderness that the baron offered her. She knew. She knew Preston's character, his life, who he was. She had likely been right at his side. A regular Bonnie and Clyde.

He wanted to tell her to leave them alone. He didn't want to see her right now.

"He gives orders to kill," Surrey confessed. "He's given orders for…ehm…families to—"

"No!" Charlotte stepped forward and grabbed hold of the bars to stare into the baron's eyes. "You're lying, Sebastian! If you think Preston would do such things, you don't know him."

She didn't know. At least, she didn't know everything that her ex-boyfriend/childhood friend did. That was good to know. Either that or she was a very good actress.

The handsome baron's gaze was full of pity for her. Michael thought he even saw a tear or two glittering off the dim candle-light.

"'Tis you who doesn't know him," the baron countered. "He keeps great and terrible secrets from your delicate ears. You thought what he was doing was for good. 'Twas never about the good of anyone but Preston."

"No," she cried. "It takes a certain person to—"

"He gave deVille the order to burn Rosie's village."

"What?" she gasped. Her eyes were wide on her friend. Wide and horrified. "Sebastian, please don't deceive me in this."

"I didn't know of it until a few hours ago. I was having an afternoon drink with Preston when deVille came to speak with him. He confessed to everything, burning the place, killing Rosie's husband, seeing both of you together in the middle of the night. Preston was enraged and ordered your death. John deVille was to kill you tonight."

"You said he was dead," Michael reminded him. "Who killed him?"

"Preston had him brought to the courtyard and shot," the baron told him.

Charlotte let go of the bars and stepped away with tears filling her eyes.

"Why did Preston have him shot?" Michael asked him.

The baron yawned and leaned his back against the wall. "I put into Preston's useless head the idea that deVille was a spy for you. He had to be on your side since you didn't kill him last night after you killed everyone else who was with him." He stopped to grin at Michael. "It doesn't take much to sway him."

Good to know, Michael thought. Maybe Surrey was the brains behind everything. Michael would be careful with him.

"Are you going to bring him here?" Charlotte demanded, staring at him.

"Not yet," Michael told her in a deep, low voice she almost didn't recognize. "There isn't enough proof. It's your say against his. He has a lot of influence. I don't want him walking away."

Surrey nodded. Charlotte let out a breath she'd been holding and turned away.

Michael knew this had to be hard for her. Was Preston that good of a liar? Had he fooled her so completely? It had to hurt. But...she wasn't dumb. Something would have slipped eventually. Did she know? Was this an act?

"Charlotte," he said more softly. "I'll be fair. If you can be, too, then you can help me, yeah?

She smiled, and man if she was faking it, she was truly a viper. He remembered her mother's words and then rejected them. Charlotte wasn't a snake.

"Yeah," she agreed, and then laughed at using his word. "I can be fair."

"Michael!" came Colin's urgent voice on his way down the stairs. "We're under attack!"

"And now it begins," said Surrey with a fading smile and slid down the wall to sit and close his eyes.

◆‑‑• •‑‑◆

CHAPTER TWENTY-FOUR

M ICHAEL BOUNDED UPSTAIRS. Was it Preston, his friends?
"Who knows we're here?" he called out to his men,
surprised to see there were so many. At lease fifteen more than
yesterday and ten more than the day before. Any one of them
could be working for Preston. There wasn't time to welcome or
warn them. They still didn't have enough weapons and whoever
was outside seemed to have a lot.

"Everyone in town and at the manor house knows we're
here," William told him, appearing at his side.

That meant Preston Bristol knew as well, Michael thought.
He turned to find Charlotte, certain that she had been behind him
a moment ago. Had she stayed behind with Surrey? Were they
talking right now?

It didn't matter. He turned to William. "The duke sent weapons—"

"In the gatehouse. Come, 'tis attached."

He hurried with William through another door and saw
more men running from the gatehouse to the small parapet to
fight. Good. The men were already fighting back. Michael pushed
William to move faster. When they arrived at the gatehouse,
Michael found about a dozen flintlock pistols left, everything they
needed to fire them, swords, arrows, axes. He grabbed another
pistol and a few handfuls of bullets, or round balls. They did the
same damage. He loaded two and shoved them into this belt.

William took two as well and did everything Michael did.

When they returned to the keep, Colin rushed to him and took him by the arm. "I had to subdue Lady Charlotte. She was trying to leave. She wouldn't hear of not going out there. She said he wouldn't shoot at her."

"Where!" Michael almost took him by the shoulders and shook him.

"In the kitchen."

Michael dashed forward, then realized he didn't know where the damned kitchen was. He ran from room to room and then called out. She answered and he followed. He found her tied to a beam going up the wall to a rafter overhead.

He pulled out his knife and began to cut her loose. "Where do you think you were going?"

"Preston won't kill me, Michael," she insisted.

But he shook his head. "I'll lock you up with Surrey. Don't step foot outside, Charlotte. Do you hear me?"

"She won't listen, Investigator." Preston's voice came from the doorway. He limped into the kitchen with three men behind him. They were all pointing their pistols at Charlotte.

Michael threw his pistol down and put his hands up. Where were William and Colin? His other men? If Preston or his men had killed them, Michael wasn't sure he could control himself and not kill the guilty without a trial.

"Where are my men?" he demanded, stepping in front of his wife, blocking their aim.

"If he takes another step, shoot him." Preston ordered. "I will deal with him next. Untie her."

"Preston." Charlotte remained calm, but the set of her jaw told Michael she was not okay. "What are you doing? Why are you attacking this keep?"

"Because you're in it, Charlie. I've come to take you back from this stranger and break the spell he has over you. You have ignored me long enough. You succeeded in showing me that I need and want you in my life. Are you satisfied? I threw Amanda out and prepared my bed for you. I will give you everything you want."

Michael listened, aching with every fiber of his being to punch Preston's teeth out. But she had to hear these things once and for all and know where her heart truly stood.

"Preston," she began. "Tell your men to stop pointing their pistols at me."

He ordered it and they pointed them at Michael instead.

"Not on him either," she demanded.

"You overreach," he said, narrowing his eyes on her. "The pistols stay aimed where they are."

"Then I will not speak to you."

"It doesn't matter. I will still kill everyone here and take you back."

Michael smirked slightly. He wanted to see him try.

"I don't want to go back with you," she told him. "You're too late. You should have stayed with Amanda. I'm sorry but I'm in love with Michael—"

That was all Michael wanted to hear. Her choice, when offered it, was him. He didn't need to hear anything more. With a lightning quick movement that no one saw, he pulled his second pistol free from his belt with one hand and a knife from his jacket with the other. He flung the blade and shot the pistol at two different targets and hit them both.

Weaponless, he leaped for Preston but was stopped by the last of Preston's men. They fought and Michael landed the last, jaw-breaking blow.

But more of his men rushed in. Michael recognized some of the men from earlier. They were the men who had joined his force. Apparently, they had just done so to gain entrance into the keep.

It angered Michael and he fought harder. He fought for Charlotte, to keep her out of the madman Preston's grip. Setting his gaze on the viscount, now holding Charlotte by the arm and a knife to her throat, Michael punched and sliced his way—using his dead opponent's swords—through Preston's men until no more stood against him.

"Take a step closer and I slice her pretty throat," Preston promise. "Let me pass."

"What's this?" Came another voice. Michael looked to his right and saw the Baron of Surrey standing in the kitchen doorway, arms outstretched, palms up. "Preston, just what do you intend to do with that blade?"

"You were supposed to kill him, Sebastian. What happened? Why did you betray me?"

"Who says I betrayed you?" Surrey's dashing smile appeared as genuine as if he were talking to a beloved brother. He stepped into the kitchen and his gaze settled on Michael. He slipped a knife out of his sleeve and pointed it at Michael, then laughed.

Michael's belly sank. Charlotte had released Surrey and now Michael was going to die in front of her. How could she defy him yet again? He wanted to shout at her. He wanted to live and save her.

"You let him go," he said, forgetting the baron and sounding more defeated by her than angry. He would never have all of her heart, and it broke his. She was the first person who'd ever made him forget all his ghosts. She made him want to abandon everything and start his life over with her here.

She looked as if she were about to say something in her defense, but Preston stopped her.

"Sebastian, were you this man's prisoner?"

"I was. Use caution with him, for he knows how to make do without a pistol. When I went to Croydon to kill him, he nearly killed me instead! With his bare hands!"

Michael didn't know why the baron was lying through his teeth, but it was good to believe he wasn't being betrayed by a man who could be his...brother—his head was spinning from it all.

Why was he lying to Preston now?

"She remained quiet until he left to deal with you, and then she released me. Tell Pres about it, dearest."

Charlotte looked about to spit bullets at him. Behind her, Preston lowered the knife. "You remained loyal, Charlotte?"

"Of course. Pendridge is a stranger. I was not *choosing* to stay with him. I was a prisoner under my father's orders. I waited for you to come, Preston, but you were too busy with Amanda."

Michael stopped breathing. What? What was she saying? She was lying, too. She *did* choose to stay with him.

"She means nothing," Preston argued. "I sent her away. Forgive me for doubting you, but you also must remember that I could not come to you. He had shot me."

"Hmm, I should not forgive you for inviting Amanda to you to begin with."

Her pout earned her an indulgent smile from Preston that make Michael sick. He was going to kill Preston if he didn't step away from his wife.

Everything happened in a split second after that. Preston turned his back to Surrey for a moment and, in that moment, the knife the baron had been flipping up in the air, landed hilt first in his hand and then flew through the air, the blade sliced into Preston's back.

Charlotte screamed, alerting more men. Michael hurried to her where she knelt over Preston's body. "Charlotte, are you with me?"

She looked at him with tears running down her face. Seconds passed on endlessly until she spoke, "Aye. I'm with you, my love."

"Come," he said, gently pulling her from her friend. He knew how it felt to be pulled away from a dead friend.

Clements grinned at him, the way he used to when he and Michael were off duty and at a club, and Michael walked away with a woman hanging off him.

"You love this one, Mick?"

"Yeah, Jimmy, I love her."

"It's about time!" Clements laughed, covering his mouth with his hand, like he used to do because he had a crooked front tooth. He was walking away backward. "Have fun on the journey, man."

"I'm going to try," Michael promised as Jimmy disappeared.

"Captain?"

Captain? It was William.

"We should leave, Captain. There are more men coming."

"Yes," Michael said and smiled at him. He took Charlotte's hand and, together, with the baron already gone, they raced out of the kitchen.

"Do we have any men left?" he asked Will as they ran down the hall.

"They'll be back, Sir. Most of them grew afraid when they saw Lord Sutton and his men."

Michael hated that Preston and his buddies had been strong-arming the people for so long. Well, no more. Preston was dead and it was all going to stop. He eyed the baron while they ran out the back door to the keep's inner courtyard. What was Michael to do with him? And Charlotte...how far would she go for her outlaw family?

"Can we get to the garrison from here?" he asked William.

When William nodded, Michael told him to lead the way.

"We are not leaving?" asked Charlotte.

"No," Michael told her. "I'm not running. Whoever wants to come against me can try. But they won't be victorious. If I run, what am I showing them?"

"That you are clever enough to live another day."

He frowned. "You have no faith in me."

"I do. Forgive me." She smiled and leaned up to kiss him.

"Why did you release Surrey from his cell?"

"I didn't," she replied. "I don't know who did."

"'Twas me," Colin said, coming to stand with them. "Most of us follow him. Not Preston."

This was getting ridiculous, Michael decided and stormed toward Colin and punched him in the jaw. The younger man went down like a sack of potatoes. He remained on the ground, out cold. Michael looked up at William. "You, too?"

"No, Captain."

"Good. The garrison?"

Still staring in shock at his friend on the ground, William hesitated one more instant and then ran.

Michael and Charlotte followed him to the smaller garrison and stormed inside. They gathered all the weapons they could carry and brought them to the parapet.

"What if we cannot beat them?" she asked him, looking worried.

He smiled, reassuringly, while he handed out more weapons to the men already up there. "We'll do fine. How good are you at shooting that thing?" he asked her, eyeing the arrow she was nocking to a bow.

"Good enough."

"You would shoot your friends for me?" He didn't want her to have to.

"You have no faith in me."

"I do." He smiled and kissed her. "Forgive me."

"I did, too…once."

Charlotte turned to the voice behind her and screamed. The arrow fell limply from her hands.

Preston stood with them on the battlement. Surrey's knife was still in his back. In his hand, he pointed a pistol at Michael. "Tell your men to stand down or I will kill you. Follow her example and drop your weapons and live."

"Do it," Michael told William and the others and then led them by example.

"Preston," Charlotte said softly. "Put that pistol down and let me have a look at your wound."

He smiled and shook his head. "So you can twist the knife in deeper, Charlie?"

"I never wanted to hurt you, Preston," she told him. "You were all I thought I had."

"I was," he whined, "and then this piece of rat scum—"

"I had my father, Preston. You never wanted me to see it, but I had my father. He wanted to be there for me, but I never let him because of you. You used me for years. I was an oddity. A girl thief who—"

"Who is a Horseman."

The parapet grew quiet.

"What?" Michael turned to her. "What is he saying? You're a Horseman?"

"Aye," she said so softly he barely heard her. But he did.

Well, that was it. What more was there to say? She'd lied to him about everything. She was a Horseman. If he didn't arrest her, what good was he as a lawman? No. It was over. He would give it all up. They all knew. Preston, Surrey, probably all the men. They all knew, and they were laughing at him.

"She's the Dark Horseman," Preston continued happily.

Michael stared at her with cool detachment in his half-hooded gaze. "You're the one who killed that earl."

No. Please. He didn't want her to be guilty of murder. She would hang.

"No, Michael," she insisted. "The earl pulled down my mask and saw who I was. Sebastian killed him to protect me."

"Oh, well that makes all the difference, Charlotte," he told her harshly, disgusted by them all. "A man lost his life to keep you from jail, where you belong."

"Aye. Aye, you're correct," she admitted with tears forming in her eyes and falling over the rims. "I told you, did I not, that you would end up caging me. Oh, I wanted to tell you the truth, Michael. I—"

"What is this?" Preston interrupted with a biting edge in his voice.

Michael noticed the dark red stain flowing down his hose. He was losing blood. A lot of it.

"You speak like this stranger means something to you." In his hand, the pistol shook. His face was pale. He was dying.

Michael thought the viscount might not have the strength to pull back on the trigger, but he wasn't about to test the theory.

"Preston, I have loved you for so long I don't know what it's like not to love you. I will remember the good parts of you."

She was trying to comfort him. She knew he was dying. He'd been her friend. Michael expected nothing less from her.

Preston nodded and tears fell from his eyes. His knees gave out. He fell on them.

Rushing to him, Charlotte took him in her arms. Almost instantly, he pulled the trigger. The pistol was fired, and Charlotte collapsed to the ground.

No! She wasn't just shot! No! Michael couldn't move. He couldn't breathe. He couldn't lose her! NO!

CHAPTER TWENTY-FIVE

"MICHAEL?" SHE MANAGED lightly. Michael held her close so she didn't have to make much noise. "'Tis my side. See? A flesh wound."

He hovered above her, his sapphire eyes examining her wound. He looked mildly relieved. "What kind of doctors do they have here?"

Mr. Simeon appeared beside them and had a good look at her wound. "Not anywhere near as skilled as when you come from, but she will make a full recovery."

Michael was so relieved he thought he might cry. He looked around quickly. It wouldn't do for the men to see the captain of the police cry. Then again, maybe *not* crying when his friends were killed was the reason he used to wake up every morning and put the barrel of a gun into his mouth.

She'd changed everything. She brought happiness back into his life. She made him feel human again, alive.

"I'm going to have you taken care of, my love," he promised her, then looked at Simeon, realizing that the time traveler had appeared in front of William. He didn't care. "Go to the duke, tell him what happened and where we are—"

Another voice came up from behind him. "What are you going to do against all the men coming upon the keep in the meantime?"

Surrey. For some crazy reason, Michael smiled. It was help.

That's why when the baron asked for Michael's coat, he gave it, not realizing what he meant to do.

Surrey put on the coat and pulled the hood up over his head. Then he heaved Preston's body off the ground, walked to the edge of the wall, and hurled him over the side.

In Michael's arms, Charlotte cried out and buried her face into his chest.

"That should take care of that," Surrey said, stepping away from the wall while Michael comforted his wife. "If you could kill the leader of the Horsemen, and the overseer of all the crime in southern London," the baron continued, "you can do just about anything."

"But it was you who killed him, not me," Michael corrected.

"They don't know that. They just saw *you* throw him over."

Michael shook his head. "I won't take credit for stabbing a man in the back."

"Even if it was to save your wife?" Surrey asked with a challenging smile that went warm after a moment. "Tell me why I like you even after you punched my friend, Colin, in the jaw?"

Because we're brothers and you sense it. We have a sister.

"Can I have my coat back?"

Surrey winked at him and then handed over the garment.

Michael saw Simeon standing with Colin and William near the edge. "What's he still doing here?"

"He followed me," Surrey explained. "When I saw that he'd been hit—"

"I'm talking about Simeon. Mr. Simeon!" he shouted. "Go get her help from the duke! Now!"

The time traveler gave the two men he was with a sheepish look before setting his large dark eyes back on Michael. "Now?"

"Now!"

He disappeared. The men thought he fell over. William screamed out and looked over the side.

Surrey stared in utter astonishment and then walked over to where Simeon had just been. "How did he do it?"

"Do what?" William's voice shook. "Where did he go?"

"Ask him." The baron pointed to Michael.

"He can travel through time." Michael didn't care who knew. He had no time for notions about King Arthur and time travel and being the brother of one of the most infamous bad guys in fiction. Only, he was real. He wouldn't tell them that he was allegedly Arthur's son since, according to the duke, lives were at stake.

He gazed at Charlotte, so thankful he didn't lose her. "My love, just a little longer now."

"Michael, Preston must be buried."

"He will be."

"What do you mean?" Surrey demanded. "How can he travel through time?"

"He was cursed by some witch to travel through time, never to settle down. Something like that."

"Hmm, that's quite interesting."

Michael realized what he'd done. He'd just given Mordred a possible way to find his father. He cast Charlotte a worried look and then glared at the baron.

"Don't get any ideas, Surrey. No one can go in his place and he can't bring anyone with him."

"There are ways around everything, Investigator," the baron said with a smirk.

Michael sure as hell hoped not.

"Where, exactly, did you say you came from, Pendridge?"

"Captain?" William asked, sounding nervous, still shaken. "I heard Mr. Simeon say to you that the doctors here were not as skilled as the ones from *when* you came. What did he mean? Are you one of them, too? Can you travel through time?"

"No." Michael tried to sound convincing, but Surrey's un-blinking gaze was unsettling.

"You don't sound like anyone from around here...in Eng-land." Surrey said. "Is black magic at work here?"

Michael laughed. "Listen to yourself—"

"You said your Mr. Simeon could travel through time and you want *me* to listen to *myself*?"

Simeon popped in again, scaring William and Colin out of their skin. "The duke is on his way and so are a few others."

"Who?" Michael asked.

"Can you truly travel through time?" Surrey asked.

"Mr. Green, for one," Simeon told Michael, ignoring the other question. "We should all disperse."

Colin looked over the side. "The men are still down there."

"You should go speak to them, Investigator," Surrey advised. "I'll handle this Mr. Green person."

The baron was clever…and curious. Michael had to get rid of him. "No. You go down there and let those men know reinforcements are coming. Take Colin and William with you."

Surrey smiled and bowed to him. "As you wish."

He surrendered too easily but there was nothing else Michael could do short of knocking him out.

"Michael?" Charlotte said, still in his arms on the ground. He wouldn't leave her unless he had to fight to save her life. Then, he wouldn't lose.

"Yes, my love?"

"I'm happy it was not your hand that killed Preston."

Yes. He knew she would be. However he felt about the viscount and the things he did and had done, Charlotte had her own feelings and they were different than his. He hadn't wanted to be the one who took her oldest friend's life, no matter what Preston deserved.

"So am I, love."

The air behind Simeon began to sparkle. A breeze from the south filled Michael's nose with the scent of apples. He thought it odd and turned to Charlotte to remark on it when he saw two men mounted on great warhorses appear from out of the shimmering clouds above her. The horses wore trappings depicting a dragon.

Michael recognized the two of them, though he couldn't

believe his eyes. They appeared more primitive now in their leather armor and fur jackets, with two-edged swords dangling from their belts.

"You heard him," said *Luke*. "'Twas the same as before. They were sent for love. The brooch has been tampered with for certain."

His companion, Sir Gawaine, eyed Michael with the same dark eyes that had looked at him through glasses in an office once before. "By Merlin." They both turned their gazes on Simeon.

Michael's eyes opened wide. "Merlin?"

Simeon shook his head. "I would know."

"We have been trying to find you, Traveler," Sir Luke told him. His destrier snorted beneath him. "You are difficult to pin down."

"Well, you can thank the one who cursed me for that."

"Who was it?" Gawaine demanded.

"A witch."

"What witch?"

"How am I supposed to know what witch? They have names? I never believed in them before, so I didn't ask questions. And why have you been trying to find me? Who told you I was Merlin?"

"She wants you found," Luke told him. "She wants the spell broken and Mordred found."

"Why are you questioning me about this?" Simeon demanded. His voice sounded a bit shaky. "I'm not Merlin!"

"We think the witch was Morgan Le Fey," Sir Gawaine overrode his voice. "And part of the enchantment is that no one remembers who they are, or who anyone else is. I could be Arthur, and none of us would know it."

"You're not Arthur," Simeon said with a smirk. "And I'm not Merlin."

Luke reached for him, but he disappeared. Michael hid his smile.

The way Gawaine glared at him, he figured he hadn't been all that successful at hiding it.

"You cannot just disappear and escape," Sir Gawaine warned.

"Escape what?" Michael asked him.

"Notice," the knight said. "You are talking too much, telling too many people too much. You're not even supposed to be here. Someone tampered with the brooch. You were supposed to lead us to King Arthur."

Michael wanted them to continue to believe the brooch had nothing to do with the king. But, of course, it did. He was one of three people who knew who and where Arthur Pendragon was. He looked at his wife and tried to reassure her with a smile. He wasn't going back. "Oh, so you think you're going to send me back without my wife?"

Luke slapped his forehead and turned his horse away, mumbling about Morgan skinning them alive.

"We're not leaving you here," Gawaine promised. "You're too much of a risk. You all are. I don't know why we must keep doing this. Here!" He was shouting by now. "Take the brooch. If you don't, we will take you to Morgan and let her deal with you."

He tossed the charred brooch to Michael. This was it. His chance to go back home.

But this was his home now, where he wanted his home to be. With her.

Michael let the brooch fall into Charlotte's lap.

Someone else snatched it up.

"What do I do?" the Baron of Surrey asked without taking his eyes off the brooch. "Where will I go?"

"No!" Michael tried to grab it from him, but the brooch began to shine as if it were new. It was already enchanting Surrey. The name of the king appeared in the stone. Michael turned away and then heard Surrey say one word. Pendragon.

He disappeared. The brooch fell to the ground. No.

No! Michael stared up at the two riders. Were they working with Morgan? Were they dangerous to Arthur? He didn't know. He only knew what he'd read in books. Mordred kills the king.

"You better go find him. And you better hurry."

"We do not know where he went," Gawaine told him. "The brooch appears to send people to their true love. The last time someone used it without authorization, she went to the twenty-first century. It took us a month to find her."

"Ah, aye," said Luke, smiling. "Elia. We should pay her a visit and see how she is doing with that Charles Lancaster fellow."

Charles Lancaster? Michael's heart raced. Yes, they knew of him. They were the ones who had sent Kestrel to the past. They had no idea how close they were to King Arthur.

"Why do you express such urgency about us finding the rogue?" Gawaine demanded, pulling him from his thoughts. "Who is he?"

"He's Mordred."

CHARLOTTE RESTED IN her bed at the manor house. It had been three days since Preston shot her. She liked to believe that the pistol fired accidentally, that Preston hadn't meant to shoot her, but she knew he likely had.

She would miss him, but she was glad he was gone. As for Sebastian, what madness surrounded him and Michael. Brothers! Sons of King Arthur! She'd never believe it if she hadn't met Mr. Simeon, and if her father didn't believe it. Oh, she had quit defying him. He wasn't so bad. He sent for the best physicians and paid for her constant care. Even after she'd confessed to being the Dark Horseman, he promised that she would receive a fair trial. She hadn't truly done anything as a Horseman. It had been Sebastian who'd killed the earl. Laws weren't as strict here as in the twenty-first century. Because she'd been there did not make her guilty. Still, she vowed to put in as many hours as she could in a day to doing things for others.

Her mother hadn't been home in four days. It was the longest she'd been gone. Charlotte didn't think she would be back. And she didn't care. Charlotte would have liked a relationship with her, but it was up to her mother now. If she ever returned. Her father didn't seem overly concerned, and he knew his wife best.

Rosie and the others were doing well, helping her father and Michael's men rebuild in the village. Charlotte would like to live among them eventually.

With Michael. He'd forgiven her. She thought she might go mad if he hadn't. She smiled, thinking of it all. Her, the pampered daughter of a duke, who had learned years ago how to use her wiles to their best advantage, had lost her heart to a stoic stranger who'd appeared in her life like a flash of light, leading her toward true happiness.

"Time for your medicine, my lady," Old John said in his gravelly voice as he entered.

"The nurse is to bring it to me, John. You have enough to see to. And I think 'tis a bit early."

He handed her the small cup he was carrying and waited for her to drink it. The moment she put it to her lips the smell of whiskey assaulted her nostrils. She eyed the butler and smiled then downed the drink. It was the good stuff. She knew because it burned her eyeballs.

"Ah, that will help, old friend."

He smiled proudly. "You could drink with the best of them, my lady."

The sound of a man's deep laughter settled around her like a favored blanket. Michael appeared at the doorway and gazed at her lying in bed. "What more will I learn about you in the days to come?"

"I cannot wait to get out of this bed."

His smile remained as he stepped inside. "Why? I like you in it."

John slipped out of the room with a smile on his weathered face.

"I can carry you to our bed, where you belong. Your wound

is no longer bleeding."

"I can walk." She smiled at him, and if she ever thought her smiles didn't affect him, she was greatly mistaken. He seemed to go soft. Maybe she hadn't seen it because he hadn't gone soft with anyone else.

He reached the side of the bed and bent to carefully scoop her up. "No wife of mine will walk after she's been shot."

She laughed softly into his neck. "I miss you at my side in bed."

"I'll jump in beside you when we reach our bed," he promised, kissing her forehead.

"Ah," breathed Mr. Simeon, popping in in front of them and blocking their path to the bedroom. "It is wonderful to see the brooch succeeded yet again."

"Simeon," Michael muttered, though Charlotte knew he was happy to see him. "Then the knights haven't found you?"

"No," the traveler laughed and actually wrung his hands together. "I am enjoying leading them on a merry duck chase."

Michael didn't bother correcting his use of the term but smiled and stepped around him.

Simeon hurried in front of him again. "I probably won't be around much."

"Oh?"

"The brooch went out again yesterday. To a woman in New York City yet again. Another of Arthur Pendragon's relatives called Camelee Pendrey. She's an actress who is making a name for herself. Well, she *was* making a name for herself."

"Right," Michael agreed. Pendrey. Another Pendragon. Who was she? Another sister? An aunt, niece? "Now she'll be another missing person case on someone's desk. Do me a favor and keep your eye on her if you can."

"I intend to," Simeon informed him with a smile. "I'm now invested in all this, so I want to see where it leads."

"Any word on Lord Surrey?" Michael asked. "If you're right and he's Mordred..." Should he tell Simeon about Charles

Lancaster? No. He was warned to tell no one. Simeon might not be Arthur's magician friend. But he had a strong feeling that Mordred would find his way to Arthur. "Look in my time, in New York City, for Mordred. You have to find him."

"Why? What do you know? Quickly, tell me! I must leave."

"Will we see you again, Mr. Simeon?" Charlotte asked him. "You have become a trusted friend."

"Have I?" he asked.

"New York City," Michael told him quickly not sure if he heard. "Arthur's there."

Alone again, Michael and Charlotte looked at each other and smiled.

He carried her to their bedroom and set her down gently on the bed, then jumped in beside her.

He told her the latest about Preston's men and to how many he'd given second chances. Many joined the force, thankful that Preston's constant hand was off them.

"You're a good man, Michael," she told him softly as he began to undress her. "If what I have read about King Arthur is true, you are sure to be his son."

He kissed her mouth, snatching up her breath. "It's you who makes me a better man. I intend to kiss every part of you and show you how grateful I am."

She shook her head. "You were good before you got here, or the world from which you came would not have affected you so."

"Maybe, but that's all over now." He scooped her thick tresses off her shoulder and kissed his way down her arm, her fingers and sensitive palms. "Every day is a new day. And I want to start all my fresh, new days with you."

EPILOGUE

SEBASTIAN ALEXANDER, BARON of Surrey, landed in the middle of absolute chaos to his senses. Sirens were going off, pistol fire was being exchanged more rapidly than anything he'd ever heard. He covered his ears with his hands and opened his eyes, then closed them again. They stung from the almost blinding light above him. Was it the sun? He squinted and shielded his eyes with his hand. It wasn't the sun, but a dozen little suns just above him, though they didn't burn. He waited and as his eyes adjusted to the light, he realized they were lanterns of some kind, meant to give light, not heat. The noise shattered his thoughts. He stared, astonished, at the dozens of small, rectangular boxes all around him, no bigger than his hand, and a dozen more, larger, fifty-two inches or more by Sebastian's estimation, picture boxes hanging on the walls around him. The sounds had come from them. Suddenly, the pictures changed and all of them showed the same thing. A beautiful woman outside somewhere, talking into a stick.

She was talking about "shootings" and "bombings" in the ever-changing world they lived in. The boxes all changed again and metal monsters with wings flew through the sky dropping…cannon balls or something he'd never seen before. Remarkable.

This was the future. Pendridge's blackened brooch had worked. Well, he either lived or died here. Best to live. He turned around to leave all the picture boxes and the noise and walked through a sheet of glass. He never saw it. It was completely see-through! Amazing. He swiped the glass bits off the shoulders of his justaucorps and looked up.

The woman from the picture boxes stood staring at him. A man carrying a big, black piece of metal with a short telescope attached stared at him as well. He had no idea how to describe things he'd never seen before.

"Sir," the woman holding the stick called out.

Sir? He was no sir. He was a lord. He—

The man holding the bulky telescope turned to him.

"What were you just doing in that electronics store?"

"I was lost."

"Inside the store?"

He shook his head. "What is a store?"

She smiled, but after experiencing Charlotte's array of well-practiced grins, he knew she thought him dull-minded.

"What year is this?"

She blinked her almond-shaped green eyes. "Excuse me? Ladies and gentlemen," she said, looking at the man with a telescope on his shoulder. "We have some kind of looter here. Sir, what did you steal?"

"The year, dear lady?" he asked again, not caring what she thought. He wanted to know when he was.

"It's twenty nineteen."

His eyes opened wider. Was it possible? He turned to look at the picture boxes behind him for proof on the far-advanced world. He saw himself and the woman on all the boxes. "What are—"

"Okay. Who are you?" she asked, tugging on his sleeve. "What did you take from that store?"

"I took nothing," he vowed, holding out his hands. "I came here from—" He turned again toward the picture boxes. "How are you doing this?" he pointed to the all the moving pictures of himself. "Are you a witch?" He remembered Pendridge talking about his time traveling friend being cursed by a witch. This woman was certainly beautiful enough to be a witch.

"No." She laughed a little.

He smiled watching her. "Are you certain?" he asked softly.

She cleared her throat and looked into the telescope with a slight smile. "Reporting live for TTN, I'm Noelle Upton. Back to you, Janet."

Another woman appeared on the screen. Sebastian looked around for her but didn't see her.

"Turn off the charm, buddy. What were you doing in the store?"

Sebastian took a deep, cleansing breath. He didn't want to lie to her and have her find out and curse him with boils. "I came here from the past. Two hundred and ninety-five years to be exact. I was—" His words came to an abrupt end when the air behind him shimmered and two knights appeared on horses trained to trample and kill.

They had come for him. He had to run...but first—he put his fingers under her chin and lifted her mouth to his and kissed her.

She opened her eyes and broke free. Sebastian made the mistake of looking into her eyes. There was a fire burning inside. She pulled back her hand and cracked him across the face.

He took a moment to appreciate her saucy nature, and then he ran.

"This is Noelle Upton live on eighty-fourth and eighth where two...men just appeared..."

Sebastian didn't hear the rest. He kept running, into alleys and up metal ladders hanging from gigantic brick structures with windows. Were they castles?

It didn't matter. So, they were going to chase him down. He didn't blame them. He'd heard things they'd said when they had come for Pendridge. Things about Merlin and King Arthur. Mad things. But then who was he to say what was mad when he'd just traveled almost three hundred years into the future? Thankfully, they didn't know he'd heard them. Still, he guessed stealing their brooch was a good enough reason for them to hunt him down. Good. He liked a challenge. He also liked Noelle Upton and how she looked in her hose and coat, with her red hair spilling loose around her shoulders. If he was staying here, he wanted to see her again.

He was running and thinking of her pretty face when a metal beast on four wheels smashed into him and knocked him out cold for a few moments. When he opened his eyes again, he saw a man and a woman bending over him, concern was etched in their faces.

"Don't try to move," the woman told him.

"Help is on the way," the man said.

Sebastian stared at him. Had he seen him before? "Who are you?"

"Charles Lancaster. Here. Here's my I.D. I'm insured."

Sebastian shook his head. Did he just hear the thunder of horses' hooves? "I must go," he told them. As much as it pained him, he got up.

The man took hold of him. "You need to go to the hospital. There's an ambulance on the way."

"What is an ambulance? Armed men who fight for you, I hope?"

The man stared at him as if he could see inside his soul. Sebastian didn't like it. "Did the car hit your head?"

Aye! Hooves! He heard it again. Closer!

"Not my head. No." He pulled away. "I really must go." He broke free and ran, disappearing into the shadows cast from the monstrous-sized forts around him as the sun went down. He was careful not to run into any of the moving creatures on wheels. Were they alive? Or machines controlled by the men and women inside them? He couldn't think straight. He felt somewhat ill. He turned into a dark corridor made of what felt like mortar. He coughed and tasted blood. He spit it out and held on to his stomach with one arm.

The alarming screech of a siren blared through his ears making him feel dizzy. Finally, it stopped. He listened for the horses and heard nothing. He decided it was best to sleep here—wherever here was. He'd worry about his condition and those damned knights in the morning.

He curled up on the hard ground and, after finally falling asleep, he dreamed of a beautiful red-haired witch speaking spells into her wand. Her name was Noelle.

And he was going to find her.

End

About the Author

Paula Quinn is a New York Times bestselling author and a sappy romantic moved by music, beautiful words, and the sight of a really nice pen. She lives in New York with her three beautiful children, six over-protective chihuahuas, and three adorable parrots. She loves to read romance and science fiction and has been writing since she was eleven. She's a faithful believer in God and thanks Him daily for all the blessings in her life. She loves all things medieval, but it is her love for Scotland that pulls at her heartstrings.

To date, four of her books have garnered Starred reviews from Publishers Weekly. She has been nominated as Historical Storyteller of the Year by RT Book Reviews, and all the books in her MacGregor and Children of the Mist series have received Top Picks from RT Book Reviews. Her work has also been honored as Amazons Best of the Year in Romance, and in 2008 she won the Gayle Wilson Award of Excellence for Historical Romance.

Website:
pa0854.wixsite.com/paulaquinn